THE

THE FOREVER BUG

CREATED & WRITTEN

BY

"FRANK JULIUS" CSENKI - AUTHOR

www.frankjulius.com

This book is a work of fiction. All the characters, organizations, and events portrayed in this novel are either product of the author's imagination or are used fictionally.

Published by

FRANK JULIUS BOOKS

978-0-9959718-9-9

JANUARY 2021

FRANK JULIUS BOOKS

www.frankjulius.com

BLOOD DICE

Book #1 Hotel/Casino Adventure Series

THE RED JEWEL

Book #2 Hotel/Casino Adventure Series

INN FORMATION

Book #3 Hotel/Casino Adventure Series

BORDER HOUSE

Book #4 Hotel/Casino Adventure Series

THE FOREVER BUG

Science Fiction

MOSAIC LIFE TILES

Autobiographic Anthology Series 1

THE FOREVER BUG

CAREFUL WHAT YOU WISH FOR

Humanity had finally gotten its wish. At least, that is what we all believed and perhaps still believe after almost thirty years. But do we really have what we've always wanted?

Everything had changed—our values, our principles, how we conduct our daily lives. How we look at one another, what we see in each other's eyes, and feel in our souls, or do we still even have souls? We now live; we no longer die. Oh sure, there are those amongst us who just cannot take it any longer and kill themselves or die in accidents, but yes, we no longer die. We have our children, but they, except for a rare few, are now adults too, no matter how young they've become. The birth of a newborn human baby makes the news. Yet, the human race soldiers on into a future that no one could have imagined. When will it end? Perhaps with the stellar death of our life-giving sun as it runs out of its nuclear fuel. But until that time comes in this sector of our galaxy, it looks like nature has provided us, humans, with a pathway to eternity if we so choose to take it. Will humanity be able to find its way through this evolutionary change or devolve and disintegrate without the steady infusion of new blood? Only time, of which we now have plenty, will let us know.

***

CHAPTER ONE
2049

MORRY CALLED

Dateline: Friday, May 7th, 2:41 PM 2049
Toronto Canada – CHYI Radio Studios

"We have Morry on the line from Syracuse, New York, our second international caller this afternoon. What's on your mind this open line Friday Morry?"

"Hey *Westernman*, thanks for taking my call.

"I get that, Morry, but really it should be me thanking you for calling in. Without people like you, Morry, listeners, and callers, I would have no show. So let me thank you today for calling *The Westernman Show* on CHYI," Wes replied with genuine gratitude in his delivery.

"That's what we do here, Morry, take calls and talk the living crap out of each other; God knows we have plenty of time to do that now," Wes replied.

"You know I'm a long time listener and first-time caller."

"So, how long have you been a long-time listener

Morry?"

"Well, *Westernman,* I guess this year will make it forty years!" Morry replied.

"Morry, my man, that is when I kicked off the *Westernman* talk radio program, forty years ago! I am so impressed, and you are still listening after all these years from Syracuse?" Wes asked, astonished as he was but kept right ongoing.

"I have to tell you, Morry, I'm just going to have to meet you in person. May I ask how old you are? But before you answer that question, I'm going to have to ask you to hold on for another thirty seconds after these forty years. Can you do that for all my listeners and me across this great land?"

"Okay, *Westernman,* I'll hang on; I do have something to tell you that I'm sure you will find interesting."

"You're listening to Wes Ternman, and you've got the *Westernman* show coming at you from above the 49th parallel direct from atop the CN Tower in the land of the free and the greatest city in the great white north and North America; Toronto Canada. We're broadcasting around the globe on FM, AM, shortwave, and globalnet sat-systems. A special shoutout to our Canuck listeners on moonbase 5 beaming at you with laser-line radio."

"All right, back on with Morry from Syracuse, he's been listening to the Westernman show ever since day one. Can you people believe that!" Wes said.

"Yes, Westernman, I was 74 years of age when I

first caught your show back in 2009. Monday, June 1st, I believe it was. Since then, I have had onset macular degeneration. My vision was fading. In fact, my driver's license was pulled. So not being able to watch and enjoy as much television as I used to, I started listening more often and regularly to the radio. That is when I stumbled on your show on opening day, which was forty years ago, Westernman. But you know what the exciting part of this story is?" Morry asked.

"No, what's that, Morry?" Wes replied.

"The best part is that I'm now 114 years of real age. My *Bug age* is 66. I turned 90 when The Bug kicked in for me in 2025; that was twenty-four years ago. I've been reversing for twenty-four years, so that makes me 66 in Bug years. My macular degeneration had completely reversed back to normal vision 20/20, just like when I was 66, even better. My Bug, twenty-four years of age reversal, has given me a second life, Westerman. I suppose I was one of the lucky few who managed to live long enough to catch The Forever Bug, and now, well…the rest is history for all of us, isn't it Westernman?" Morry finished saying.

"Absolutely, Morry, The Bug had changed everything, putting you in the small minority who happened to catch it just before you were ready to check out, I would imagine. You caught The Bug at age 90. Can I ask how you were doing at that time?"

"Yeah, not good, and when you say I was close to checking out, you couldn't be more correct. I think I was heading for palliative care when The Bug kicked in just in the knick of time. Yeah, I was one of the lucky buggers in that nursing home, Westernman. The Bug saved me, and now, well, I'm back to whom I used to be, thank the good lord," Morry said and then paused with a tone of gratitude in his voice, unmistakable even on radio.

"Oh, and of course, I've had my driver's license reinstated many years ago. But who needs one of those any longer, right Westernman? The funny thing is, New York state here still requires that I have a driver's license when all the damn cars just drive themselves," Morry said laughingly.

"Well, the fact that you've regained your sight and still tune in to my show every day says volumes to me! Especially having been able to watch television again and back to how you were at sixty-six. Morry, I want to meet you!"

"You know, Westernman, it hit me pretty much the same time or maybe a month or two after most of the world was already infected. I guess that would have been sometime in the tenth month of 2025; yeah, October of 2025 is when I noticed that my vision was clearing up, Westernman."

"That's right, we all remember 2025. The whole world remembers 2025. That is when humanity's destiny took a dogleg to the left, and we've never looked back since. 2025 sure took care of 2020 and the following five years of misery for the planet with the Nouveau Coronavvirus - Covid19. Yet here we are, humanity now stronger but more perplexed than we could have ever imagined," Wes replied.

"Morry, that is quite the story, shared by only a few

of you elderly folks who managed to outlive Covid19 twenty five years ago. You know, I, too, was tested in 2025. It's the same thing with me as millions of others around the globe. The Bug had manifested itself into my DNA. I proved positive in 2025 for The Bug.

But as we all now know, The Bug had already commandeered our DNA a long time before 2025. Apparently, according to the WHO (World Health Organization), it took Covid19 to activate it. By 2025 the entire planet was infected. Morry, I'm not sure if the term *infected* is even applicable to The Forever Bug; I guess so, but it's been an infection the whole world has welcomed," Wes said with a tone of certainty in his voice.

"Morry, I was just thirty-two when the Westernman show debuted on CHYI back in 2009. When I tested positive with The Forever Bug in 2025, I was 48 years old. Nothing unusual happened in the following years except that I haven't been sick for even one day or one minute of my life since. Just like the millions and billions around the planet now. In the year 2037, when I turned 60 is when The Bug kicked in for me. I noticed becoming more spry and energetic with each passing day, week, and month. It is twelve years later, and although my real age is 72, my bug age is 60 minus the last twelve years of age reversal makes me 48 years old in Bug years. As we all have known for the past twenty-four years, The Bug virus makes itself known in a good way, around 60 for most of us men worldwide. For women, it's closer to 64. Then there are the *Forever Youngers*, those born around the year 1980 or later. For them, The Bug seems to kick in at age 40 and reverse fifteen years to 25, but this is a topic for another day, yes, *the Forever Youngers*, how interesting that is," Wes said, trying to recall his own Forever Bug history.

"I'm proposing you come for a visit, Morry. All expense-paid by the Westernman show. I would like to have you as a special guest for one of my upcoming programs. Can you do that, Morry?" Wes asked.

"Westernman, I'd be delighted to come for a visit to Canada. I could take the hypertube to Buffalo and connect to Toronto. The whole trip is under an hour even with a switch and transfer thrown in at the Peace Hyperlink," Morry replied.

"Okay then, Morry, stay on the line, and I'll have my producer Luke Stenner arrange the whole thing with you. That was Morry from Syracuse, a dedicated, loyal listener for the past forty years. Morry was gracious enough to accept my invitation to Toronto and the CHYI studios as my guest on the Westernman program. That wraps it up for me this Friday. May everyone across this land, this planet, and beyond have a splendid weekend. You have been listening to the Westernman show. Stay healthy and stay young."

***

WHAT THE BUG DID

Globally speaking, The Forever Bug virus had begun making its mark on humanity a few years before the war on Covid19 was underway in 2020. However, The Forever Bug did not make its presence felt until three years later, in 2023. That's when strange things started happening around the globe. Even as early as 2023, the ratio between births and deaths was beginning to change. It had held steady at 7.7 deaths for every 19.4 births. That translated into 2.5 births for every death, but that now was changing and changing fast!

By the year 2025, The Forever Bug had infiltrated the entire population of the planet. Natural human deaths were declining to the point whereby the year 2028, no one died of old age or natural causes. The Bug had eliminated all known human diseases and sickness. By 2030, the world was fully immersed in a transition period that changed how we did everything. Changes to the global economy were fast, furious, and epic.

Banking and healthcare were the two aspects of human life that were affected the most. Diseases that once were considered death sentences no longer configured in daily social living.

Cancer no longer existed; heart disease was eliminated. Parkinson's, ALS, Dementia, and Alzheimer's were all in the past and long forgotten. The Forever Bug cleared all that up and took out most of the medical community with it. The need for family physicians, general practitioners, doctors of all sorts faded dramatically. Most hospitals, nursing homes, and assisted living facilities were turned into condominiums and apartments.

Hospitals could still be found but were staffed only with doctors who tended to patients involved in accidents needing first aid and surgery. The medical profession had taken a massive hit along with everything associated with medicine. The hardest-hit companies were those in the pharmaceutical industry. Drugs other than pain medication were no longer required…people just weren't becoming even mildly sick. Someone with a fracture or a burn would require pain medication, but that was about all.

The medical profession still existed but refocused and redirected to concentrate on reconstructive surgery, prosthetics, human bionics, and linking machine to man. Medicine was centered on linking with artificial intelligence advances, linking the brain with digital memory and instantaneous learning concepts. These studies and advances then subsequently led to the rethinking and justification challenges to traditional notions of education. The process of learning and education systems throughout the world was under review.

Governments worldwide were examining the need for education as we once knew it when a student now merged with machine language in a wireless cerebral link. One now could learn and understand calculus or quantum mechanics in an afternoon session with a digital self-image in the form of a hologram as his or her own personal teacher. AI artificial intelligence had permeated virtually all aspects of daily life in the modern world. Robotics had become so ubiquitous in everyday life that bionic and robotic pets had started becoming commonplace. By 2033 dogs and cats, birds and reptiles, whatever you wanted were replicated indistinguishable from the real animal with programmed personalities and dispositions. The best part was that pet food was no longer needed, just a quick recharge once a month. Still, real live pets were preferred but at sky-high prices.

There were other changes, many. One example was that now everyone on earth could afford their own home if they so chose. Banks and lending institutions were now issuing one-hundred-year mortgages; time was no longer an issue. This led to both the banks and the borrowers benefiting. The banks raked in the money, and everyone owned a home. Some banks were bold enough to gamble and go the full two-hundred-year mortgage. A dwelling now costing one million dollars could be paid off with a low monthly payment that everyone could afford over a two-hundred-year term. But this was just the tip of the iceberg.

The Forever Bug brought seemingly everlasting life to humanity. This did not sit well with the clergy. No, the scriptures and the world's religions were not in tune with this new evolution wave. Rumblings were felt from the Vatican to Mecca to Islamabad to Mumbai and across the spiritual landscape.

Along with renewal, there came a frightening change, and that change was no human births. The Forever Bug brought with it the end of natural new blood. Shortly after The Bug had made its presence felt and known throughout the world, further pregnancies were becoming fewer and fewer. Once The Bug had settled in on the global population, human birth declined to where no new babies were born. The reason: The Forever Bug had given renewed life to humanity but also brought with it a premature ovarian failure. Women worldwide could no longer become pregnant because the ovaries could no longer produce the required amount of estrogen to release eggs regularly. The real kicker came when weeks after discovering premature ovarian insufficiency (POI) in women, men were also being rendered infertile around the globe. The Forever Bug had triggered the immune system in men to produce anti-sperm antibodies, and the circle of human infertility was complete.

The Bug had robbed humanity of becoming naturally pregnant and voluntary procreation. Society grappled with these changes in lifestyle and living until we came to terms with our newfound fate. With no naturally occurring deaths and no births, the problem of overpopulation was instantly solved. Surprisingly births and deaths still occurred but brought about in entirely different ways. The Bug had changed everything, and now we live on in this new utopia while it can be perilous for many.

On the surface, one would have thought The Forever Bug brought with it much joy. No more diseases, no more sickness, no more human suffering. Yes, one would have thought these were all for the betterment of the human race. Everyone on earth enjoyed the same benefits that The Bug brought with it, but some had significant problems with this newfound freedom from death. The Bug had manifested new problems for humanity and now had arrived at our crossroads…do we choose life or death. For many, it was death, but not for themselves, for others. Even those who only want the best for their families and friends, and loved ones will risk it all for one act of love: an essential requirement that cannot be taken away. What is that one act of love and ultimate human desire, one might ask? The answer: babies, but babies were big trouble in the era of The Bug.

***

CHAPTER TWO
2025

CAM CALLED

Dateline: Friday, August 29th, 3:10 PM 2025
CHYI Radio Station Toronto Canada

Sylvie was teetering on edge, consumed with anxiety, almost trembling. She tried everything to maintain her composure as she pulled up in front of the CHYI radio station to pick up Wes. She was determined to break it gently and didn't want to come across as freaked out about it all.

"That was one hell of a strange show you had today, Wes," Sylvie said to her husband of eighteen years. "You must have had at least a dozen callers all saying how great they felt. Not just from here in Toronto but all over the country! What do you think is happening, Wes?"

"Yeah, kind of strange how everyone is suddenly in such a feel-good mood," Wes replied, glancing over at his wife in the driver's seat of their SUV.

Wes and Sylvie were on their way to see Wes's Dad at Willow Woods home for the elderly. The plan was to head out of Dodge right afterward and hit the highway for the drive to Algonquin Park. This was the

Labor Day long weekend making for a much-needed trip away from it all. In three more days, it would be September 1st, which was also the first Monday in September this year, making an earlier than usual Labor Day weekend. The traffic, the noise, the congestion, the city, they both needed a break. Yes, this was the weekend to see some moose, deer and make love in their tent underneath the stars of Algonquin. The trip to see Wesley's father would only take an hour or so, and they'd soon be on their way to God's country.

Sylvie then looked back over to Wes and once again said, "No, really, what's going on with those crazy calls? And talking about calls: Cam called today," she finished saying.

"What? What do you mean Cam called today, my Dad? He called today, he called you?" Wes asked with a bewildered look on his face.

"You mean someone from Willow Woods called for him, right?" Wes insisted.

"No, Wes, he called; it was your Dad; he called me and actually told me he didn't want to disturb you during your show," Sylvie replied.

"Okay, babe, this is getting too weird for me. First, you ask me what all those callers were talking about, and now you tell me Dad called! Well, hell, he doesn't even know his own name, let alone know how to use a phone!" Wes replied.

"You got it, my-talk-show-sweetie, your Dad

called me! Yeah, yeah, I know that sounds impossible, but there you have it, and you want to know what he said?"

"What he said? You mean you had a conversation?" Wes asked, being totally flabbergasted.

"I know, babe, I know, I wanted to call you right away, but I couldn't believe it myself. Wes, he was talking to me on the phone like a normal person. He said he remembered my number, borrowed his nurse's phone, and called because he wanted to hear my voice," Sylvie said, trying to maintain her calm.

"Wes, your Dad is having some sort of a reversal. My God, Wes, he sounded normal, called me by my name Wes, and told me on the phone how much he misses us and that he could hardly wait to see us this afternoon. Just hearing his voice on the phone and knowing it really was Cam, well, he made me cry!"

Sylvie started to cry again as she recalled the conversation with Wes's Dad. Anticipation filled her heart. She knew Wes would have felt the same if he could have heard his father talking on the phone. Sylvie was so overcome with emotion that she had to pull over.

"Put the car in park, and let's switch; I'll drive to the home from here, Sylvie, come on babe, let's trade places," Wes said as he was opening the passenger side car door.

Having traded places, Wes buckled up his seatbelt, pulled back onto the road, reached out to take Sylvie's hand, raising it to his lips, kissing her fingers. He looked over at his wife, smiling with hope in his eyes.

"Wes, I told your Dad we'd be there at 4 o'clock this afternoon. You know what he said?" Sylvie asked.

"No, Sylvie, what? Jeez, I still can't believe this!"

"He said, yeah, he knew because he read it on the visitor schedule sheet early on in the day. He said he was excited to know that we'd be coming in to see him! Wes, he's reading now and talking like a normal person!"

"Okay, Sylvie, I believe you, but I can't believe what I am hearing! I just can't. Babe, he's almost comatose for God's sake!" Wes said, looking over at his wife, confused but listening.

"We're only a few minutes out; let's just see what this is all about. This has been one strange day. Listeners from across Canada, calling in to my radio show just to tell me how great they felt, and then this… Dad has his brains back! Holy crap!" Wes replied.

"I see you packed all the equipment and gear for Algonquin. If everything is good with Dad, we should be heading to the park in the next hour."

"Wes, honestly, hon, I don't think we will be going anywhere," Sylvie replied, looking over at Wes and wiping tears away from her eyes.

Wes pulled into the Willow Woods lot, parked the SUV, looked over at Sylvie, reached out, pulled her in close, and kissed her.

“Let’s go see how Dad’s doing,” Wes whispered as he pulled away from Sylvie’s lips.

Wes wrapped an arm around Sylvie, and they walked up the pathway. Arriving at the front door, Wes reached out to punch in the entry code. The door opened, and they entered the lobby. Sylvie and Wes had blown right through the hall, not noticing the chairs off in the corner or anyone sitting in them. They made their way through the lobby, heading for the elevator when a voice from behind called out their names.

“Wes, Sylvie, I’ve been waiting for you,” came a familiar-sounding voice just as they were about to step into the elevator.

Suddenly hearing their names, they both turned around and were stunned at what they saw. There standing not ten feet away, was Cameron Ternman, Wes’s Dad. Both Sylvie and Wes were flabbergasted to see Cam.

Not in five years had Cam been able to stand without a walker, and yet, there he was. Not only was Cam freely standing, but he was dressed to the nines! Cam was wearing his freshly pressed double-breasted navy blue suit, polished oxfords, white shirt, and silk red tie. He was clean-shaven, hair nicely styled, even had a splash of cologne, and with the twinkle in his eye, he was looking oh so handsome and vibrant, debonaire and dignified even! Most incredibly, Cam wasn’t shaking or showing any signs of his Parkinson’s disease. Cam was by himself, no attendant or minder by his side.

"Wes, Wes, my son, oh Sylvie, come here and let me hug you both; I've missed you so much. I've been waiting all afternoon!"

Wes's jaw dropped, his eyes went wide open. Sylvie teared up again and ran over to Cam, hugging him, crying from overwhelming joy. Wes, having given up years ago on his father ever recovering, was shell-shocked. He couldn't quite believe his eyes.

"Dad! Dad, you're walking, and…and talking. Dad, you're wearing a suit! You're not in slippers!" Wes said, looking at his father, astonished with disbelief as his eyes too glazed over with tears.

Cameron Ternman, 69 years of age, standing six feet three inches tall, opened his arms wide to embrace his son and daughter in law. "Come to me and let me hug you both; I feel like I have been granted a second life by the good lord." And with Cam having said those words, the three of them hugged one another, holding on tight with both joy and bewilderment.

"Son, I'm getting out of here today. Do you think you have a place you can put me up for a while?" Cam said with love coming from deep within his heart and soul.

"Oh, Dad, you're back! Dad, welcome home; we've missed you so much all these years," Wes said as he backed up, wiping his eyes, still in disbelief that his Dad was back! "Dad, what's happened? How is this possible?"

"Wes, my son, I know, I know this is crazy but such

good crazy, isn't it? I heard earlier on in the day, others like me, men and women, were suddenly feeling great. Wes, no one in this place is using a walker any longer. Things started happening about a week ago when we noticed subtle changes, and then it took hold like wildfire. Now here we are. It's like we've all been suddenly cured!" Cam explained.

"So this is what my callers were talking about earlier on today. Dad, this is sweeping the country; it's like a light has been suddenly turned on to instantly wipe away all the darkness. My God, Dad, what is happening?" Wes exclaimed.

"I have no idea what is going on, but whatever it is, I'm in! I'm still 69 years old, but Wes, Sylvie, I'm feeling twenty years younger and all within the last two or three days."

"Come on, Dad, let's get out of here; they can forward your things later if you even want them," Wes said as he wrapped his arm around his father's shoulder.

"You see, Wes, I told you we wouldn't be going anyplace this weekend. We're spending it with Dad at home!"

"That we are, babe, that we are. We've got five years of catching up to do; God, it's so good to have you back, father," Wes said.

Sylvie moved in close to Cam's other side, lovingly hugging her father-in-law around his waist as the three of them walked out of Willow Woods

Long Term Care Center for the very last time.

***

CHAPTER THREE
2036

PANIC

Dateline: April 1st, 10:AM 2036 – Toronto Canada

Toronto Civic Stadium – International Medical Convention

The elimination of all diseases and general sickness the world over would have one thinking that utopia had finally arrived on earth. Nothing could have been farther from the truth, however. With no one falling sick in the past eleven years on the planet, epic industrial and business catastrophes were breaking out in every corner of the world. The global medical profession was in a freefalling spiral into total collapse, with no-way-out. Not only that, but it was about to take several other industries down the tubes with it.

Mark Canning MD – President North American Medical Association – "Good morning, ladies and gentlemen, fellow doctors, specialists, researchers, and academia, we have a problem. It would appear that the world and humanity no longer need us or our skills," Mark said, addressing the crowd. A deathly silence fell upon the gathering overcapacity thirty thousand plus physicians, physiologists, nurses, and scientists, as Dr. Mark Canning said those words.

"Yes, my fellow colleagues, we are facing an international disaster in the medical community. In the past eleven years since The Bug has saved humanity, it has managed to wreck our industry and driven thousands if not millions of doctors, nurses, and health care workers into virtual poverty. I need not tell you how specialists in oncology, cardio, endocrinologists, dermatologists, and every discipline of our profession face financial ruin not just here in North America but throughout the world." Mark stopped for a moment to let those words sink in.

Every person in attendance this afternoon at the Civic Stadium was well aware of their dilemma but hearing it being said loud and clear by the President of the North American Medical Association added certain weight to the crisis facing each of them.

Mark Canning continued. "This Bug is wiping us out! What is it we are supposed to do? That is the number one question I'm continually being asked by colleagues. I've been a physician my whole professional life, and now I'm asked to seek a second career as what? Perhaps I can learn to be a carpenter? Perhaps I can be an accountant? Well, no, I can't be an accountant or a plumber or a forklift operator! I am a physician!" Mark shouted into the microphone. The stadium erupted with resounding applause and cheers. Mark waited the two minutes for silence to once again ensue.

"Ladies and gentlemen, The Forever Bug, yes, that is what the world is calling it now, is saving humanity but will end up doing us in. Most everyone in this stadium has lost their hospital jobs, closed their clinics, fired their staff, have gone into bankruptcy, some sad to say have chosen suicide," Mark said, stopping again for a while as the crowd went silent.

"Are we going to stand for this?" Mark asked loud and clear into the microphone.

The crowd erupted in a resounding reply in unison, "No, no, we will not!"

Mark Canning then waited and spoke into the microphone again. "That's right, we will not stand for it, and let me assure you all here gathered today that we are looking for a way out. A way out to get us back in. Back into our professions and back into turning sick people healthy again. That is what we do! We heal the sick!"

Mark then fist punched the air above his head repeatedly and, with each thrust of his fist in the air, yelled into the microphone, "*a way out to get back in, a way out to get back in,*" several times before leaving the podium.

The entire stadium of doctors and health professionals then erupted into a chant, *"a way out to get back in, a way out to get back in."*

The crowd repeated the chant over and over, becoming their battle cry to resolution. The convention was underway.

A dozen or so CEO's of the largest pharmaceutical companies were in attendance at this medical convention. The heads of Argus, Merit, Unihealth, and Granger, just to name a few. Companies whose stock prices had plummeted like rocks sinking to the ocean floor. These companies not only represented the most powerful and influential drug companies in the world but had an obligation to its millions of shareholders to make a profit. The Bug had robbed them of that pledge and catapulted them into survival mode. Survival mode had brought about worldwide hatred of the pharmaceuticals. Because the need for disease-fighting drugs had been virtually wiped out, the only remaining drugs produced by these few drug manufacturers were pain killers and anti-rejection drugs used in organ and body parts transplants.

The feeling of pain was only experienced by people who were involved in some sort of mishap or accidents, bodily injuries. Body parts no longer malfunctioned, organs no longer became diseased or failed. Sure, legs were broken, eyes were still being injured, and reconstructive surgery was as strong as ever. But no more were there patients needing care for diseases. Essential inexpensive pain killer drugs like acetaminophens, ibuprofen, even acetylsalicylic acid (ASA), also known as aspirin, were priced sky-high in the hundreds and thousands of dollars just for a few pills. That was how the drug manufacturers were getting by and staying afloat, honoring their commitment to the shareholders. These gouging price policies fostered bad blood between the public and the pharmaceuticals. War with these once drug giants had broken out. People were actually going without the medication just to eventually bring the prices down, and it was working!

Something had to be done; this utopia thing wasn’t working for them, not one bit, and they weren’t about to pass up a chance to act while many in the medical and pharmaceutical field were of like minds. The Bug had become the friend of humanity but the enemy of the pharmaceuticals and the medical profession. Doctors who at one time had taken an oath to do no harm were now faced with doing the opposite so they could get back to honoring their commitment to do no harm, but could they beat The Bug? The drug manufacturing giants of the industry harbored some sinister ideas that they weren't afraid to try. The problem with some of these wicked ideas was they'd be dabbling into both physical and spiritual territory where they did not belong. Would they be able to beat or maybe modify The Bug? That still remained to be seen, and The Bug would prove to be no easy egg to crack.

***

CHAPTER FOUR
2036

IT'S A BUGGER!

Dateline: April Fools Day. 12:00 PM 2036 – Toronto Ontario

"Good afternoon to everyone tuning in to the Westernman program and welcome. You have got CHYI in Toronto, Canada, coming at you five days a week Monday through Friday from noon to 3:PM on 101.1 FM, 1040 AM, shortwave, and Globalnet-sat systems. This is Wes Ternman, your host for the coming three hours," Wes spoke into his mic to do the program intro, paused for a moment.

"Regular listeners to the Westernman show know that we cover all topics that need covering no matter how weird, crazy, controversial, or dangerous a case might be. I am Wes Ternman, and I hold nothing back. The Westernman show has been on air since 2009, making this year number twenty-seven of informative, provocative, and crystal clear, honest radio.

We have a unique program set up for you this afternoon. This might be April 1st, April fools this Tuesday but let me assure you, there will be no fooling around today. Before I introduce my two guests, Westernman wants everyone out there in radio land to know that I will not tolerate any B.S. on this program. The policy and acumen of this broadcast have been to maintain integrity. I will always get to the heart of the issue; that is the aim of this program and has been since its inception.

The Westernman show has had more than its fair share of charlatans and snake-oil salesman over the years. While on paper, they may look great when we sign them up but then disintegrate on-air. We have had them trying to spread conspiracy theories and straight B.S. promoting their beliefs, charging up their base for nothing more than a little bit of fame. In the end, they carry no substance and usually get kicked off my program before the show is over. You know we've had a few on-air incidents for those of you who have been listening over the years. I will not have my listeners lied to or be swayed into some crazy cult by peddling preachers looking to line their own pockets," Wes took another break just seven seconds, but on radio, seven seconds of dead air can seem like an hour.

"Today, however, is not one of those days. My two guests have impeccable credentials and are highly respected worldwide. Today they will share their expertise. Ladies and gentlemen, the Westernman show will attempt to shed shining light on what The Forever Bug is and just exactly how it came about. Stay with the Westernman show for the next three hours and be enlightened. I know I am certainly looking forward to clearing some things up in my own mind; let's see if we can get some answers.

With the North American Medical convention in Toronto this week, the Westermann show successfully booked our two world-renowned guests for this afternoon's broadcast.

My two distinguished guests are Drs. Lillian Eavers and Nigel Fohr. Dr. Eavers and Dr. Fohr are Nobel Prize winners in medicine/physiology and chemistry. Like I say, not only are they doctors, but they are scientists extraordinaire. Ladies and gentlemen, physiology is the science dealing with organisms' living functions. Their research led to the discovery of The Forever Bug.

Dr. Eavers is head of the Department of Epidemiology at McMaster University Medical Center and Health Sciences in Hamilton, Ontario. Dr. Fohr is the Director of Biochemistry at McGill University in Montreal. Needless to say, The Forever Bug, as the world now knows it, is named after Drs. Fohr and Eavers (Fohreavers) coining the phrase Forever Bug, and ironically how appropriate it turned out to be," Wes said, introducing the doctors.

"Welcome to you both, and I want to thank you for taking this afternoon to clear up some questions we as a nation have collectively, I'm sure. We are going to take questions from callers in. But before we start in with all of that, I would like to ask you both to give us a quick overview of your respective fields of discipline. We are looking for clarity in helping us understand what is taking place on our planet. Has humanity indeed been given a fountain of youth to drink from, or are we on the brink of something totally different? Dr. Eavers, if you be so kind," Wes finished.

"Sure thing, Westernman. It is my pleasure to offer some insight, but to help us better understand, Dr. Fohr should lay down the building blocks of how all this came about. I will hand it over to Dr. Fohr, and he will lay the groundwork of how and then I can fill in the cracks, so to speak, on why all of this makes some sort of sense and what we are looking at in the next few years," Dr. Eavers said.

"I'd be happy to, Dr. Eavers." Dr. Fohr replied. "Let me first start by explaining in layman's terms just precisely what biochemistry is all about and what a biochemist does. In a nutshell, Westernman, in biochemistry, we examine the bits and pieces at an atomic level of life. We break down, analyze, and identify the parts that fit together in our human DNA that make us who and what we are. We aren't so much looking at the *why*, but more to do with *how* things come about if that makes sense. Dr. Eavers in epidemiology is more so in the *why* lane." Dr. Fohr said.

"Okay, that is very interesting already; you have my undivided one hundred percent attention; I am so glad we were able to book the two of you for today's program. I have a feeling we will be clearing up a lot of questions this afternoon," Wes said. "Please continue, Dr. Fohr, and sorry for the interruption; I'm all ears as I'm sure all my listeners across Canada are as well," Wes added.

Dr. Fohr then started in again. "So, where to begin? Over the past thirty-five years, we humans have had some real global pandemics to deal with. We all know what Covid19 did to us back in 2020 and 2021. Many of us dealt with the H1N1 swine flu pandemic of June 2009. Then, of course, we go back a few more years to 2002, when the world experienced the severe acute respiratory syndrome commonly known as SARS. We know these are all certain types of viruses that are infectious and aggressive in their nature. There is no doubt about it; viruses tend to have a pathogenic effect on their hosts. They invade our genetic makeup, taking over our cells' machinery to replicate more viruses infecting more cells and causing us illness. Well, that, of course, was the scenario ten or so years ago. Us humans no longer get sick." Dr. Fohr paused for a moment, taking a sip of water.

"But why am I bringing up viruses? Well, here's the thing. Although most viruses are bad, some viruses are good as well. And why are they good? They are good because they actually exist to kill bacteria, bad bacteria, and most amazingly, others exist solely to fight off more dangerous viruses. We know about protective bacteria, right? Many of those in our stomachs are probiotics. Like probiotics, we also have many types of viruses inside our bodies to protect us from other harmful viruses. They actually are bacteriophages or just commonly referred to as phages. Certain types of viruses infect and destroy specific bacteria types, but let's not get too complicated. The main thing to remember is that there are good and bad viruses," Dr. Fohr finished saying.

Wes had done a bit of homework over the past few days, knowing that he would have these two distinguished Nobel Prize winners on his show. But then again, Wes usually prepared himself for his guests, making sure he would be asking somewhat intelligent questions. Wes's first opportunity to test his thoughtful questions theory came at this juncture.

Wes then said, "So are you saying that The Forever Bug is some sort of a virus, Dr. Fohr? But how does just one virus, no matter how great a virus it is, just like you are saying, there are beneficial and harmful viruses, how can it stop all diseases? That has to be one super-duper virus, doesn't it, and where did it come from?" Wes asked.

Dr. Fohr listened to Wes, asking his questions. Wes could see that Dr. Fohr was impressed with Wes's questions. As Wes asked his questions, Dr. Fohr nodded his head, raising his eyebrows, looking over at Dr. Eavers with his approval, and then looked back at Wes.

"Westernman, that is precisely what I asked myself back in 2025 when suddenly everyone on the planet began shedding their diseases for apparently no reason. Neither Dr. Eavers nor I had any idea what was going on. Was this a new sort of viral pandemic in reverse? Was it even a virus that was making people well again? If it was some sort of a new virus, how could a virus do this? Then the question; where did it come from?" Dr. Fohr replied, paused for a moment, then continued.

"So let me bring you closer into the picture. Your listeners must understand the basics, the fundamentals of our makeup. First, all life on this planet is made up of cells. Next are chromosomes; all the cells in the human body except for red blood cells contain chromosomes. It becomes interesting because, on each of these chromosomes, there are hundreds and thousands of genes. By the way, Westernman, the word chromosome comes from the Greek, khroma meaning color and soma meaning body. Back in the 1800s, it was discovered that chromosomes could easily be stained with dye making them easier to study, so hence the name."

"Okay, I'm with you so far, Dr. Fohr, but I have to ask. I get cell, all right, and you say all cells contain chromosomes, but just exactly what is a chromosome? You lost me there," Wes said.

"Yes, well, a chromosome is a molecule, quite a long one in fact, with one part or all of the parts completing the genetics of an organism," Dr. Fohr replied.

"Okay, got you, please go on," Wes said.

"So, we have cells and chromosomes which contain genes. Genes are what make us look like we look. Blonde hair, hazel eyes, and these are what we pass on to our children. Genes specify the particular structures of proteins that make up each cell and define our heredity. Thus genes contain DNA (deoxyribonucleic acid), the chemical basis of heredity," Dr. Fohr said, speaking very slowly and distinctly.

"Dr. Fohr, we are talking about viruses and genes and chromosomes and DNA, whatever acid you called it. I don't think most of my listeners will ever remember what DNA stands for, but you have given us a pretty good introduction to some basics. I'm sure you are planning to lead us to understand this topic better. But during your explanation, even though I was glued to every word you said, I had this burning question in my mind; I just have to ask you," Wes said.

"Okay, shoot, what's your question,

Westernman?" Dr. Fohr said, with a little laugh to release the tension.

"Right, viruses, are they alive? Are viruses a living thing or organism? This program is all about The Forever Bug, our Bug, humanity's Bug that we now all have but like, is it alive inside us? And what if The Bug decides to die, then what?" Wes asked.

"No, The Bug is not alive. No viruses are. Not the H1N1, not the SARS, not Covid19, not even the Spanish Flu virus, the most lethal virus in human history. You know it infected about one-third of the world's population back in 1918. Five hundred million people and ended up killing fifty million by the time it was over in 1920. But even that Bug, yes, the Spanish Flu is still with us today. That too was an H1N1 type of virus, so it's still around," Dr. Fohr said and paused for a moment, looking over at his colleague Dr. Eavers nodding his head towards her. He then said, "but I'm sure Dr. Eavers will offer something to think about."

Dr. Eavers then spoke up, taking her cue from Nigel Fohr.

"When Dr. Fohr says that no viruses are alive, he is correct. But this now becomes a philosophical question, and what do I mean by that? What I mean is we must decide how we define life. What exactly is life? Some would argue that viruses are a certain type of life form and their arguments are not without merit. Viruses have been with us from the very beginning. They have evolved and mutated. They cannot reproduce or replicate by themselves, they do require a host, cells in fact, but they go on existing in their chemical states. When they were first discovered, viruses were considered poisons, then, as time went on, they were given the status of a life form. Later on in the modern era, they hold biological chemical status and sit in the gray area between living and nonliving. You see, they cannot replicate on their own. But here's the thing…they carry their own DNA or RNA. When invading a host, they take over that host's cell mechanism and replicate by the thousands, infecting the cell and moving on to infect other cells, so strangely, it's not alive until it is," Dr. Eavers finished saying.

"I see," Wes replied. "But Dr. Fohr, you just introduced another term very confusing to most of us. I get DNA, but what is RNA?" Wes asked.

"Right, well, I don't want to get too stuck in the mud here with detailed biology and physiology, but yeah, good question, Wes. RNA is like DNA, but it has one extra oxygen molecule, and this is a critical difference because it makes it less stable than DNA. With RNA being less stable than DNA, organisms that need to mutate quickly use RNA to stay one step ahead of the human immune system," Dr. Nigel Fohr paused for a moment. "Let me know if I'm getting too ahead of you."

"No, I'm good, please go ahead."

"All right, and now we get closer to it all. The RNA molecule has something special about it. RNA has messaging capabilities. You will now ask a messenger to what or who? Well, it can send messages that contain the characteristics and information contained in our genes to the cells.

Furthermore, it ensures that genes are translated into specific proteins, being the cell's essential tools. One example would be hemoglobin that carries oxygen throughout our body. You see, RNA can do some acrobatics; it can fold up into shapes that are complex tools affecting the cell. The vast difference is that DNA's double helix is ideal for securely holding information, but it really doesn't do much else. In other words, DNA has no manipulation ability whereas RNA does and thereby being the tool of choice for viruses," Dr. Fohr said.

"Wow, okay, this is a lot to take in, but I never said it would be easy," Wes said, speaking into his microphone.

"Hold on, everyone, we will be taking callers' questions shortly. I think we are getting to the nitty-gritty here soon. I know Drs. Fohr and Eavers are making an effort to simplify their explanations allowing us to understand, but I have to admit, it's a chunk," Wes added.

"I hope everyone listening this afternoon is writing all this down, it's a lot to take in, but I am fascinated. Over the years, I both read and heard about viruses and pathogens, pandemics, ebola, and what have you, but I wasn't really getting it if you know what I mean. I've always really just had, how should I say, surface understanding, I suppose would be one way to explain it. I'm starting to understand this a lot better, and I hope everyone out there has been paying attention. I promised I would bring you a program today to clear up The Forever Bug world we live in, and I think we're getting there," Wes said.

Then Dr. Fohr continued. "But remember I said there are good viruses as well. Ones that fight off harmful bacteria and other disease-causing viruses. This is where The Forever Bug comes full circle and most interesting in making sense of it all. Here's the most interesting part. It was us humans that made it possible for The Forever Bug to come into existence. We were the catalysts that made it possible, and ironically we didn't know it at the time," Dr. Fohr said and paused.

"All right, that's a cliff hanger right there!" Wes then said, "Perfect time to take a two-minute break, let this info sink in, and we will be right back. You've got the Westernman show, coming at you from Toronto, Canada."

Wes then reached up and pushed his microphone to the side and away from his face. "Drs. I think we might have a record audience out there today. My producer Luke Stenner tells me that the calls have been non-stop ever since we started the program, and people from all across the country have been holding with their questions. Thanks ever so much for doing this once again. I'm sure the questions coming your way will be interesting. You know I've been on air since 2009, twenty-seven years, and our listener numbers keep growing every year. Dr. Eavers, I'm sure they want to hear more from you as well; maybe we should have Dr. Eavers join in now after the break," Wes suggested.

"I will, Wes," Dr. Eavers replied, "But I think it's

important for Dr. Fohr to put a button on the fundamentals, I think he is just about done, and then I can put a bow on it tieing things up," Dr. Eavers replied.

"Okay, that sounds good, and afterward, we can open up the lines for caller questions," Wes replied, pulling the microphone back in front of his mouth. "You're listening to the Westernman show on CHYI. We have Dr. Eavers and Dr. Fohr as our special guests this afternoon, and we are discussing The Bug. Dr. Fohr has been giving us the fundamentals of DNA structure and virus biology. Dr. Fohr, please continue; we are all anxious to hear how The Bug began and manifested itself," Wes said.

"Well, you've hit the nail on the head Westernman, that's precisely what it did, manifest itself, but we didn't know it at the time. It all started happening around the time of SARS, the early part of the century. Anyway, just to recap, DNA is on genes, and then you have genes on chromosomes, and the chromosomes are in cells. Wes, you and your listeners have most likely heard of the human genome project. Several years ago, a project was undertaken to map all of the genes and chromosomes in a human being. So before we get too bogged down in the science of it all, just keep this in mind, a virus that has been newly synthesized by the messenger RNA will travel to the cell's nucleus, and here something amazing happens. There is a special enzyme from the virus called integrase, and it is used to insert the newly formed viral DNA into the host's cell. This can happen to every cell in the human body theoretically. It will become crystal clear why this is so significant in the birth and manifestation of The Forever Bug," Dr. Fohr said. "By the way, I'm not so sure Dr. Fohr and I are so enamored about having The Bug named after us, but I suppose it's a good thing at this point," Dr. Eavers said, adding her comment.

Dr. Fohr continued on. "We are almost there, Westernman, almost. In the early part of the century, around 2002 or so, the scientific community, biochemists, and physiologists began research into human aging. Of course, we asked why we age and how we can stop it, maybe even reverse it. The human genome project we talked about earlier on, which mapped all the genes in the human body, enabled us to see the picture much clearer. We were able to work with genes, DNA, and RNA closer than ever before. Then not too long after that came another breakthrough in DNA engineering and gene editing called CRISPR; yes, you can pronounce it as Crisper. This discovery was huge, and it came about in 2017. Unknowingly it gave rise to the up to now dormant Foreverbug virus, which manifested itself in full bloom in 2025. So, getting back to Crisper, what is it?"

"Yes, I've heard of the Crisper," Wes said. "But it's not in use any longer since we no longer get sick, right, Dr. Fohr?" Wes asked.

"Well, not really, it's still in use, but not by scientists, not by genetic engineers, not by doctors."

"So who uses Crisper today, then Dr. Fohr?" Wes asked. But as soon as he spoke, he caught himself with a hugely astonished look on his face. "No!, you can't be serious…The Bug? The Forever Bug is using our human developed technology?" Wes asked, unbelievably speaking into the microphone.

A smile formed over Dr. Eavers' face as she looked at Wes and his astonishment when it dawned on him suddenly that a biological organism had incorporated human technology into its RNA composition and behavior.

Wes then asked, "You mean to say that this, this…Forcver Bug has hijacked our technology and is somehow learned how to use it to benefit mankind?"

"Well, to cut the story short, the quick answer is yes," Dr. Fohr replied. "But wait, Westernman, we need to tie up a few loose ends. Just how indeed did this happen?"

"Right, how did it happen?" Wes asked.

"We are almost there now; you and your listeners have not long to wait, just a few more minutes, and all of this will make sense finally with a clarity I am hoping. There are only two more things to talk about, so we have a clear picture and understanding. Let's get back to Crisper. Once scientists understood the DNA sequencing in cells, they then wanted or needed a way to manipulate that sequence easily. If they had such a tool, that would prove a potent tool. Their wish came true in 2017 with the advent of Crisper. Crisper allows us to change the DNA sequence in cells precisely that otherwise might cause disease. It's a bit more involved than that, but in a nutshell, those are the basics. A protein that is an enzyme called CAS9 is created, which is used as a scalpel to cut foreign

DNA. Once the DNA is cut, and the unwanted section or bad section removed, the DNA then heals itself rid of the disease, And from here Dr. Eavers will fill in the rest, and maybe shed a little of the *why* onto the *how*."

"Thank you, Dr. Fohr; I will do my best not to confuse everyone out there," Lillian Eavers said with a smile on her face.

"The floor is yours, Dr. Eavers," Wes chimed in.

"Now we move on to what Dr. Fohr mentioned earlier on, our research into aging. This is the technological breakthrough that led to us winning the Nobel Prize in physiology and chemistry.

So as we age, changes take place in our body, cells become malfunctioning and senescent. What happens inside our cells leads to the aging process. What Dr. Fohr and I discovered was the existence of telomeres. They are protective caps found at the end of chromosomes, and these telomeres become shorter the more we age. You see, every time a cell copies itself, its telomeres get shorter and shorter and eventually too short of replicating, and the cell dies. We later learned that hyperbaric oxygen therapy lengthened the telomeres and actually reversed the human DNA aging process. Our research shows that human aging is just another disease that, in theory, can be treated. It can be treated through DNA engineering and gene editing. We were at the doorstep of immortality through human intervention, but we weren't quite there yet. But it was enough for The Forever Bug to kick in and take over." Dr. Eavers explained.

"Wow! Wes exclaimed. "Just wow! You mean The Bug, the virus that was dormant all this time inside humans, was sort of woken up by your experiments, and more less, took over where you left off?" Wes asked.

"That's it, Westernman, it did just that," Dr. Fohr then added.

"But let me tell you how we think it accomplished this leap, from being dormant to granting everlasting life, it would seem at this point."

"Yes, please, how did it do it?"

"The Bug was awakened by the Crisper DNA manipulation, specifically the CAS9 enzyme. When we introduced high-pressure oxygen into the cell, and the telomeres started to grow, enabling cells to replicate endlessly, the CAS9 enzyme then triggered the Forevever Bug virus." Dr. Fohr said. He then took a long deep breath, paused a moment to indicate that the climax to his story was about to come.

"You see, Westernman, back in 2022, our experimenting with human aging and specifically our research into the new DNA splicing tool: the Crisper CAS9 enzyme gave rise to The Forever Bug, but ironically we didn't know it at the time.

Remember Wes, we weren't looking for a virus at the time. Both Dr. Eavers and I completely missed the boat on what we had unleashed. Sure, we knew that Crisper was one powerful DNA tool. Still, we had no idea that these centuries dormant H1N1 type bug hidden deep within our DNA would be awakened and manifest itself with the newly acquired CAS9 into the human DNA evolutionary progress.

Once The Bug had incorporated our CAS9 splicing enzyme, it started its Messenger RNA gene therapy on human DNA by mutating oxygen molecules into the cell as a typical human DNA element. It affected aging, but it did the same to all foreign DNA that came into the body, other viruses; it performed its own Crisper gene-splicing eradicating disease-causing DNA along with the viruses that invaded the body. We essentially became immune to all diseases and resistant to aging. The Forever Bug had accomplished what we have been trying to do, but it did it on a molecular level through natural evolution, but fast, really fast!" Dr. Fohr said.

"And you know Wes, like I was saying, Dr. Fohr and I, yes, we received the Nobel Prize for our work with DNA; all of it to do with the aging process. Our prize was for the discovery of the CAS9 enzyme to remove damaged genes using Crisper. But The Forever Bug picked up on this tool and mutated to remove all forms of invasive DNA, but Dr. Fohr and I only discovered that just a couple of years ago in 2034. Yes, until just two years ago, we, the world, had no idea how all this was happening to us. We were determined and driven to find out how this was happening. Finally, with the advances in computer sciences and quantum computing power, we hit on it two years ago. In September of 2034, Dr. Fohr and I discovered the mutated H1N1 type of virus now being called The Forever Bug, and in its RNA was our human developed CAS9 Crisper gene hijacked and assimilated as part of its molecular structure."

"Absolutely amazing!" Wes remarked. "So, here we had earth spinning and rotating around the sun for the past eleven years, and we humans had no idea why we were becoming younger or shedding all diseases. You and Dr. Fohr discovered the good virus now just two years ago with its stolen CAS9 gene-splicing tool that you and Dr. Fohr had used in gene therapy applications back in 2022! Absolutely amazing!" Wes said.

Dr. Eavers then began again, "And to button things up, as I said earlier, this is what we can say with assurance. Viruses can and do alter our human DNA. The Forever Bug is proof of that. As much as we understand how this happens, the question of why it happens is still up in the air. Perhaps it happens because it is a form of natural human evolution, a chink in the armor perhaps," she then stopped, smiled, and said, "Or maybe it's a tear in the matrix," Lillian Eavers said jokingly.

"Right," Wes replied with a smirk and a ha.

"In this case, we stumbled on the way to make us live longer. Some say maybe forever, that, of course, still needs to be seen and tested. We will know more as the years pass," Dr. Eavers finished saying.

"Well, okay, but there is the last question I have, and you probably can guess what that is," Wes said.

"Yes, I can, Westernman," Dr. Lillian Eavers replied.

"You want to know why The Forever Bug robbed

us from being able to reproduce, why we can't have babies anymore. The Forever Bug virus has, for all intents and purposes, rendered the human race non-reproductive. Yes, that is the question for the ages, and why that is Westernman, well, that is still a mystery. Perhaps in the years to come, we will have answers or maybe a way around it. We can only hope. We do need babies," Lillian Eavers said.

"Well, that wraps up our first hour of the Westernman show this afternoon. It certainly has been an exciting and educational hour. When we come back, Drs. Eavers and Fohr will be taking your call-in questions."

Wes took a breather for a few seconds. "You have the Westernman show, and we will be back in two."

Wes then pushed his microphone aside, reached out for his glass of cold ice tea. He looked across the table at the two Nobel Prize-winning doctors and asked, "So that's how it all happened, so interesting. Do you think humanity has a chance?" Wes asked his two guests.

"What do you mean Wes, does humanity have a chance?" Dr. Eavers asked.

Wes then thought for a moment and replied, "Well, with no humans dying naturally any longer, sure all of us living now are destined to live for who knows how far into the future. Without new blood, babies, are we really destined to survive as a species?" Wes asked with a confused and worrisome look on his face.

"That, Wes, is the question for the ages, God only knows, and when I say that, I truly mean it, Wes, God only knows," Lillian replied, with a smile and a reassuring touch as she reached across the table to comfort Wes.

"Some think we now have the world by the tail," Dr. Eavers added. "But time will tell; we are only in our eleventh year of age reversal and living disease-free."

"I know one thing, Wes, the world has been turned upside down, and the shaking has just started. There is no telling what will fall out of humanity's pockets when the shaking's all over with," Dr. Fohr said.

"So far for most of the world, things are looking up, but as you know, Wes, not all is good in paradise, and those who think so are fools," Dr. Eavers added.

Wes stared back at his two guests, reached out for his microphone moving it around in front of his mouth. He wondered what the next hour would bring.

"We are back; you have the Westernman show coming at you on 101.1 FM from the most fantastic city in North America, Toronto, Canada. We're broadcasting around the globe on FM, AM, shortwave, and globalnet sat-systems.

My guests this afternoon are the distinguished Nobel Prize recipients Drs. Fohr and Eavers, the discoverers of The Forever Bug. We are discussing how it came about and why it is here. I'm Wes Ternman, and I am about to take my first call-in question of the program. I have Rudy on the line from right here in Ontario. You're calling in from Hamilton on the golden horseshoe?"

"Hey Westernman, that's right, I'm calling from Hamilton just down the Queen Elizabeth Way hypertube, a few miles from you," Rudy replied.

"So what's your question, Rudy?" Wes asked.

"Yeah, I have a question for your two guests. I've been patiently waiting for the past hour to ask this question, and I am pissed!" Rudy said, yelling his response.

"Whoa! Well, you know we hold nothing back on the Westernman show Rudy; what is it you are pissed about?"

"I'm pissed at these two charlatan doctors. That's what I'm pissed about. Yeah yeah, DNA and all that crap, damn it! What about the fact that they are planning on a method to kill us all? What about that? They haven't mentioned a word about that, did they? Here we are, us older guys now starting to get younger, and we have no disease, and the bastards are working on a way to stop all of it… all of it!" Rudy said, screaming into the phone!

Wes was surprised; as Rudy ranted on and on, Wes was looking out through his studio window at Luke Stenner, his producer screening the callers. Wes looked at Luke and gave him the thumbs up. With Wes's thumbs-up action, Drs. Eavers and Fohr didn't quite know how to react.

Wes Ternman never shied away from controversy; that is what made his show. He insisted on honesty but most certainly welcomed the totally unexpected; in fact, he thrived on such callers. Wes lived for shaking up the world and sometimes his guests. Nobody walked away scot-free. If someone needed to be called out on something, well, so be it. The truth would set everyone free, except, of course, those who might want to hide it. So Wes went with Rudy's call.

"Rudy, Rudy, what are you talking about? Nobel Prize-winning Canadian scientists trying to kill us?" Wes replied into his mic. Wes then raised his right hand, indicating to his two guests to hold on and to remain calm while he got to the gist of Rudy's call.

"Why don't you ask them about the North American Medical Convention now taking place in Toronto? I'm sure your two distinguished guests were there for that," Rudy said.

"Hang on, Rudy, take a breather; I'm sure Dr. Eavers and Fohr are open to any questions our callers have, but you sound so mad, Rudy. Are you sure you want to attack my two Noble Prize-winning doctors coming at them like you just did," Wes asked, trying to bring down the tone a bit but secretly hoping Rudy would rant right on.

"Westernman, you have a couple of fakes and snake oil salespeople there with you today!" Rudy countered.

Wes then thought, *this is good, Rudy's riling up the audience out there. It always makes excellent radio when you can cast doubt on the impeccable, and his two guests were undoubtedly beyond reproach.* Wes figured, so far as he could tell. *But it sounded like*

Rudy might have another angle on this.

"Rudy, Rudy, those are some harsh words you have for my guests; what have you got to back up such outlandish accusations?" Wes asked.

"How about this Westernman – how about the convention this morning, you know that one at the Toronto Civic Stadium the medical convention taking place. The stadium was filled to capacity. Your two doctors were probably present; that's why they're in town, isn't it Westernman? Why don't you ask them to tell you what I'm talking about? They know!" Rudy said, pausing as he ran out of breath.

Wes waited for Rudy to catch his breath; he knew Rudy wasn't quite finished yet. "Go ahead, Rudy, we're listening," Wes said into his mic, looking with wide eyes at both Lillian and Nigel.

"Westernman, I'm on the maintenance crew at the civic stadium, my shift would have ended at 7:AM this morning, but because this medical convention was such a main event and priority, I was asked to work overtime. At 10:00 AM this morning, I was there when that Dr. Canning character gave his speech about bringing back sick people again. At least it was clear to me that's what he was talking about. Your two snake oil guests aren't saying much about that, are they!" Rudy gasped again after running out of breath.

"I left the stadium around 11:00 right after that Dr. Canning's speech, caught the hypertube home to Hamilton and started thinking. Westernman, I got so pissed about what I heard him say. I had remembered your promo from last week saying you'd have these two charlatans on your program today; I just had to call your show to expose these two liars," Rudy said, breathing heavily, but he was done.

Wes then thought, *okay, this has gone too far; he better bring an end to it.* Wes then looked over at the window to Luke Stenner's desk and motioned to Luke moving his finger across his throat, gesturing to mute Rudy's phone line just in case Rudy wanted to bud in.

Luke got Wes's message with a thumb's up sign.

"Okay, so what about that, Dr. Fohr? Rudy seems to think that the medical community is cooking up some scheme to end The Forever Bug and freedom from disease. What have you got to say about Rudy's claim?" Wes asked.

Drs. Eavers and Fohr looked at one another with concern as Wes asked his question.

"What do you say to Rudy, Dr. Fohr, Dr. Eavers?"

"Well, look, it's no secret that the medical field, in general, has all but disappeared. Many practicing doctors have lost their clinics, lost their jobs in hospitals. Many have fallen into bankruptcy, and some even into poverty.

This morning, Dr. Canning's speech focused only on bringing the medical community together to support one another. His speech encouraged the medical community, what's left of it, to strategize and facilitate a roadmap into transitioning doctors and specialists into other careers. But other than that, I really have no idea what Rudy is talking about. If that is how Rudy feels, I'm afraid he must have misunderstood what Dr. Canning's speech was all about," replied Dr. Eavers.

"That goes for me too," replied Dr. Fohr.

Wes then looked over at his producer and gestured to him to open Rudy's line so he could respond.

"Couple of god-damn liars you have there on your show Westernman, liars, that's all I can say, god-damn liars." Rudy hung up.

"Well, it seems Rudy wasn't buying your explanation. But never fear, we'll just download that speech from this morning and see if Rudy is totally out in the left-field or not; he did sound pretty upset," Wes said after Rudy had hung up. Wes looked over to Luke in the producer's booth, and Luke was already giving the thumbs-up signal. Luke had already downloaded the entire speech from this morning and had his assistants working on it.

"Looks like we already have Dr. Canning's speech from this morning. Our crew will pick out the highlights, and soon all of you within earshot will see what Rudy was talking about if anything at all. Let's not jump to hasty conclusions just because of one caller. Remember, ladies and gentlemen, sometimes we might take things differently or out of context. Just because I tell you I had a great day sailing yesterday out on Lake Ontario, well, it could be taken many different ways. To those of you who think a great day of sailing is gentle breezes and soaking up the rays, well may be considered boring and not great at all for someone who loves the thirty miles an hour winds and the whitecaps spraying all over the boat," Wes added.

Dr. Fohr and Dr. Eavers sat looking at Wes and then at each other, but somewhat squirming in their seats.

***

CHAPTER FIVE
2050

TRANSITION

By the time humanity marked the end of the year 2030 on December 31st, the transitions caused by The Forever Bug had become complete. Not only was the transition complete in North America but globally. The Bug had entirely embedded itself into every strand of human DNA, missing no one anywhere on planet earth. The new viral Bug had spread at breakneck speed throughout the world faster and more effectively than any other virus in human history. There was good reason for the spread to have happened so quickly, just two months in fact, to infect every human on the entire planet. Because The Forever Bug had the complete opposite effect on humans than all other viruses resulting in global pandemics, The Forever Bug was able to spread like wildfire.

Nobody knew it was there wherever there happened to be, and in this case, there was everywhere.

International travel became more robust than ever in history. Advancing technology was making it easier and accomodating for The Bug to spread virtually overnight across nations. Air travel across the Atlantic and the Pacific had been reduced to just a couple of hours with supersonic commercial airlines. The millions of people using high-speed rail and hypertube commuting contributed to the increasing acceleration of The Bug's infection. The Bug only brought about health and wellness; people worldwide felt almost euphoric in their daily existence, and the world economy hummed along like a tuning fork. But this tuning fork had some unexpected vibrations that were causing significant concerns the world over.

As we passed from 2030 to 2031, on January 1st, the youngest humans alive were not less than eleven months old. Newborn babies were not found since March of 2030, with the last humans being born in the previous month. Humanity had been robbed of its ability to procreate voluntarily and naturally. Some said it was the end of the beginning, while other deep thinkers claimed it was the beginning of the end. At first, around 2026, it was becoming evident that fewer women were becoming pregnant, resulting in fewer babies. The reduction in births had been a slow decline initially. By 2025 the entire world was already infected. Still, it took The Bug another two years to fully manifest its capabilities into human DNA and further render humans infertile. By the end of February 2030, its effect on the human race was complete; the end of babies through natural conception.

But there were other flies in this new ointment. The world had changed dramatically. Some of the changes could never have been imagined before The Bug, but now seemed perfectly reasonable and rational. The manner in which the world operated was turned completely upside down on many levels. When the year 2040 rolled around, the new world order had become commonplace, with nobody batting an eye. The Bug caused dramatic changes in civilization. Values that we once held dear we no longer did. Since no humans suffered natural deaths any longer, certain forms of crime were no longer tolerated by society. There were just a few ways humans died now, and almost all of those ways involved some sort of mishap or accidental death.

Those ways hadn't changed, people still died in fires, and people never stopped drowning. People kept falling from high places, and sadly people were even being murdered. The murder rate around the world, however, had all but come to a screeching halt. With life itself on a brand new footing and people living well into their hundreds yet getting younger by the day, life had become more precious than ever. We no longer *had* to die. Before The Bug, like it or not, we all faced the same fate when our time came but not anymore. This then changed everything when it came to murder.

Taking life in The Forever Bug era was an automatic death sentence for whoever would commit such a deed. For one human to deprive the right to virtual immortality from another human wasn't something this newly evolved planetary civilization could tolerate. This new form of thinking and rationalization took hold globally, and by 2040 all the nations had passed this new law concerning murder. The only defense for killing another human being was in the line of self-defense; no other reasons were considered justified. Many different rules relating to crimes had evolved as well. Crimes that carried sentences of ten years or twenty years in prison had been modified to thirty and sixty years in prison. With the severity of incarnation being taken to the next level, there was a marked decrease in the number of serious crimes people committed against one another. Thefts throughout communities were rare, robberies were almost nonexistent, and violent crimes, in general, ceased pretty much everywhere.

The Forever Bug had given people a new start. If things hadn't been working out for people in their lives, there was now new hope, new and endless chapters could be written. New careers could be started. Architects could become musicians, musicians could become scientists. Bankers could change careers and become surgeons. Yes, there was plenty of time now to become not just who you were, but who you could be over and over with the opportunity to reinvent yourself and see the world from different perspectives.

Ah, surgeons, you ask? Well, yes, humanity no longer got sick, but surgeons nevertheless were still in demand. People who lost limbs or fell from high places, broken arms, legs, spine, or more still had to be cared for and fixed. General practitioners, family doctors were no longer needed at all. Nurses, well, they were still around along with the places where they worked, hospitals but not many. With no humans having to be treated for diseases, no cancer wards, no more diabetes, no more anything, all hospitals concentrated on operations and recovery. People still required pain management after surgical procedures, but people no longer required drugs for headaches or high blood pressure, or fever. Those were all in the past. We still, however, needed pain medication to help us heal from surgery. The medical field, along with the pharmaceutical industry, also had to reinvent itself. Changes led to turmoil, and turmoil led to conspiracies as the years passed.

At the beginning of 2040, February, the youngest naturally conceived child alive was ten years old. Only the in-vitro conceived babies were younger, and all in-vitro births were done with by 2035. That was it; no one younger than five years of age could be found on planet earth by 2040. Profound changes in the educational systems globally had come about during these years from 2030 to 2040. Grade schools were beginning to vanish. There were no schools with kindergartens, no more grades one through five, and by the year 2050, all high schools were obsolete; only colleges, trade schools, and universities existed in the world. This, too, caused tremendous upheavals. Boards of education were folded. Eventually, teachers had to seek new careers. However, there was a saving grace when it came to the transition of teachers into other jobs. Thankfully the change was gradual, and the writing was well visible on the wall for everyone to see. As the lower grades began disappearing, teachers had time to transition to other careers. It wasn't an overnight change like the medical and pharmaceutical professions had to deal with. Teachers were inherently capable. Most experienced no problems transitioning into other occupations such as journalism, psychology, even farming; for those who had grown up on farms, many returned to their roots.

The industry that took the most significant hit of

all was the insurance business, specifically life insurance. Before The Bug, life insurance companies had a bet going with the human race. They betted that you wouldn't die and were willing to put money where their mouths were with million-dollar payouts to your beneficiary if you did, and you gambled that you would die by paying them a monthly premium to support your side. Now the tables had turned, you now betted that you wouldn't die, and they had no hand to counter in the traditional sense. People just weren't buying life insurance any longer. Not in the way they did before The Bug. Yes, there still was casualty insurance to cover accidental deaths but nowhere near what people were buying in the past. Generally, people no longer died, so the life insurance industry model no longer worked. The industry was virtually nonexistent by 2040.

Travel and Tourism flourished in the new age of The Bug. People were no longer tied down with small children; they could travel at will. No longer were vaccines required for African safaris or a boat trip down into the Amazon. People could charge charge charge and pay later. Time was no longer an issue for paying off bills for those who wanted to go that route. The credit card companies loved it, the banks loved it, and the stock market loved it. National consumer debt had been rising ever since 2025, but it wasn't considered an issue. When banks were now extending one-hundred-year mortgages and some, even more, there was no reason to not have a lovely home to live in. The middle class was becoming the upper-middle-class throughout the developed world. Some countries were still lagging behind, but catching up was in progress.

The advancement in technology was a significant factor in the ever-expanding global economic rise. From robotics in farming to robotics in manufacturing, the changes in the way the world worked were dramatic—the impact of technology on agriculture all but eliminated shortages in the food supply. Crops no longer went unharvested in the fields because no one could pick them or plant them. No longer were migrant workers in the U.S., and Canada needed to bring the crop to market. Everything had become mechanized. Men and women who used to pick the vegetables and fruit had all been long replaced by AI autonomous farming robots. Technology had advanced by 2045 to have eradicated the typical resurgence of locust plagues in Africa. An entire region radius of fifteen to twenty miles wide could have its atmosphere electrified, thereby killing the insects in flight.

Consumer high tech had taken leaps and bounds by 2035, and by 2040 the human race was living in two daily worlds of existence; that of reality and augmented reality. Human to machine brain interfaces was well underway by 2040, and by 2050 individuals were conducting daily cerebral interface with their home PCs and mobile phones. Humans were downloading life memories to their digital devices and uploading data files to become walking and talking library of congress data banks.

Daily life was, for many becoming almost much too exhausting to deal with. The digital world outstripped the real world as far as time consumption. Many people throughout the globe lived a digital life most of the day, with reality only set in when it came time to brush your teeth or eat or drink or go to the washroom. In some ways, this was becoming a huge problem. Many people lived a life of fantasy spurred on by available and affordable technology. Then in the latter part of 2047, something happened. It was an event the world had forgotten about, perhaps better said, given up on. Then on July 15th, a news headline took over the internet in viral capital letters shaking the world as it turned on its axis.

The headline read as follows:

Dateline: Montreal Canada: 10:12 AM July 15th, 2047 – Urnews.com

CANADIAN WOMAN GIVES BIRTH IN SECRET

AT THE FOHR-EAVERS RESEARCH CENTER.

(Full story to follow)

***

CHAPTER SIX
2036

DINNER

Dateline; April Fools Day. 2036
Toronto Ontario – The Ternman Home

"Sylvie, you outdid yourself again. This feast you've put out tonight looks absolutely amazing," Cam said, turning to his daughter in law.

"Thanks, Cam, it looks a lot busier than I really was. You know most of this is so automated nowadays everything practically cooks itself. Oscar helped; *it* actually carried everything to the table and even set the table as well," Sylvie replied.

"Are you still referring to Oscar as *it*? Sylvie, you gave *it* a name, isn't *it* a *he* yet?" Wes asked and then gave a huh, and a laugh. "Oscar come over here," Wes said, looking at Oscar.

The AI humanoid robot, standing five feet two inches high at standard height, walked over to Wes's chair with a typical human type gait and stood beside Wes, turned his head towards Wes and said, "Yes, Wes, what can I do for you?"

"Did you hear Sylvie, Oscar? She called you an "*it,*" are you not offended, just even a teenie weenie little bit?" Wes asked Oscar.

"I know Wes, I heard Sylvie clearly, but I am not capable of human emotions, as you know. No matter how I am referred to, the bot responds in the same way, the bot being *me* in this case." Oscar replied.

"Ah-ha! Wes said. You just referred to yourself as *me* and didn't call yourself *it*," Wes replied to his bot.

"Yes, I did Wes, that is because I am programmed to respond appropriately when interacting with different humans. You are comfortable referring to me as you would to other humans, so I responded in kind. Still, I would have used the word *it* if I was conversing with Sylvie instead," Oscar replied, all along gesturing with his hand towards Sylvie when referring to her across the table.

"Okay, Oscar, you are official as of this April Fool's day, no longer being fooled with." Sylvie declared. "From now on, Oscar, you will be *you* and not *it*," Sylvie said, looking at Oscar and Wes.

"Thank you, Sylvie, that makes me feel better," Oscar replied and actually smiled at Sylvie.

"Oscar, I have to tell you, every time you smile at me, it creeps me out a little," Sylvie said.

"Would you like me to deactivate my facial expressions when speaking with you, Sylvie?" Oscar asked.

"No, that would probably creep me out even more

if you were to say something nice and not smile," Sylvie added.

"Cut it out, Sylvie, you are just confusing Oscar; his circuits might start smoldering any minute," Cam said laughingly.

"You know that was just his AI telling you that he feels better; he doesn't really feel anything, right, Oscar?" Wes said.

"That's right, Wes, not emotionally anyway. But technically, I can feel, perhaps a better word is sense. I do have molecular nanoparticle sensors covering my entire outer shell. I can detect variances in temperature and external pressure; I can feel someone touching me, holding onto me, or hitting me. As you know, I don't have human feelings of the heart, but I am programmed to say the right thing at the right time; I am even capable of blushing if someone kissed me on my cheek," Oscar replied, flushing his silicone face, and blushing off and on like a strobe light.

"Okay, Oscar, that'll be enough; you're almost a human now, no longer an *it*. You can relax now," Wes said.

"I think you purchased the comedian version of the Oscar three series bot Wes," Sylvie added, laughing as she commented, "but I do love *it*…him."

With Wes telling Oscar to relax, Oscar's command was to assume his ready position and location. Oscar's programming instructed him to seek an out of the way position but remain in a ready response mode.

Hearing Wes's command, Oscar then walked around Wes's chair, towards the head of the table, around the back of Cam's chair, and found a spot just inside the doorway to the dining room. Oscar faced the dining room table but bent his head down so his humanoid face wouldn't be staring at the table. Oscar then switched into his standby-ready mode.

Smokey, Wes, and Sylvie's black and white spaniel then sauntered up beside Oscar and settled in. The two were friends. It was all because of technology. Oscar's features included a pet function in its software and hardware. The robot simulated a breathing rhythm coupled with human-sounding heartbeats dogs could detect. Smokey must have figured Oscar for a living human being since he reacted to Oscar's instructions whenever they played together. Sylvie thought Oscar's pet-friendly function was just perfect for her busy days. She'd tell Oscar to take Smokey to the dog park or out for one of Smokey's daily walks whenever Sylvie couldn't make time.

Sylvie's day was usually spent in her studio making specially ordered colorfully artful ceramic bowls for her online customers from all over the world.

Oscar then knelt down and softly petted Smokey, whispering to him, "good boy, that's a good boy," as Smokey rolled over onto his back, asking for a belly-rub. Oscar dutifully complied.

"That darn robot's become my buddy too, you know Wes," Cam said, pointing at Oscar with his butter knife. "Over the past year and a half since you got him, Oscar and I have become good friends. Christ all mighty, I cannot believe I'm saying these words, I've become good friends with a machine, but it's the honest truth. You know, son, I think I would trust Oscar before I trusted a lot of people I've met in my life," Cam finished saying, then he added, "Are you my buddy, Oscar?"

Oscar responded immediately, raising his head, identifying Cam, and then looked at him, saying, "That I am Cam, we are good friends."

"You see, I told you, and no, he isn't an *it*, he is Oscar! Right, Oscar?" Cam turned to address the robot.

"Right Cam, I am Oscar."

"Dad, I know what you mean about trusting Oscar before some of the people we've met in the past. The thing with Oscar is that he isn't programmed to lie or to lead you astray. It's digitally impossible for Oscar to lie," Wes said.

"Yes, honey, Oscar will not lie, so I will not be asking him if "this dress makes me look fat," Sylvie said.

Everyone started laughing, including Sylvie. Oscar did not respond; his head remained bent towards the floor; his attention focused on Smokey.

"Cam, you were saying that I outdid myself today with dinner. But I think the person who really outdid themselves today was Wes. Wes, that was one hell of a show this afternoon with Dr. Fohr and Dr. Eavers. My God, Wes, I thought the crowd outside was about to storm the CHYI studios building and break down the doors!" Sylvie said. "Your radio program turned into a television breaking news event. I was afraid something really horrible was going to happen."

"Yeah, the program sort of went off the rails after I played Dr. Canning's 10:00 AM speech to the attendees of the convention on air. I decided to play his nine-minute speech, which completely changed the program's tone," Wes said.

"It sure as hell did son, I don't think you took more than three or four more callers after that, and none of them were friendly to the doctors."

"No, Dad, none of the callers were calling in to congratulate our Nobel Prize winners. Rudy sure poked the hornet's nest with his call this afternoon. He set the citizens of Toronto on fire. Yeah, about an hour after Rudy's call, it became apparent that my two guests were going to need evacuation from the studios before the crowd outside grew larger, louder, and more aggressive. Their ability to leave the building was becoming more dangerous as the minutes ticked by. It was a good thing that the Toronto Police department acted as quickly as they did with crowd control measures," Wes said.

"I was blown away watching it unfold live. It was around 2:00 PM, the street was cleared of traffic, the cops had pushed back the crowd with riot police, and then that chopper landed in front of CHYI to pick up Dr. Fohr and Dr. Eavers," Sylvie said with bewilderment in her voice. "Wes, that's the first time anything like that's ever happened because of your radio show!"

"Yeah, that was a first. I think the crowd outside was ready to lynch the two doctors, which is very sad—unfortunately, Drs. Fohr and Eavers were caught in a trap that they unwittingly created for themselves," Wes said and paused a Moment when Cam then commented.

"I was on my way over here when all that was happening. My car was driving me over as I was listening to your show. I had tuned in right at the beginning of the program and have to tell you— I thought the two doctors were fabulous. But yeah, they both screwed up Wes, they screwed up big time," Cam said.

"Yeah, they screwed up all right, Dad but look, cut them some slack. Rudy's call caught them both off guard. There is no doubt about that. The doctors didn't lie; I believe they tried to sugar coat that speech Dr. Canning made, and the sugar turned into salt instead. Unfortunately, my listeners immediately labeled both of them as liars attempting to cover up some sort of conspiracy the medical community has in store for us. I don't think Dr. Fohr and Dr. Eavers had the foggiest notion of what Canning was talking about. That whole chant thing that went down after Canning's speech, *a way out to get back in*, thing. That was powerful, with the entire stadium chanting those words over and over in unison. Sounded like the doctors wanted us all to get sick so they could start making money again. I just don't believe Fohr and Eavers had any idea that was coming, but it came all right," Wes said.

"Pass me that thousand island dressing, will you, son?" Cam asked.

"Here you go, Dad."

Just then, as Wes was reaching for the salad dressing, Wes's phone rang.

"Oscar, answer that call for me, will ya with speaker on," Wes said.

Oscar reacted instantly. He stopped rubbing Smokey's belly, raised his head, stood up, focusing on Wes, and picked up the incoming call.

"Wes Ternman," Oscar answered in Wes's voice.

"Wes, Dr. Lillian Eavers here."

"Dr. Eavers, this is unexpected. Are you safe and back home?"

Oscar's built-in directional microphone was able to pick up Wes's voice from across the dining room as clearly as if Wes had been holding onto his phone.

Wes put his knife and fork down, leaned back into his chair, and looked at Sylvie and Cam, shaking his head, raising his shoulders, gesturing that he had no idea what this call was about.

"Look, Wes, I wanted to call you to tell you how much Dr. Fohr and I appreciated your hospitality today. We understand that you have a radio program, a very effective program with a wide variety of loyal listeners. Naturally, that is why we agreed to come on your program. Wes, you do a wonderful job as a radio personality and talk show host like no other. Dr. Fohr and I know you look for controversy to bring issues into the light." Lillian said. Wes just listened, as did Sylvie and Cam.

"I'm afraid the controversy today wasn't caused by you or your first caller Rudy; it was caused by Dr. Fohr and me. When Dr. Fohr said he didn't know what Rudy was talking about wasn't a hundred percent accurate, but we were both caught off guard by Rudy," Dr. Eavers paused, "And good on him, Rudy was right. But Wes, yes, we heard Canning's speech, but honestly, we don't really know what Canning was talking about. The thing is, Wes, you would have needed to be at the Civic stadium this morning to appreciate our position.

To be honest, I don't think anyone there, not one of those thousands of doctors and nurses, really expected Dr. Canning's emotionally stirring speech hitting at the heartstrings and pocketbooks of all those doctors and nurses. Yes, he got our interest real quick. Even Dr. Fohr and I were somewhat caught up in his words that made them all long for the professions they all lost not too long ago. It was like a wave that swept the crowd over, and when they started that chanting, well… it just took on a life of its own.

The doctors are suffering Wes, it was a moment they easily got caught up in. As things turn out, it seems that Canning heads up some group that's looking to put an end to The Forever Bug. But Wes, this is just a theory that Dr. Fohr and I have come up with; we have no proof.

We think that Canning has some secret group he's

heading up, and this was his chance to get a good chunk of the North American Medical Association members on board with him and his group whenever they decide to go public. Wes, this is just a theory, but something you might want to look into. Dr. Fohr and I put this idea together by just listening to his speech. Think it over, Wes, and if you think what Dr. Fohr and I are proposing makes sense, then call me back, and maybe we can have another one of your radio shows to explore this further," Dr. Lillian Eavers said.

Wes sat at his dining room table, looking at Sylvie and Cam. Everyone heard Dr. Eavers clearly as a bell. Sylvie and Cam looked back at Wes, waiting for him to respond.

Wes was thinking…*Dr. Eavers had just proposed a conspiracy theory that made sense. If Dr. Eavers and Dr. Fohr were coming up with something like this, there was bound to be many more people putting two and two together.*

"Dr. Eavers, you know we had no choice but to evac you out of the studio by chopper before things got out of hand. We couldn't risk anything happening to you and Dr. Fohr. You two are much too valuable to Canada and the world for anything to go wrong. And you understand I had to protect my radio program as well. In these times of pesky litigious lawyers lurking for any opportunities, I had no choice but to protect my program and the CHYI studios," Wes replied.

"Yes, I understand, we understand perfectly. We are all professionals in our fields, and we all have certain responsibilities that we must honor," Lillian replied.

"So, Dr. Eavers, let me say this. I am thrilled to do another Westernman show with you and Dr. Fohr as my special guests, but the next time we will schedule the show and announce it to be from an undisclosed location. That will prevent the crowd gatherings like this afternoon, and we will avoid any crazies out there who might have you in their cross-hairs. And having said that, I hope you are both under 24-hour protection," Wes said.

"We are Wes; we are, in fact, both Dr. Fohr and I have been for the past two years, ever since we discovered how The Bug works," Lillian said.

"I was wondering what those two undercover looking guys were doing waiting around at the station this afternoon, so they were your protection; neither one of those guys really looked like Uber drivers, okay, makes sense," Wes replied.

"You see, Wes because we know how The Bug works, we are under protection from people who might think we also know how to make it not work, but we don't. When it boils down to it, that is where I am going with Dr. Canning and his theory if you get my drift," Dr. Eavers said, hoping that Wes understood what she was trying to tell him without coming right out and saying it.

"I hear you loud and clear, Dr. Eavers, loud and clear," Wes said.

"Look, I will be in touch again just as soon as Dr. Fohr, and I have something for you. We are on the front lines with this thing, you know," Lillian said.

"I know you are Dr. Eavers; I know you are. Be careful out there. I think some people might want to harvest your brain," Wes said.

"Well, they're not going to get it, Wes, not mine or Dr. Fohr's. Be well and talk to you later, and once again, thanks for your understanding Wes, talk to you later."

The call ended.

"Oscar, did you record that call?" Wes asked.

"Wes, you know I record everything. Would you like me to play it back to you?" Oscar asked.

"No, it's okay; I just wanted to make sure you got that call," Wes said.

"Oh, and Wes, even if I hadn't recorded the call, I remember every word, but then again, I remember everything, which really is no different than having the call recorded. I'm just a remembering machine, Wes," Oscar said.

"Okay, Oscar, that will be enough with the jokes; you can relax now," Wes said,

"Wes, I feel that something sinister is going on in the medical community that is just coming to light now," Sylvie said with more alarm in her voice.

"Something sinister!" Cam commented, "Hell, it sounds like some sort of *Star-Chamber* made up of rogue doctors and heads of some pharmaceuticals, that's what I think. They're probably planning to take over the human race and make us all sick again so they can have their God complexes back. That's what I think!" said Cam.

"Well damn, after twenty-seven years in this business, it never gets old, does it?" Wes said.

"No, Wes, it never gets old, and neither do we," Sylvie answered.

"Ditto that!" Oscar all of a sudden said.

"Shut up, Oscar," Wes replied, shaking his head with a long, loud sigh.

***

CHAPTER SEVEN
2047
THE BUG CHAMBER

Dateline: October 4th, 1:00 PM 2047
Kawarthas Ontario Canada – Buckhorn Lake

The vibrant red and orange-colored leaves of Ontario's Sugar-maple trees carpeted the rolling hills landscape around Buckhorn Lake's shores as far as the eye could see. Off the beaten path and deep in the forest was Dr. Canning's ten acres Kawarthas hideaway. The hideaway's main building was a large and beautifully constructed majestic five thousand square feet log home with several on-property luxury cabins serving as guest houses. This Thursday afternoon saw the arrival of The Bug Chamber members.

The group comprised of Dr. Stephen Bird, CEO of Merit Pharmaceuticals. Dr. Michael Dern, CEO of Granger Pharma, Willy Hollman, CEO of Permacare Health, Keith Shultz CEO of Durham Chemistry, and Dana Blackman, the only woman, and CEO of Finacare, the largest hospital health care company in the USA with private clinics and trauma hospitals now established in Canada. Rounding out the group and the seventh member was Ernst Heiko, CEO of Steiner Corporation of Germany, the largest drug manufacturer in Europe before The Bug hit. Steiner now only manufactured painkillers.

These six individuals had been arriving sporadically in secret over the past two hours, with Ms. Blackman being the last to come, but just in time for lunch. Mark Canning was sure to be present upon his guests' arrivals. He was there to meet Dana Blackman at the front door when she arrived at 12:35 PM at Mark's Kawarthas hideaway cottage.

"Dana, I'm so happy you were able to make it," Mark said, greeting Dana Blackman as she stepped out of her rented Lexus. Dana came close to Mark and pecked him on the cheek in a friendly manner but very appropriate. Dana Blackman was on her own, like every other CEO attending this deep woods private meeting.

"Well, Mark, this is quite the place you have here," Dana remarked. "I've been to cottage country in Ontario once before, but that was in the Muskoka region. This is my first time in the Kawarthas and Buckhorn Lake area; I must say it's stunning this time of year; the colors Mark, the colors are spectacular!"

"Dana, if you think the colors are great, wait till you taste the maple syrup from those beautiful colors. Our maple trees in the Kawarthas provide for the finest maple syrup you can find anywhere in Canada," Mark replied. "And how was your flight up from Massachusettes Dana?" Mark asked as he walked Dana into the foyer.

"Flight was good, Mark. It was my pilot's first time landing at Peterborough International Airport; we made good time from Nantucket," she replied.

"Oh, that's right, you spend most of your time out on the island, I recall," Mark said.

"Yes, it is a bit inconvenient, but you know, with 3D virtual holographic conferencing nowadays, I can't really tell the difference any longer whether I'm in Boston at a boardroom meeting in person or at my cottage on the beach. I do prefer being oceanside," Dana replied.

"Sounds like you have the best of both worlds, Dana. So, this is the foyer, but here is a keycard to cabin number two. I'm sure you will find it most comfortable. Come with me Dana, I'll show you to your cabin where you can freshen up or take a breather if you like before we meet with the others for our luncheon. That'll be in about twenty minutes or so. We will meet here in the foyer, at 1:00 PM," Mark said.

"Perfect timing then," Dana Blackman replied.

At 1:00 PM, Mark's six guests gathered in the spacious foyer of his majestic log home. The building's entrance would have been considered a lobby if Mark ever decided to turn his home into a hideaway lodge or resort retreat. The group was together again for only the third time since first having been formed back in 2036. Depending on how things went this afternoon, today's meeting may prove to be the final time and disbandment of The

Bug Chamber, but Mark held out great hope that wouldn't be the case. Mark was onto something, and he needed his group of six colleagues' buy-in.

"So, shall we? Lunch is ready, and I'm sure we're all looking forward to sampling the tasty Canadian cuisine my chef has prepared for us today," Mark said.

Lunch, or perhaps better said brunch was buffet style. The large round dining table was equipped with seven chairs and place settings. Mark selected a round table to host the luncheon; it made for a natural icebreaking atmosphere. The conversation was light, casual, and topical, covering family updates, current events, and even lighter talk concerning the weather.

Lunch was designed to take the edge off of what was about to occur afterward; The Bug Chamber meeting was why everyone was here, but this was nice. This preamble of sorts provided everyone the opportunity to rekindle personalities and take bearings of one another. Meeting only for the third time in the past eleven years does not easily afford one to just pick up from where they left off so quickly. The passing of the years brought about changes, especially in these years of upheaval; Mark was well aware of that.

After brunch, Dr. Mark Canning had his group of seven reconvene to the boardroom, at which time everyone morphed into a severe tone of getting down to business. The boardroom was warm, with oak walls. One wall held a vast seven feet by twenty feet flat wood carving mural of the lake and surrounding countryside. A sizeable long oak boardroom table with room for a dozen chairs occupied the center of the boardroom. Only seven were currently placed, leaving ample space between The Bug Chamber members. Mark Canning took his place at the head of the table. A minute or two after entering the boardroom and when everyone was seated comfortably, Mark wasted no time and started in.

"I'm glad we all agreed to meet again. I, for one, have been holding on to that one little smidgen of hope that our 2042 meeting in Bavaria wasn't the last," Mark said as his opening statement.

"I figured that was it, Mark, The Bug had won*, The Bug beat us all*. I recall saying that to you before you left, remember?" Ernst commented.

"I do, Ernie, I do, and I replied, *keep the faith,*" Mark said. "You know I haven't been to Germany since that time we all last met in 42. But I don't think any one of us thought we'd be getting back together as a group again, and yet, here we are," Mark added.

"Yeah, here we are, the seven of us all over again," Michael Dern of Granger Pharma said. "When Mark called me eight days ago and said he was looking to get us back together again because of the recent new developments, I had to admit I was skeptical, but Mark convinced me we should try again."

"Yeah, it was a tough sign back-on for me as well, but why not give it another shot? Besides, if we stand a snowball's chance in hell of getting our foot back inside The Bug's front door, well, I want my company to be among the first-in," said Stephen Bird of Merit Pharmaceuticals.

"Exactly, gentlemen, and that is precisely why we're all here," Dana Blackman commented. "Finacare Health Systems is the largest hospital and health care provider in North America. I am proud to say that somehow, we managed to weather this Forever Bug storm over the years. We had no choice but to reinvent ourselves. When The Forever Bug finally infiltrated all of North America, it became abundantly clear that nobody was becoming sick any longer; we soon realized big changes were ahead.

All our patients in every one of our 682 hospitals in 2025 were suddenly getting better. Soon after that year, our company took action, and we changed. Our business plan changed dramatically. We went from 682 hospitals across the USA to just 34 in a matter of three years. We migrated from full-service long-stay hospitals to becoming trauma centers. We now mainly only look after accident victims and injuries from violent acts. Oh, and I can't leave out all the attempted suicides; those have been on the rise like crazy lately. From physicians to janitors and office staff, thousands of our employees were furloughed, laid off, and retired. What saved our asses as a corporation was that we acted fast, almost overnight.

But I'm not alone in the way our company met the challenge head-on. Everyone around this table did the same. And we survived, but now, we may have a chance to grow again. We may have an opportunity to bring some of those skillful doctors, surgeons, internists, and neurologists back. The human race may need our services like it did 25 years ago, and I, for one, couldn't pass up this opportunity. If Mark says he has a theory that's' worth a flight to Canada to hear him out, well I'm not about to say no, and that is why I am here, just like the rest of you," Dana said, looking around the table at her peers.

"Generally speaking, our industry has adjusted. Over these past number of years, mainly the last two decades or so, many have gone by the wayside. Many folded for good. In some cases, the larger conglomerates took the hardest hits; they were too big to change. The upheaval was too great and quick to deal with. The tsunami brought on by The Bug came at us out of nowhere, taking most healthcare and pharmaceutical sectors of the world economy with it.

How did we all survive? I will tell you. We learned to mutate with The Bug; that is what we did. The Bug taught us how. We learned quickly that we couldn't fight it; hell, nobody wanted to fight it! Who in their right minds would want to fight a virus that was wiping out all known diseases mankind had ever had to deal with? The Bug was our savior and sadly our despair also," Dana added.

"All right, we are here to see what we as a group can do to revive our industry and how we can get ahead of whatever might be coming down the pipeline; I think we are all in agreement with that. Our mission hasn't changed; it's only been delayed. If my theory is correct, we could all be in for rebirth, so to speak. A new beginning with a new challenge which would put us into a totally unexpected partnership, with The Bug," Mark said.

"Partnership with The Bug?" Keith Shultz of Durham Chemistry remarked.

"Yes, Keith, let me explain; after all, that is why we are here," Mark added.

“Please do, please do,” Keith replied.

Mark then said, “*Sandi*, play holo 04-01-2036.” Mark’s voice-activated his boardroom digital management system named *Sandi*, projected the 3D holographic imager in the boardroom table's center in full three-dimensional view for the group. The action hologram video was of the Toronto Medical Convention of 2036. Mark replayed his speech so that everyone could get refreshed and how this all started.

“We remember that well, Mark,” Ernie said. “Christ, who could forget? You caused a freaking meltdown in Toronto that afternoon. Drs. Fohr and Eavers barely escaped from that radio program and station that day.”

“Right, that medical convention was supposed to be a high-bar job-fair for professionals in our industry. At first, I tried talking about doctors, physicians, nurses, specialists finding and moving into other professional life fields, other careers. God knows we now had the time to do that, but somehow I got overwhelmed. A speech I prepared about taking on new horizons and jobs turned into something quite the opposite. But while speaking, I felt the desperation on the faces looking back at me, and I caved. I told them what they wanted to hear instead. I turned a new horizons speech into a battle cry instead, and the rest is history. Let’s face it, our fellow physicians, clinicians, medical brothers, and sisters didn’t really want to do anything else. Medicine was their life’s work; it flowed through their veins; not one of them in that stadium that afternoon was excited about changing jobs. Nobody wanted to become an accountant or a heavy equipment operator! Nobody!

Look, after the seven of us had our meeting the day before, I really thought we might have a chance to bring something about. A change in the way The Forever Bug worked.

I honestly thought we were on the verge of undoing some of what The Bug did to our human DNA. I dreamed of seeing our doctors back, our pharmacies up and running as they were just a few years ago. I had fooled myself to think we were within inches. When I told that crowd that we were working on something and working *on a way out for them to get them back in*, well, I meant it.

I believed it. I went with it. We had pooled our resources focusing on R&D. Everyone around this table was convinced we were on the edge of a breakthrough in discovering a weakness in The Bug's ability to mutate our DNA. I need not remind you that we were all getting ready for the global reversal. Sadly and much to our chagrin, it never came.

The Bug proved to be resilient beyond our expectations! Our dedicated prep work was in vain. By 2030 all the world's sperm banks had depleted their inventories of cryogenic sperm and harvested human eggs. The in-vitro babies brought into this world after the no baby years, they too caught The Bug rendering them disease-free. The whole thing was a bust by 2036. I personally had given up and pretty much retired after our meeting in Bavaria. That was it." Mark said.

"Okay, I'm with you Mark, we thought we might have a breakthrough with DNA engineering, but it was oh so sinister, Mark. What we were thinking of doing, I now believe, was unconscionable. I lost sleep over it for many months, and in the long run, I personally am glad we failed in our efforts. What we as a group were thinking of, well, I'm just glad we all came to our senses," Dana said. "And Mark, let me make it clear, that whatever your theory is, if it even borders on manipulating The Bug's effect on human DNA and causing people to be sick again so we can get back into business, well count me out! I can't imagine where my head was initially to entertain such a plan back in 2036.

"Yes, Dana," Michael Dern of Granger Pharma piped in; Michael Dern was the one and only *Forever Younger* in this illustrious group of seven.

"We were just trying to save your industry and restore the livelihoods of our fellow scientists and the entire global healthcare industry, along with all the rest of the global industries the medical field touches. The Bug had all but wiped out one-third of the world's economy. When you think about it, we only wanted to restore things back to how it was. I, for one, was convinced that we weren't meant to live forever. I liked being in an industry that brought hope to people. I loved knowing the drugs we made at Granger gave people second chances, that we could cure certain types of cancer; I loved being able to put smiles on children's faces. I believe that one must know what suffering is to appreciate your good fortune. The Bug has taken that all away," Dern said.

"Look, back in 2025, I had just turned 40," Michael Dern said and paused for a moment to get everyone's attention.

"I, along with billions of others born after 1980 for some reason, began our age reversal early in our life cycle. Here I am, twenty-two years later; real age 62.

My age reversal kicked in at age 40, back in 2025. I started reversing back to 25 years old. We all know now why The Bug changes us, everyone, not just *Forever Youngers,* back to 25 and then stops there and begins aging us again.

We've discovered that The Bug works on optimum age cycles. Age 25 for both males and females is our optimum physical condition, our strongest point in human development. When The Bug reaches this pinnacle, it starts the process repeatedly, and we all start getting older. The cycle will repeat over and over. For us, *Forever Youngers,* it's 25 to 40 and back again to 25. Right now, twenty-two years later I'm, actually 32 in Bug years. I was 40 when it started; take away fifteen years to bring me back to 25 and add seven to complete the twenty-two years that have passed since 2025, making me 32 years old in Bug years.

I suppose I am one of the lucky ones. I will always be at or near my optimum. In fact, we are 59.2% of the world's population. When The Bug hit us in 2025, the world's population was 8.1 billion people. Today, in 2047, the world was projected to have 9.59 billion, but what's happened instead?

I'll tell you. We were on target to average 140 million births per year or 3.2 billion additional births. Deaths were to average 76.3 million per year over the last 22, or 1.7 billion, netting to 1.5 billion people. But none of that happened. Other than the in-vitro deliveries, really insignificant numbers, there were no births. Of the 1.7 billion who were projected to die, only ten percent died. All of those were due to accidents. That still means we dropped in global population by 170 million. Today the global count is 170 million less than in 2025, bringing our population to 7.9 billion. For 40.8% of our world's population or 3.2 billion people, The Bug doesn't start its magic until they are old, 65 or 70 even. I want to change that. Bug or no Bug, I, as CEO of Granger Pharma, have been pushing my people for the last ten years to find a way to make us all, every one of us *Forever Youngers*. If people are to live forever, wouldn't it be amazing to have us all stay young!" Micheal let that sink in.

"Mark's theory about being in a partnership with The Bug, well, Granger's goals line up perfectly with Mark's description. To bring everyone into Forever Young status would be one form of partnership, and I don't think that's a bad thing.

We at Granger want to make that happen. Even with The Bug now well established, it still sucks getting old. Sure we no longer get sick, but the 60 and 65 year-olds are always looking for ways to look younger, waiting desperately every day for their Bug to kick in. Some can't wait. The stress of waiting and waiting is too much to bear for some people, and they choose suicide.! I want to put a stop to that or help as much as we can. That is our goal at Granger, and I will never ever apologize for joining this group in the hopes of making older people younger again sooner! That might not have been the mission statement for us all, but it was mine," Michael finished.

" So we know now what Micheal's angle on this was. He joined our group in the hopes of finding a way to shorten the aging process and turning that into major profits, I'm sure for Granger. Maybe as a bonus from our collective research efforts, and that's fine. We do have a dilemma, don't we?"Dana commented.

"Michael is right, but like Dana just said, we do

have a dilemma. We ought not to be ashamed for trying to bring things back as it once was. You see, it's not that we want to make the world sick again; the way I see it is we want to take part in making people well again, each and every day, for eternity. Unfortunately for that to happen, people need to get sick, and that is where worlds collide," Mark said.

"No, I didn't have you all fly into my little hideaway here to get you to buy into some lunatic bizarro Dr. Evil plan to make the world sick again, no nothing of the sort. Thankfully we all came to our senses and abandoned such ideas. But I do think I am onto something.

I want to bring your attention to something from that radio show, that Westernman program from which Drs. Fohr and Eavers had to be rushed away. I have the program; I retrieved the recording as it unfolded on the afternoon of 2036. I've listened to it a few times now. You know how sometimes you pick something up, just from someone having said something, it kind of catches your ear. At the time, you don't think much of it, but it somehow occupies a particular slot in your memory banks, staying with you and keep going back to it," Mark was saying,

Everyone around the boardroom table was listening and nodding their heads.

"Well, it finally hit me like a locomotive. No, really, it did; it's something that Dr. Eavers said to Wes Ternman during the show. Mind you, when she said it, it sounded perfectly normal, but it was profound. Foretelling almost and yet such a natural thing to say. It was a comment she added at the end of answering Wes Ternman's question about The Bug, making humans sterile – no more babies. But it only hit me ten days ago. To me, it makes perfect sense, and this is why I have you all here today," Mark said with conviction in his voice. Mark could tell that everyone was on the edge of their seats. He had set them up just right.

"Okay, Dr. Canning, let's have it!" Dana commented.

"And you shall," Mark replied. "Sandi, play Westernman radio talk show program, start in at 49 minutes 22 seconds," Mark added.

"And you know Wes, like I was saying, Dr. Fohr and I, yes, we received the Nobel Prize for our work with DNA. All of it to do with the aging process. Our prize was for the discovery of the CAS9 enzyme to remove damaged genes using Crisper. But The Forever Bug picked up on this tool and mutated to remove all forms of invasive DNA, but Dr. Fohr and I only discovered that just a couple of years ago in 2034. Yes, until just two years ago, we, the world, had no idea how all this was happening to us. We were determined and driven to find out how this was happening. Finally, with the advances in computer sciences and quantum computing power, we hit on it two years ago. In September of 2034, Dr. Fohr and I discovered the mutated H1N1 type of virus now being called The Forever Bug, and in its RNA was our human developed CAS9 Crisper gene hijacked and assimilated as part of its molecular structure."

"Absolutely amazing!"

"So, here we had earth spinning and rotating around the sun for the past nine years, and we humans had no idea why we were becoming younger or shedding all diseases. You and Dr. Fohr discovered the good virus now just two years ago with its stolen CAS9 gene-splicing tool that you and Dr. Fohr had used in gene therapy applications back in 2022! Absolutely amazing!"

"And to button things up, as I said earlier, this is what we can say with assurance. Viruses can and do alter our human DNA. The Forever Bug is proof of that. As much as we understand how this happens, the question of why it happens is still up in the air. Perhaps it happens because it is a form of natural human evolution, a chink in the armor perhaps, or maybe it's a tear in the matrix."

"Right."

"In this case, we stumbled on the way to make us live longer. Some say maybe forever, that, of course, still needs to be seen and tested. We will know more as the years pass."

"Well, okay, but there is the last question I have, and you probably can guess what that is."

"Yes, I can, Westernman."

"Sandi, pause here for a Moment," Mark interjected. "This next part, the next five sentences, is what prompted me to rethink everything. It gave rise to my theory with enough variables coming in line to justify me calling this meeting suddenly. Listen carefully to how Dr. Lillian Eavers anticipates Westernman's question. But especially the last couple of sentences. Her reply to Wes was the game changer for me. See if you pick up on what I think we might have on our hands," Mark said, egging his colleagues on.

"Sandi, resume playback," Mark said.

"You want to know why The Forever Bug robbed us from being able to reproduce, why we can't have babies anymore. The Forever Bug virus has, for all intents and purposes, rendered the human race non-reproductive. Yes, that is the question for the ages, and why that is Westernman, well, that is still a mystery. Perhaps in the years to come, we will have answers or maybe a way around it. We can only hope. We do need babies."

"Sandi, stop playback," Mark then paused and sat looking at his colleagues. He could tell the wheels were turning. He was curious as to who would speak first.

Mark sat silently; the seconds passed by. Mark held out hope that it would be his close friend Dana who picked up on it and was able to marry it with the recent news that had taken the world by storm just ten days ago when Mark first called everyone for this meeting at his Kawarthas hideaway. His colleagues sat in silence for the next twenty seconds or so, and then Dana Blackman spoke.

"Mark, you are a genius; your perception in putting two and two together is marvelous. More incredibly because one half of your equation took place eleven years ago. Yes, in light of the earth-shattering news that took the world by surprise ten days ago, I'm with you on this Mark, totally!" Dana finished saying. Dana then looked around the table at her colleagues, the five men who sat there; they all suddenly clued in, having heard Dana's response.

Mark thought enough time had lapsed and was about to let them off the hook. His presentation this afternoon wasn't an exercise trying to embarrass anyone; it wasn't necessary; Dana did that for him. She was as shrewd as they came. Mark and Dana were on the same wavelength, knowing precisely how to respond. She avoided anyone becoming embarrassed while bringing everyone along at the same time.

"All right, I think everyone is in tune with what I am trying to say. Dana laid it out nicely, but allow me to elaborate and set the markers for my theory," Mark said.

"I'm with you Mark, I think we all are. I really feel you might have something here, but go ahead," Willy Hollman of Pharmacare Health said.

Apparently, Willy was in tune with Dana, Mark thought, *hopefully so were all the others now.*

"Since 2036, there hasn't been one human baby born on this planet, not even the in-vitro babies. The world's supply of human sperm and eggs have all been used. There were only a couple hundred thousand anyway, and in the six years from 2030 to 36, well, the world went through those pretty quickly.

I'm sure there are a few dozen cryo sperm and eggs held in storage by the WHO and CDC, maybe even a few at certain universities and research centers, and that's fine. We know that nothing we can do will prevent those babies, if ever born, from catching The Bug. The thing is that in-vitro babies don't make the news; there is no reason for them to any longer. But an ordinarily conceived human baby, well, well… now that is a totally different situation and one that I assure you will make the news!" Mark said with a tone of revelation.

"Yes, my friends, did you pick up on Dr. Eavers's statement to Wes Ternman? Remember that was back in 2036, in-vitro babies, hell all babies were no longer being born. The human race was at a standstill, and what did Dr. Eavers add to her answer, which I believe she didn't mean to?" Mark posed.

Dana then interjected, "it is now a *eureka moment* to me, now clear as a bell! It's in her last three sentences, she said, *perhaps in the years to come, we will have answers or maybe a way around it. We can only hope. We do need babies."*

"Bingo! Exactly! This is no in-vitro baby!" Mark exclaimed. "I have no doubt in my mind that this baby was conceived lovingly, through intercourse resulting in normal pregnancy and childbirth. Somehow the fact that this baby's development was being kept a secret for the past nine months alone is proof by itself that this is no in-vitro conception! And to find out now that all this was taking place in secret, and only announced through a leak, and then to top it off, it all happened at the Fohr-Eavers Research Center. Well, that's it, it all makes sense," Mark said, feeling vindicated for keeping everyone in suspense.

"But hang on, there is something we are missing. It is staring us in our faces, and yet we are missing it. It just dawned on me as well a few days ago," Mark said. Mark now had everyone on the edge of their seats again.

"We are so focused on the baby that we completely forgot about the parents! I believe the government wants it this way. In-vitro parents never made the news before either, and they didn't make the news this time. It was leaked out that a woman gave birth, but all in-vitro babies are carried to term by mothers or surrogate mothers. I'm thinking the government is either treating this like another in-vitro, or…or something's happened to the parents! You'd think if this was a natural pregnancy, as I believe it was, that the mother and father would be continuously sought after for interviews. But no, they're nowhere to be found, apparently. Something is going on my friends,!" Mark finished.

"Absolutely," Dana added. "Absolutely! Listen up, everyone; back in 2035 or maybe 2036, the last in-vitro baby was born to mankind. What did Dr. Eavers say in 2036 on the Westernman show? She said that perhaps in the years to come, they will have found a way around it or will have the answers. Well, that is precisely what Drs. Eavers and Fohrs have been concentrating on since 2036, enabling humans to reproduce naturally, bug or no bug!. I believe in Mark's theory; that they have done it!" She exclaimed, then added.

"But wait, I believe they have done it, but with exceptional circumstances involved or special conditions, unexpected results may be changes in The

Bug or changes to our DNA that they needed to keep under wraps. Changes that need to be addressed by the government, or better said by the various governments around the globe.

Let's face it, there would be no reason to keep an in-vitro birth secret; there's nothing secret about it, but a natural birth, now that is a game-changer for the world, but I bet it comes with some caveats! Something is going on, and that is what we need to find out! Am I right, Mark?" Dana asked.

"You are absolutely right!" Mark answered loud and clear.

Everyone around the table started shifting around in their chairs and looking at one another. It all made sense. Mark was onto something, and it had the potential to change things in a big way. Changing things not only in Canada and the USA, but this had global implications.

"I'm sure, Drs. Eavers and Fohr were already challenged by the Canadian government to conduct research into bringing back natural childbirth. Let's face it, my dear friends, once The Bug had robbed us of procreation, it would be just a matter of time before humans disappeared altogether, whether we had immortality or not. Eventually, the human race would deplete itself to a few hundred million and over the ages to a few hundred thousand and then perhaps down to Omega man himself," Dana said. Everyone began nodding in agreement.

"Sandi, what was Canada's national population in 2035?"

“According to Stats Canada, the national population in the year 2035 was forty-one million two hundred three thousand,” Sandi answered.

“And what was the population projected to be by today’s date in 2047 if The Bug had not ended all human births?” Mark asked.

“If humans had retained the ability to procreate, the projected population in Canada would have increased to forty-four million six hundred thousand Canadians,” Sandi replied.

“And what is the actual population of Canada today?” Mark asked.

“Since 2035, the national population of Canada has consistently been on a decline. Canada started the year off with forty-one million two hundred three thousand people. Still, by the end of 2035, twenty-four thousand six hundred and two Canadians perished in accidental deaths. Another eight thousand one hundred sixteen deaths by suicide brought the population down by thirty-two thousand seven hundred and eighteen,” Sandi replied.

“And Sandi, what about immigration,” Mark asked.

“All the 196 countries of the world signed a joint United Nations agreement imposing a moratorium on all international immigration,” Sandi replied.

“And why was that?”

"According to the UN resolution, every country wanted to hold onto the people they had. With no new humans being born and only depleting currently held populations on the horizon, immigration was banned worldwide."

"What is the current date population of Canada compared to December 31st, 2035, Sandi?" Mark asked.

"The current population for Canada as of yesterday's date stands at 40,962,000, two hundred and forty thousand less than in 2035."

"What is the projected population for the year 2099?" Mark asked.

"The projected population for Canada on December 31, 2099, is thirty-eight million sixty-two thousand people," Sandi replied.

"In what year will Canada have depleted its population beyond its capability to ensure the survival of the species?" Mark asked.

"In three hundred years, the population will have decreased by fifteen million. The global population will have declined much faster, and it is projected that in five hundred years, planet earth will be void of human beings altogether," Sandi replied.

"So, The Bug that has given us eternal life ends up doing in the human race, is that it?" Ernie asked, almost in disbelief.

"Well, if we stay on the current projection and we have no new babies, no new humans, yeah, that's the sad ending Ernie, our inability to procreate will do us in even if nobody dies a natural death. Eventually, we will all die from some sort of accident or other. Who knows, maybe you will be one of the last remaining humans roaming the empty streets of Bavaria. It's not a pretty picture, my friend." Mark said.

"And let's not even talk about the declining economy. Remember, declining populations mean declining profits and declining incentives. When industries start projecting mega drops in sales, there are bound to be mega drops in jobs as well…the domino effect ensues, resulting in economic collapse. Declining taxes bring on declining services, and pretty soon, it spirals out of control with a potential social crisis, eventually leading to anarchy. Yeah, it's a lot to swallow, but we need to start chewing on this now!" Pausing for a few seconds, then added, "And that is why Dr. Eavers said so profoundly to Wes Ternman, *perhaps in the years to come, we will have answers or maybe a way around it. We can only hope. We do need babies.* Mark then looked around at his colleagues one by one pausing for another few seconds.

"Our mission is to find out how this new baby was born. I'm sure the government will have Drs. Fohr and Eavers keeping a lid on it. They will probably say they're experimenting with a few leftover in-vitro births, but that will be a lie," Mark finished saying.

***

CHAPTER EIGHT
2047

OUR SHOOTING STAR

Dateline: October 4th, 2047
Algonquin Provincial Park Ontario

The first week of October in Northern Ontario brings on a magical time of the year; it was fall. All seven thousand six hundred square kilometers of Algonquin Provincial Park was beaming with fall colors as far as the eye could see. The air was crisp, wildlife throughout the park was busy preparing for the long cold winter, and Wes and Sylvie were on their way to sleep under the stars of Algonquin. It would only be a two-night camping trip with a four-hour canoe paddle down and back up on Costello Creek.

Sylvie was in front of The CHYI Radio building to pick up Wes as he walked out after signing off the Westernman show. Sylvie brought Oscar along. Oscar was only too happy, not that it could actually be satisfied, but was programmed to understand camping. Oscar could be used to gather fallen branches and sticks to build a fire, and most importantly, he could stand to watch guard all night in case a bear decided to check out their campsite. A bear, no matter how big, wild, or aggressive, stood no chance against Oscar. Oscar could turn into the Hulk in a split second if the situation required.

It was just 3:07 PM, and an hour later, they were

already north of Barrie on Highway 11, only two hours south of the park's west gate. Wes and Sylvie sat back enjoying the trip but were engrossed in planning their two-day canoe paddle on Costello Creek. Their car's AI maintained live trip updates on highway conditions, detours, or whatever unusual events their vehicle detected on the way. Traffic turned lighter once they passed through Barrie, and they didn't expect any slowdowns until entering the greater Huntsville area.

"Yes, babe, I had the park two-day camping passes downloaded into the car. We won't need to drop into the visitors' center; we can continue right on to our designated campsite. I bought the *camp-anywhere pass* within our quarter-mile designated radius along the creek," Sylvie said.

"Great, I'm sure we'll find a perfect spot, and we've got great weather this weekend, Sylvie."

"I planned it, Wes, just for you and me, but you know what I love about camping in the fall and winter, Wes? No freaking bugs!" Sylvie added.

"Yeah, I'm with you there."

"I didn't even pack any bug spray this time."

By 9:00 PM, it was pitch black—a moonless night and not a cloud in the sky. Wes had picked a clearing to pitch their two-man tent, and now the wonder was about to begin. This was just not possible in the city. Wes positioned their air mattress to stick out the tent's entrance, and they snuggled together in their made for two sleeping bags. With their heads sticking out of the tent, laying back, they gazed upon the constellations and the milky way.

"Oh Wes, I've waited for this all summer, and now we're finally here; just look at all those stars Wes, just look at that. Oh my God, Wes, it's the most beautiful thing I've ever seen; I never get tired of this, ever!" Sylvie said, gazing at the Milky Way.

Wes just lay beside Sylvie quietly, listening to her and hearing her breathe as they both looked and marveled at the heavens above. Sylvie had something on her mind that she wanted to talk to Wes about, and this was the best possible time and best possible place she could ever imagine broaching the subject. She would do it, here and now beneath the stars.

"Wes, this is 2047," Sylvie said.

Wes wasn't sure what Sylvie was getting at, but he knew something was coming; he replied, "Yes, it is Sylvie, and…?"

"You know I love you with all of my heart, don't you, Wes," Sylvie said, but not asking. She said it more as a statement than a question.

"Of course I do, and you know I love you back with every breath I take," Wes replied. Wes was curious now where Sylvie was going with this.

"Shortly after we met back in 2005, remember two months after that in October, right around this time we camped here in Algonquin, remember hon? I was only

27 back then, and you were just 28. Oh, Wes, how the years have flown by. Here we are forty-two years later. Wes, you're now 70 in whole years, and I'm 69, Wes, neither one of us looks a day over 40. Yeah, The Bug had started making us younger for you almost ten years ago, and I started reversing about six years ago, but we look much younger, Wes. Wes, I don't think I looked this good since I was in my early 40's. And you Wes, well you look like you're in your late 30's Wes," Sylvie said.

"I know, babe, I know, what are you getting at Sylvie?" Wes asked. He then rolled onto his side, facing Sylvie, pulled her in against himself, and kissed her gently on her lips. "Tell me, Sylvie, what are you getting at?"

"We have a second life, Wes, we have a second life! Who knows, we may even end up having a third life!" Sylvie said with a sense of wonderment in her voice. "Before we had gotten married, we made a pact with one another; you remember what that pact was, don't you? And you remember the reasons we decided to make that pact, don't you, babe?"

"Yes, baby, I remember that pact, and I think about it from time to time. I'm not really that surprised you're bringing the subject up."

Sylvie then turned onto her side, facing Wes and bent in to kiss Wes and said, "I love you so much, I love you to the ends of the world, to my dying day, whenever or if ever that occurs," Sylvie then paused for a couple of seconds. "Remember the news back on July the 15^{th,} Wes? You remember, don't you? We brushed it off, back then but there hasn't been another peep about it, Wes. That baby that was born to that lady, that baby, I bet that was a natural baby," Sylvie said, now becoming excited. "We made a pact not to bring a child into this overpopulated world, but things have changed now. The world is being depopulated. Wes, we have a second chance. I'm getting younger; you are too. Okay, I may not have a baby yet; I'm still too old, but in another few years, or even sooner. I feel like I'm 30, I might not look that young on the outside, but maybe I could bear a child sooner than we think. I want a baby Wes, I want a baby, baby!" Sylvie was so excited now that she started crying.

"Oh Wes, I love you so much, and I want a baby!"

"Sylvie, we don't know what is going on. That baby, that baby might have been just another late in-vitro baby," Wes said, trying to calm Sylvie down.

"Maybe, maybe, but what if it wasn't? What if your two friends Drs. Fohr and Eavers, what if they found a way to make us fertile again? What if it was a natural birth? Maybe they found a way, Wes. Why else would this be kept hush-hush?" Sylvie asked.

"Sylvie, Sylvie, you know I love you too, don't you? Don't you?"

"Yes, I know that I know, babe," Sylvie said.

"Trust me, I've been thinking about that too. I've been thinking about no further news regarding that birth; it's extraordinary. I thought by now there should have been an update on the baby's progress, but there's been a total blackout. And you know something, baby, I'm with you on this all the way. Our pact no longer needs to stand. If there is a way for you and me to have a baby, I'm with you, Sylvie. I, too, would love a baby girl or boy, or maybe two or three!" Wes said, turning to Sylvie and kissing her again.

Sylvie was so happy to hear Wes's response that she started crying again, turning in towards Wes, hugging him as tightly as she could, and crying with joy hearing that Wes too wanted a baby with her.

"Sylvie, we can't be sure; it might be nothing, babe, it might be nothing, just an in-vitro kid."

"I bet it's not; I bet those two genius doctors found a way! And our government is keeping it a secret! Why, who knows, but somebody Wes, maybe you, you should try getting to the bottom of it. I think Westernman should delve into this Wes, what do you think?" Sylvie asked.

"Sylvie, I have to tell you, I've been thinking about this ever since the beginning of September. When the news first broke back in mid-July, well, it was news, yeah, and it was special because it happened at the Fohr-Eavers Research Center, and it was leaked! But after that, things went quiet. Because the blackout was still in effect a month and a half later, I started thinking about it more and more. In fact, babe, I spoke to Luke Stenner about contacting Drs. Fohr and Eavers, about doing another Westernman show with them. We got no response from their front office. The two doctors have apparently been muzzled by our government until further notice." Wes replied. "But babe, I only found out last week, just a few days ago, that it's a national security issue, and all further inquiries are being ignored."

"You see, Wes, you see! Something is going on! I just know they've found a way for humans to make babies again; I just know it!" Sylvie stopped for a bit and gazed up into the milky way.

Just then, a bright shooting star streaked across the Algonquin sky, leaving a light trail as it swept the milky way.

"There Wes, there, did you see that? That shooting star? Did you see that, Wes? That was our baby coming to earth, Wes; that is our sign from God Wes," Sylvie said.

"You are a romantic, Sylvie; I'll give you that!" Wes said.

"You know Dr. Eavers and Dr. Fohr. Dr. Eavers even called you and was very gracious, forthcoming even that evening after they had to be helicoptered out to safety. Why don't you call Dr. Eavers yourself? You have her private number. See if she or both of them will talk to you."

"I don't know, Sylvie, it sounds like something I could do. But if it should somehow leak that I'm trying to coerce confidential, national security, secret information from protected sources, we, I, could be in a heap of trouble. Sylvie, even just an attempt could get the show canceled. Our country has passed some pretty strict and crazy laws regarding state secrets and national security procedures since we no longer procreate. Our population is diminishing, and the government is playing things close to the vest," Wes said. "But Sylvie, I promise you this, I will call Dr. Eavers and ask her to come by the house; how's that? I think a private civil visit is still allowed in this day and age. We just need to be very careful, Sylvie. Dr. Eavers might take me up on our offer to invite her over for dinner, but you can rest assured she will be followed and her every move made a note of. We are entering dangerous territory Sylvie, are you sure you want to go down this path with me?"

"Wes, I will follow you down any path you ever walk, and that's a promise!" Sylvie replied, kissing Wes as she straddled him.

Wes looked up into the constellations above Algonquin as their love for one another took them deep into the starry-starry night of passionate lovemaking.

***

CHAPTER NINE

2047

A LEAK

Dateline: October 4th, 3:00 PM 2047
Kawarthas Ontario Canada – Buckhorn Lake – (finishing up)

By 3:00 PM, Dr. Mark Canning had the six members of Bug Chamber pretty much in the palm of his hands. He believed they were all on board with his presented theory so far. In fact, Dana Blackman had bolstered his theory helping to bring the others along. Mark felt he was almost there but still needed something extra; one additional variable to bring home. He was pretty sure he had it. Mark's theory was all based on circumstantial evidence put together through conjecture. His last piece of evidence to be added had to do with the original headline that swept the internet that 15th day of July. Mark had his one final nail to hammer in, and so he went with it.

"That headline on the 15th of July. It went viral on the internet around the globe," Mark said. "But there was something extraordinary about it, wasn't there? Who broke the news? Did we all notice? It certainly wasn't one of the majors, was it? No, it was an online-only news outfit called Urnews. I did some digging, and it turns out they're a small news gathering organization with one little office in Kanata, a suburb of Ottawa. These guys mainly deal with street news and local events. They are so small on the international news scale that they could fit through any crack without being noticed, and I think that's just what they did at the Fohr-Eavers Research Center in Montreal. Someone in that tiny internet news organization has an *in* with either Dr. Fohr or Dr. Eavers, and one of them wanted the news to get out. But guess what, it didn't. It was squashed. But enough got out, just barely enough to create the headline," Mark added.

"What do you mean, Mark?" Asked Stephen Bird of Merit.

"What I mean, Stephen, is this, Sandi, project to screen, baby born to Canadian woman headline of July 15th, 2047. Look at the footer under the headline Stephen; it reads, full story to follow," Mark paused for a moment or two and then said, "There was no full story to follow! The headline broke at 10:12 AM and still no full story that day or any other day since," Mark finished.

"It was quashed. Either that or it was false, and an end was put to it," Dana commented.

"So what are you saying, Mark?" Ernie asked.

"What I am saying is this; it's not false. A baby, in fact, was born. Remember, in-vitro births didn't make the news. The world well understood that there were a few thousand in-vitro births after we all became sterile, so that wasn't news. But having a news story stating that a baby was born in secret and then not following up on it well, there has to be something going on. Also, in-vitro babies weren't even born in secret; they were all celebrated births! The first and last time we heard about that birth was July 15th, and the subsequent news blackout about it has accomplished what it was meant to; everyone just forgot about it. One other thing, Dr. Fohr and Dr. Eavers are nowhere to be seen. No more TV spots, no more interviews, and the end to all news coming out of their research center.

That small online news organization, Urnews.com, out of Kanata, I bet you they've been ordered to keep quiet by the RCMP. Maybe even CSIS, the Canadian Security Intelligence Services, our country's spy agency, has a hand in this. In my opinion, Urnews.com has been muzzled by our government under a national security order. Urnews was small enough, just a handful of reporters for the government to shut them up, all of then.

There is no way the feds could have done that with one of our national news outfits or one of your network news organizations out of the US. They'd have been all over it like white on rice. But Urnews, they probably stopped it dead in its tracks the same day. Threatened everyone with national security violations or whatever scare tactics worked the best. The mention of the word prison probably did it. I bet you they've imposed similar restraints on Drs. Eavers and Fohr as well." Mark finished saying.

The Bug Chamber members sat in silent contemplation.

"That's quite the theory you've put together,

Mark," Dana replied. "It's a hell of a jigsaw puzzle, but you've made the pieces fit. I'm going to need a few days to mull this over. I don't know what anyone else thinks. But if Mark's theory of natural conception proves correct. There will be qualifying circumstances. Perhaps serious enough to affect the evolution of The Forever Bug and our double helix DNA. That, my dear friends, would be reason enough for the RCMP and CSIS to get involved. I know our FBI and Homeland Security would most definitely have their noses in there. I don't imagine your security services up here in Canada are much different when it comes to national secrets," Dana finished saying as she looked around the table at her colleagues.

"The thing is, and it's straightforward, basic even. The news of a newborn, the natural way, would be wonderful news for humanity. People worldwide would rejoice in becoming mothers and fathers once more, holding their bundles of joy. The laughter of little children once again would be the greatest gift to mankind. I think we all agree with that as well. But it seems our government wants no part of it, no part of that joy. We need to find out why it doesn't," Mark added.

"I think one of us ought to contact whoever runs that Urnews organization and see if we can get something out of them," Kieth Shultz of Durham suggested.

"Keith, sometimes the direct approach pays off, but let me assure you, if CSIS and the RCMP have told this news outfit to be quiet, trust me, they'll be scared shitless. Breaking the CSIS order could land them in jail for life, and life now days could mean a few hundred years behind bars. Yeah, they'll keep quiet. Already they are being watched day and night by Canadian authorities; they're just not going to respond," Mark replied.

"You're probably right, Mark, so how do we get to them, how do we find out, and how can we prepare for what may be coming down the pike? If something new is about to happen, I want our company to be prepared, to be ready to go on day one," Keith replied.

"Right, here's what I suggest. First, I don't have the answers; I only had what I presented, that something is up. I think we are all in agreement about that. I think the best course of action now is for us to think about this over the next few days, weeks, maybe months. One of us will figure things out or at least come up with a plan we can test. We can stay in touch via Global Medi-Secure but even on that, let's not talk specifics. If one of us has something solid, we can always call another meeting," Mark said.

"I agree," Dana commented. "What about everyone else?" Dana asked.

All the other five men of The Bug Chamber nodded in agreement.

"All right then, we have something to think about. If major changes in the world are about to happen, my friends, we need to be in the front row when they do," Mark said. "And one final thing, we have what we have or don't have at the moment. It may just turn out that in days or weeks, everything we are seeking to find out may just suddenly land in our laps without any one of us having to raise a finger, but we nevertheless need to stay vigilant." Mark then stood up, indicating a close to this Kawarthas hideaway meeting of The Bug Chamber.

***

CHAPTER TEN
2047

CRISPER CALLED

Monday, October 14th, 2047 – Canadian Thanksgiving Day
CHYI Studios Toronto Ontario Canada

"You've got the Westernman Show this Thanksgiving Monday in Toronto, Canada coming you from above the 49th parallel direct from atop the CN Tower in the land of the free and the greatest city in the great white north and North America; Toronto, Canada. We're broadcasting around the globe on F.M., AM, shortwave, and Globalnet sat-systems. A special shoutout to our Canuck listeners on moonbase 5 beaming at you with laser-line radio," Wes said in his opening remarks for his Thanksgiving day listener audience.

"Today, on this holiday, the Westernman show is thankful for being able to bring to you five exceptional and unique individuals who are here to give thanks. To give thanks for what you might ask? The answer, my dear friends, is to give thanks for their lives. We have with us today from across Canada five people, one of whom appears via 3D full-motion hologram beaming in from Banff Alberta, Canada's premier Rockies resort. Imre Lajos from Banff will occupy the chair directly across from me. His full-body, full-motion holographic image will be coming to CHYI studios via Global sat-systems. I will be able to see Imre perfectly, but I will also see right through him. No, I don't mean as a person, I mean as a person! You get my drift? Yeah, his image is transparent, but I can see him and even put my hand right through him, but I won't, well maybe I will, might be a bit freaky." Wes said. "Today, we have Imre Lajos, Mick Lawson, Jimmy Horowitz, Donna Waltz, and Jenny Chow. I said my guests are unique and that they are. All five of my guests are Forever Youngers," Wes paused and looked across his radio host interview table at his five guests and then said, "Or are they?" He paused again. His five guests looked across Wes's table, smiling and ready to be interviewed.

"Imre, Mick, Jimmy, Donna, and Jenny, I'd like to welcome all of you to The Westernman Show, and I would also like to thank you for coming. I am thrilled you could make it on this Thanksgiving Day to share your stories of thankfulness. If you do so, I am also hopeful that my listeners can take something away from your stories, and we as a nation can be thankful for everything this good earth provides each and every day we walk upon it," Wes said. "Once again, welcome, so let's get down to it," Wes then asked each one of his guests when they were born. "So Jenny, in what year were you born?"

"I was born in 1992," Westernman

"And how old does that make you, Jenny?"

"I'm 25 Westernman," Jenny replied.

“Mick?”

“I was born in 2022, and I am 25 years old.”

“Donna?”

“Same 2022, I’m 25 as well.”

“Jimmy?”

“Born in 1989 Westernman, I’m 32,” Jimmy replied.

“And that leaves you, Imre, in what year were you born?” Wes asked.

“I was born in 1981; that makes me 28,” Imre replied.

“Hang on, if Jimmy was born in 1989, eight years after you, how can you be four years younger? “Explain,” Wes countered.

“Basically, Westernman, I’ve had eight more years to become younger, well four really, but I’ll get to that. I was born in 1981. As you know, The Bug acts differently on those born in 1980 or later from those born before 1980. Us Forever Youngers, we begin our age reversal processes at age 40. So I turned 40 in 2021, but The Bug didn’t kick in until 2025 when I was 44 years old. My reversal cycle started at age 44 in 2025, and for the next 19 years, I kept reversing until I was age 25 in 2044. Having reached my pinnacle year of physical excellence, I started aging again for the next three years to today’s date, 2047, making me 28 years old. And that is how we Forever Youngers live."

"So we actual real ages and years since your birth, along with Bug ages," Wes replied. "Now we've all been living The Forever Bug years since 2025. It's been twenty-two years so far, and for some of us, it's still hard to grasp, especially for the folks out there who haven't started their age reversals yet. All of you are as old as you are straight years. But my guests today are five Forever Youngers, all of them born after 1980 and all of them reversing or will be flipping at age 40, we think. The Bug is keeping all our recently born, young and vibrant. We can thank The Bug for that.

But ladies and gentlemen, let us not jump to conclusions. Yes, it is now common knowledge that anyone born in 1980 or later belongs in the Forever Younger camp, but it is not yet proven that those not having yet reached 40 and are still in their one-directional years will, in fact, start reversing at age 40. We know those who already reached forty have, but those people born after 2025, the year The Bug kicked in, well, we don't know if they too will reverse at age 40; it's only been twenty-two years, and another eighteen to go to find out.

So the human race is waiting, but The Westernman show wastes no time. I wanted to get these Forever Youngers in here and on the record.

"So now the real ages, Jenny is 55, Mick is 25, Donna is 25 as well, Jimmy is 58, and Imre is 66," Wes said.

"Imre, I have to tell you, I can't take my eyes off of you! Your 3D holographic image is mesmerizing. You're sitting there in the chair just like you are in

Banff right now, and yet I can see right through you. It's strange as hell; I guess I'm still not used to seeing a live living ghost. Well, you know what I mean," Wes said. Then he asked Imre, "What are you thankful for this Thanksgiving, Imre?"

The 28-year-old, 66-year-old Imre Lajos then replied, "Westernman, I thank the good lord my every waking moment that I was born long enough before The Bug stopped my wife and me to have my two children. My son Shawn who was born in 2014, is now 33. He will be reversing in seven more years, and my daughter, Sarah, born in 2016, is 31 and will be reversing in another nine years. You know what that means, don't you Westernman?"

"What?" Wes asked.

"It means Westernman that in seven years, when my son is 40, I will be just turning 35. I will still be younger, and two and a half years later, we will both be the same age! He'll be 37 and a half, and so will I. Now ain't that something to chew on!" Imre remarked! "Yeah, Westernman, I am glad I have my two kids, that I am thankful for with every breath I take. I say that because I know how devastated most of the world is today for not having children anymore. Humanity lost its one great joy, giving life, to see ourselves in our children's eyes. That is something we seemed to have lost forever. The Forever Bug took care of that!" Imre said.

"Okay, you're listening to CHYI in Toronto, Canada, and you've got The Westernman show. My guests this afternoon on this special Thanksgiving

Day broadcast are five Forever Youngers. Ladies and gentlemen, if the rest of the program is as engrossing as this first half-hour has been, then we're in for a real treat and revelation. We'll be back in four minutes." Wes said.

He pushed his microphone away from his mouth and said, "Hey guys take a four-minute break. I'll be right back."

Luke Stenner, Wes's producer, then called in on Wes's earpiece. "Wes, there's a guy here outside my door wanting to see you. He says it's urgent and that he has a message for you from Crisper." Luke said.

"From who?"

"He said you would understand, from Crisper," Luke repeated.

Wes thought for a moment. *Crisper? Who…then the bell suddenly rang loud and clear! Crisper! It had to be Dr. Eavers!*

"Okay, Luke, I will be right out."

Wes's heart jumped a beat or two. Suddenly he was taken back to the night under the stars in Algonquin. Sylvie and babies. The whole news story about the secret baby at the Fohrs Eavers Research Center. His heart was racing as he came out to meet this person with a message from Crisper.

Wes stepped out of his Soundbooth and came around to Luke's area where an elderly man, elderly, in these days of The Bug. He might have been 64 or

66 even and hadn't yet started reversing.

There were the few odd-balls, so to speak, born after 1980 for whom age reversal didn't kick in till later years. Most of those were people in tip-top condition, pictures of health from Scandanavian countries. The man was sitting, apparently waiting for Wes.

"Hi, my producer says you're looking for me? I'm Wes Ternman, and you have a message?"

The elderly man, well dressed and looking very distinguished, stood up, did not introduce himself, but reached out and handed Wes an envelope. He then tipped his hat and left without saying a word.

Wes was so overtaken he didn't know what to do, and before he realized what had happened, the elderly man was out the door and gone.

Wes looked around almost as if to check and see if anyone else had witnessed this handover taking place. There wasn't anyone around from the station; it was just Luke and him. Thanksgiving Monday, all the other radio staff were off for the day; even the receptionist was given the day off. Wes was by himself. He opened the envelope and read it. It was handwritten, in cursive on unlined paper.

Dear Wes:

First, my apologies for the dramatics. I had no other way of contacting you without drawing attention to myself, Dr. Fohr, or to you for that matter. Wes, something has happened with The Forever Bug, something big. The story needs to get out; the world must know. But we are in danger. If we were to talk about this, Dr. Fohr and I might never be heard from again. However, the world must know.

You are in the information business, and Dr. Fohr and I trust you. This will be the most incredible piece of news in human history, and you have the chance to break it to the world if you have the courage to meet with us, our group. If you so choose to follow through, just say so on your radio program. On October the 21st, one week from today, on your Monday program, after your program intro, say the words, The air sure is crisper now that fall is here. I will be in touch again with you if you decide to follow up. Either way, destroy this note, not in five minutes. Now!

Lillian - Crisper

Wes's heart was racing. But he did what Dr. Eavers instructed him to do. He was in a semi-state of shock but had the presence of mind to follow through. Wes understood that this was no game.

He also knew that he would have to act totally normal for the next two and a half hours of this Thanksgiving program. Wes only wished this elderly man had shown up at the end of his Westernman show and not the beginning. Wes walked to the men's room, entered a stall, ripped the note into tiny pieces, and flushed it down the toilet. His heart was still racing.

"Okay, we are back! You've got the Westernman show, coming at you....

***

CHAPTER ELEVEN
2047

CANADIAN DILEMMA

Dateline: September 15th, 1:15: PM - 2047
CSIS HEADQUARTERS – OTTAWA CANADA

"I want to make sure that both you and Dr. Fohr understand the severity of these new developments, Dr. Eavers. Are we clear on that?" Prime Minister Peterson asked.

"We are, more than you can imagine, Mr. Prime Minister. The severity is unparalleled in all of human history; we realize how our new findings add another dimension to The Forever Bug's impact on our survival," Lillian Eavers replied.

"Right, but I want to hear it from both of you individually," Frederick Peterson countered. "Dr. Fohr?"

Nigel looked over at his colleague Dr. Eavers. Nigel took a deep breath, exhaled, and paused. Looking back at Canada's prime minister, he then said, "All I can tell you, Mr. Prime Minister is that today, I do. But I'm not sure how I will feel tomorrow. That is the best answer I can give you," Nigel Fohr replied.

"Well, that's not good enough, Dr. Fohr," Prime Minister Peterson replied, then added, "But I suppose it will have to do. I have to admit that is the most honest answer I've heard from anyone for a long time," Peterson added.

"I'm in the same camp as Dr. Fohr on this one Mr. Prime Minister. I understand today, and I am with you on your orders concerning the lockdown. Still, I may have a different feeling on this whole thing as time moves on," Lillian Eavers said. Looking straight at Frederick Peterson and then over at Hal Woods, the Director of Canada Security Intelligence Services, Marsha Collins Commissioner of The Royal Canadian Mounted Police (RCMP), and Beth Richardson, the Honorable Minister of Health, to make sure they all understood her position.

"Look, Drs. Fohr and Eavers, Canadians hold both of you in the highest regard for the work you have done over the years. Your contributions to mankind's scientific knowledge in medicine, epidemiology, chemistry, and biology are acknowledged worldwide. We recognize, not we, the world concedes your invaluable discoveries that have led to our projections of man's longevity on this planet," Prime Minister Peterson said and then paused.

"I also understand and appreciate that you are scientists and not politicians. You operate with different rules and different priorities. Your goal in research is to discover new realities, and you have done that; I understand that. And I'm sure you understand my responsibility as Prime Minister of this country is to appreciate the impact of your new discovery on the people of Canada if this information becomes public," Peterson added and then waited.

"We're on the same side here, Mr. Prime Minister. As scientists, we have a responsibility to ethics and the human race while you, as politicians and leaders of this nation, have the task of organizing it all; we don't. You need to decide how to apply it all to Canadians' lives." Lillian said.

"Lillian and Nigel," Prime Minister Peterson now addressed the two distinguished scientists by their first names to appeal on a more personal level hoping to invoke a direct level of trust. "Let me assure you I was ecstatic when I first heard about the birth of the baby but then became immediately alarmed. The news broke, as you know, through unapproved methods; in other words, it leaked. I'm not blaming you directly, but somehow the Fohr-Eavers research center had a security issue that allowed the information to spread. I became immediately concerned when I saw the news on the internet. We had no choice but to act within the coming hour, locking down all further information from your research center."

Lillian Eavers then cut in, risking alienating the prime minister. "With respect, Mr. Prime Minister, cybersecurity, as well as property-wide surveillance security for the research center, is provided by the RCMP. Dr. Fohr and I have no control over that area," Lillian said, directing her gaze at RCMP Commissioner Marsha Collins.

"Yes, Mr. Prime Minister, we too were unaware of the information leak. It wasn't until Dr. Eavers, and I saw it come through on our personal devices that a baby had been born *in secret* at our facility. We were not yet ready to release any of that news to the public,' Nigel replied.

"Noted," Prime Minister Peterson said. "I instructed Director Woods of CSIS to immediately implement the lockdown of Fohr-Eavers to prevent further leaks. All outgoing communication from your research center was terminated. Fortunately, we were able to cut the information flow before it turned into a raging torrent. Unfortunately, we had to place a complete lockdown on that small internet news organization Urnews.com out of Kanata. Commissioner Collins is still investigating how they managed to infiltrate your research center or come by your discovery. I also appreciate that you acted per procedures in informing Beth Richardson immediately upon your new discovery. And I don't have to add that we prevented a worldwide rush to action and potential calamity. Thank God we caught it in time!" Peterson finished.

Nigel Fohr then spoke up, "Mr. Prime Minister, you did catch it in time for now, but Dr. Eavers nor I can guarantee that this information isn't already out there. Remember, we weren't at the time under any information flow restrictions. Our research results and progress were not meant to be shared with the general public until Dr. Eavers and I was ready to do so. In light of that, there was a breach of protocol. Urnews agency somehow got wind of our work and decided to go public, hoping to win a scoop. But our work and data may already be out there. When I say out there, I mean the scientific community. Yes, we are bound by the rules and laws covering our research in what we can disseminate amongst the international scientific community. Dr. Eavers and I prioritize our discoveries to be cloaked in security measures directly linked to Minister Richardson eyes only protocol. We were preparing to do just that, but unfortunately, the baby's birth was leaked and how that leak happened is still to this day being investigated. Thankfully as you have said, the consequential details have not leaked since you imposed complete information lockdown on our research center, but…" Nigel stopped for a moment, taking a deep breath.

Then with a more appealing tone to his voice, he continued. "Mr. Prime Minister, Director Woods, Minister Richardson, Commissioner Collins, you must also understand that we scientists do not work in a bubble. This type of scientific knowledge, experimentation, research, in general, is a global effort conducted every minute of every hour by research centers around the globe.

The advances and successes at the Fohr-Eavers research center came about because of the global cooperation and information sharing from scientists worldwide. We have benefitted from them, and they have benefitted from us; that is how this is done. No scientific research center is an island in the stream. There are no islands, only flowing information. Sometimes that stream gets blocked with dams. Everyone living along that river of information takes note of the low water level. But when an information tributary flowing into that mainstream is wholly cut off, that tributary being the Fohr-Eavers Research Center, the global scientific community takes note. That is what the imposition of this lockdown has accomplished," Dr. Fohr replied, trying to bring further understanding to the government officials staring back at him.

"Explain, Dr. Fohr," Prime Minister Peterson replied.

"Go ahead, Lillian; you usually can do a better job at something like this than I can," Nigel said, looking at his colleague.

Lillian then took the reins from Nigel. "Mr. Prime Minister, and all you dedicated servants to the Canadian people, what Dr. Fohr has been trying to say is this. Just because the Canadian government has imposed this lockdown on our research center does not mean that we've shut the door on this. In fact, what this has caused is a global mystery to be solved. We've drawn more attention to ourselves by shutting the door than leaving it wide open. This situation presents another problem we and now you will be forced to deal with," Lillian Eavers said. Lillian now sensed an uneasiness descending on the four government officials, including Frederick Peterson.

"Go ahead, Dr. Eavers," Peterson said, nodding his head and motioning with his hands.

Apparently, Lillian had his interest and ear, she thought. "Right, it's been two months since the birth of Baby Alpha. We called her Baby Alpha since this is the first baby to be born on this planet through natural conception since 2030. It was a historical event. But like I said, you can rest assured that things are happening in the scientific community and the corporate world. I mean the pharmaceuticals and the major medical centers that still exist. They're all mainly trauma hospitals and special hospital centers dealing with human to machine interplay. These centers, as you know, mainly address bionic body functions and limb replacements, cerebral interfaces, and the like, but that could all change in the coming years with new hospitals sprouting up worldwide, and that would be both good and bad," Lillian said.

"Now this is what we must and I stress must anticipate in the coming weeks. First, the medical and scientific community out there, much like our research center in various countries, already possesses enough scientific data to put together experiments much like we did. It will only be a matter of time before they arrive at experimentation leading to the same results. Soon enough, the world will have Baby Beta, the second human conceived naturally, and then my dear friends, the cat will be out of the bag, and it will surely be too late, but that's not the worst of it!" Lillian paused again.

"Not the worst of it?" Peterson exclaimed. "What do you mean? Once the cat is out of the bag, it's game over!" Peterson added.

"No, Mr. Prime Minister, the game will be over before that second child is born; born in public, that is," Lillian added emphatically.

"You see, Sir, what will happen is this. Other entities, unscrupulous ones, countries, and organizations out to make money from this will emerge, underground, albeit. Still, it will lead to the human baby black-market industry. This is something RCMP Commissioner Collins knows too well; we are not breaking any news to her, I'm sure. But what it will cause is an acceleration of the population decline, and that we are here to bring it to your attention and offer a warning. You think we have a problem now! This is just the tip of the iceberg Mr. Prime Minister, and I'm afraid there will be many cats out of many bags in the coming few months. Yes, we are the first, but like I say, there is enough information out there already for other smart research centers to duplicate what we achieved," Dr. Eavers finished saying.

"Is that it?" Prime Minister Peterson asked.

"Almost, it," Lillian replied. "It will take time, Mr. Prime Minister, for these other entities, governments, private institutions, maybe even drug companies to find what we've found, yes, it will take time. It might be another few weeks; it might be a few years. With quantum computing power and the right formulas, they will eventually get to discover what Dr. Fohr and I did. What we have on our side right now is time, not a lot of time, mind you, but we do have some," Lillian replied.

Peterson then spoke, "You understand that the new law that came into effect last week was done in the spirit of good faith and for the good of the nation, don't you, Dr. Eavers?"

"I do, Mr. Prime Minister, I do. I hope we find a solution to this dilemma; otherwise, we are doomed and much sooner than we thought. You know it's difficult for a nation to obey laws legislating morality. The government is walking on quicksand regarding legislating ethics and delving into religious domain areas dealing with the right to life and death. When it boils down to it, the only thing we are guaranteed in life is death, and even that has been taken away from us. But now to legislate certain restrictions on procreation, now we've entered a new realm of ethics sure to be challenged by common Canadians," Lillian said.

The Prime Minister then replied, "Governments have legislated morality laws for centuries; it really isn't anything new. The one constant thing about them is that they're always controversial. Yes, I'm talking about Canada and its liberal laws on abortion, which by the way, have never changed. Many other countries in the civilized western world still outlaw abortion, and we may look at that still in the future. God knows we need a law like that if this moves forward. So talking about laws legislating births and deaths, don't forget we had that too, right to death, etcetera, etcetera. Now we will have a law that deals with births, limiting births to what end? Limiting births to limit deaths. When Canadians hear about this and your new findings, we will have entered The Forever Bug's new era. Make no mistake about it. The world will change again." Frederick Peterson said with conviction in his voice.

"I think we as a government have done the right thing, and I believe that Canadians will understand," Peterson replied. "When we lay out the circumstances and the consequences, logic will prevail, and people will calm down. A great amount of faith will need to come into play. I'm wondering at this stage how the religions of the world will take these new findings. With some luck, the United Nations will take our lead and follow suit," Peterson concluded.

"It's going to be a rocky road; that Dr. Eavers and I can assure you," Dr. Fohr added.

"So, we are in agreement then. For now, the lockdown remains, and when the time is right, you and Dr. Fohr will join us in a press conference to announce your findings. At that time, the government will also announce the National Baby Lottery program. The baby lottery program is the only way we can provide a fair and balanced way for Canadians to procreated since it's all tied to and dependent on the number of annual accidental deaths, do we agree?" Prime Minister Peterson asked.

"We do, in terms of practicality, but we have other views on regulating natural human reproduction," Lillian replied.

"Yes, on that basic right, we are of different opinions," Nigel added. "Neither Dr. Eavers nor I believe that a global lottery system on parenting is ethical."

The meeting on Parliament Hill came to a close at 3:17 PM on September 15th. Nigel and Lillian were on their way home. Nigel lived on the campus of McGill University. He caught the hyperlink from Parliament Hill to Montreal and was back home by 4:03 PM. Lillian caught the Hyperlink from Ottawa to Hamilton. By 4:29 that afternoon, she was back home in her highrise overlooking Coot's Paradise. Lillian was only a five-minute bicycle ride away from McMaster University and her lab at Hamilton Health Sciences. With the Fohr-Eavers research center being temporarily under lockdown, Lillian saw no reason for her to remain in Montreal at the center for the next while, at least not until something more was coming down the pike.

It wouldn't be long before that happened.

***

CHAPTER TWELVE
2047

PROBING

Datcline: October 4th, 6:00 PM
Peterborough Aiport - Kawarthas Ontario Canada

"Dana, Dana!" Michael Dern, CEO of Granger Pharma, called out.

Dana was Momentarily startled to hear her name being called. She turned to see who was calling her name, and there in the terminal was Michael Dern, obviously trying to catch up to her.

"Michael, what are you doing here?" She asked as the Granger Pharma CEO finally caught up.

"Oh, I'm glad I got you before you flew out. I actually flew in here, but yesterday, my pilot should be showing up soon but not for another hour. We'll be back in Philly about the same time you land in Nantucket, most likely. But I was hoping we could have a few minutes together before we both flew back to the US."

"What's on your mind, Michael?"

"I thought I would have an opportunity to speak

with you in private before we left Mark's place on the lake, but it just wasn't happening. My next option was to catch up with you here at the airport before flying off back home. Dana, I need a secure place to talk."

"Okay, well, there doesn't seem to be any place around here that I can see," Dana replied.

"No, there isn't, but my plane is just right outside that gate leading to the tarmac just twenty yards from here. My pilot, like I say, isn't scheduled to file his flight plan for another hour. I think that will be plenty of time to tell you what I've wanted to talk to you about all afternoon."

"Well, okay, Michael, but I will have to let my pilot know I will be late. Let me just call him."

"Sure, sure, give him a call," Michael responded somewhat nervously.

"Follow me; my Learjet is just down the hall."

Dana Blackman followed Michael Dern, CEO, onto his Lear.

"I'm going to have a scotch on the rocks. Can I get you anything?"

"No, Micheal, I'm good, so what is it you have for me that you couldn't talk about around the table with everyone else present?" Dana asked.

"Look, I don't blame you for thinking this is a bit weird, but you will understand."

Dana sat in one of the Learjet's swivel chairs across from Michael. She leaned back and nodded. "Okay, go ahead."

Mark, too sat back in his chair, now having calmed down and sipped on his scotch on the rocks. "Dana, you, as CEO of Finacare, oversee the most important and largest health and hospital network in North America, and my company, Granger, as you know, is the king of the hill when it comes to pharmaceuticals and human to machine interface procedures. You know we also manufacture the bionics now for millions of people around the world. Most of the bionic surgeries and interface procedures are carried out at your facilities, from Houston to Philly and Boston."

"Yes, Michael, so what are you saying?"

"What I am saying is that you and I have the most to lose if we're not front and center on this thing. We need to be ahead of everyone else. For one, I only agreed to come to this meeting today to see if I could glean anything from it. Mark confirmed my hunch in a big way this afternoon. But Dana, I was already ahead of him. I already acted months ago; to be precise, I acted on the afternoon of July 15th when the birth of that baby was announced."

"You acted?" Dana asked. "Acted how?"

"And this is what I wanted to talk to you about earlier today but just didn't have the chance until now. You know I have the greatest respect for our colleague

Mark Canning; I think all six of us around that table this afternoon feel the same way."

"Yes, I'm sure they'd agree with you. Mark is a proven leader; I trust him," Dana replied.

"Precisely, precisely, and that's why I couldn't talk about this in the open. I wanted to protect Mark."

"Protect him from what?"

"Dana, the last thing I want is to cast some doubt of any sort on Mark's professional standing, I didn't want to have even the slightest chance of him being involved, so I acted alone to leave him out of the loop. The only reason being that he is Canadian, Dr. Fohr and Dr. Eavers are Canadian, and so is Wes Ternman," Michael said.

"What are you talking about, Michael, Wes Ternman? You mean the radio talk show host?"

"Yes, the radio talk show host, exactly. Listen up, Dana. This afternoon, we agreed that the Canadian government has undoubtedly put the kibosh on any further information coming from The Fohr-Eavers Research Center. Contacting either one of the doctors would be a fool's errand. I'm sure they've been muzzled and will not talk. But not Wes Ternman. He might know something. It's a long shot but a shot worth taking," Michael said.

"Okay, go ahead; where are you going with this?"

"I believe that the two doctors have a relationship

with Wes Ternman, the radio talk show host. Dana, I've listened to his entire program of April 1st when he had Fohr and Eavers on for an hour before they had to be choppered out for their safety. Even over the radio, it sounded to me that there was more than a cordial interview going on there. I believe Wes Ternman has a close relationship with Dr. Fohr and Eavers, an off-air relationship if you will, a trusting one to be specific."

"Yeah, so what, how is that going to help you?"

"Dana, if we are to find out anything before anyone else and be ready to take action, I think Wes Ternman may be our avenue," Michael Dern replied.

"And what makes you think he will talk to you and spill the beans about what his two friends can't talk about?"

"Well, he won't, I know that, but he might give up information without him even knowing that he's' giving it up," Michael replied.

"Dana, I've had him followed ever since the news of the baby broke. If he knows something, I think his activities will expose him in ways he's not aware,"

"You're having him followed? You've been tailing him for two and a half months?"

"Yes, that's right, and I plan to continue doing so until I know for sure there is nothing there," Michael said emphatically.

"And how are you protecting Mark Canning and the whole group by having Wes Ternman, a talk show host, followed since the 15th of July?"

"I'm protecting him because he doesn't know, and neither do any of the others in our group. They cannot be held responsible for something they don't know anything about. You see, Dana, if I would have suggested this course of action back when the news of the baby's birth broke, Mark would probably have agreed that it was a good idea if not the only view we had at the time. I think that he would have initiated this himself, possibly placing himself in some serious jeopardy with Canadian authorities. I need not worry about such things, I'm American, and I hired my surveillance people without Canadian involvement.

Dana wasn't so sure that Mark would have agreed about having the talk show host tailed. Dana's trust for Michael Dern had just taken one step down on the ladder of integrity. *If he was having Ternman followed, who else was he having followed?* A sour taste was starting to develop in her mouth. "Michael, what made you think that I would be on board with this?"

"Honestly, Dana, I didn't think you would be, just as you are hesitating now; I anticipated your initial reaction, but let me explain further. I believe you will see the logic and value of my approach," Michael added.

"All right, Michael, I have to admit you are convincing, but I need to hear how you intend to close this sale before I decide to buy in."

"Here it is, Dana. Should my persistence pay off and Wes Ternman's actions prove valuable, we could both benefit one another through our joint cooperation to move on the information. We may need to build the infrastructure to meet whatever comes down the pike in drug production, facilities upgrades, staffing requirements, and general medical preparedness buildup. Dana, my first priority as CEO of Granger Corporation is to remain number one in the industry. Part of that responsibility requires me to minimize my competitors' impact on our industry. In other words, I need to form partnerships that will benefit my company going forward. I choose to stay with your company, hopefully enhancing our positions. There would be no need for me and you to waste time explaining how I acquired the information. You would already know that the advanced information and knowledge were credible, and we could act in unison. Do you see now?" Michael asked, waiting for Dana's reaction.

"Okay, Michael, you closed the deal with me. Except for one caveat."

"Whats' that?"

"It's two parts. First, this conversation never happened, and second, with your thugs following Mr. Ternman, you better make absolutely certain that no harm comes to him or any of his family members. Do you understand me?" Dana Blackman replied. "I can also tell you this, Michael, that what you are doing and have been doing so far as I can tell is not illegal. So I personally have no stake in this game when it comes to illegalities, but I do have to tell you that it leaves a nasty taste in my mouth nevertheless."

"I understand, Dana, but if I find something of value, and I come to you for cooperation, you will know where I'm coming from, and I will have the ability to prove it," Michael replied.

"What I don't like about this is the undercutting of the rest of our group Michael. I feel like you've gone rogue on them, and now I'm suddenly part of it. I'm not happy about it, but now that I know about it, there's not much I can do, is there?"

"I don't mind pulling the rug from under my competitors if I must to remain on top. But don't worry, Dana, it's possible and most probable that nothing will come of this. It's a long shot, Dana, but I think Mr. Ternman at this stage is our best hope."

"All right, Michael, I had no idea you could be this ruthless. We'll play this out, but only because so far, nothing illegal has taken place. And if that changes, I'm out," Dana replied reluctantly. "Are we done?"

"Yes, we're done, have a great flight back to Nantucket," Michael said and showed Dana off his Lear.

***

CHAPTER THIRTEEN
2047
SPY NOVEL

Monday, October 14th, 4:15 PM - 2047 - Canadian Thanksgiving Day
Toronto Ontario

The air sure is crisper now that fall is here. Wes must have run those words repeatedly through his mind a dozen times on his way home from the radio station. *One week from today; Monday's show, October 21st.* He wasn't quite sure how he'd break the news to Sylvie, so he waited till bedtime.

"You know Wes, I have to tell you, babe, you've been acting a little strange since you've walked through the door this afternoon," Sylvie said as she lay beside Wes in the darkness. She then turned onto her side, facing Wes, gently caressing his face. "I caught some of your show this afternoon. You seemed to dial it down a notch or two after the first half-hour. Are you feeling all right, Wes?"

Wes then turned onto his side to face Sylvie in the darkness. "Sylvie, something happened today during the show," Wes said softly.

"What do you mean," What happened, Wes,

something bad?"

"Remember I told you that I would call Dr. Eavers? I promised you up in Algonquin."

"You called Dr. Eavers, Wes, and something bad happened?"

"No, Sylvie, I didn't call; she called me. Well, not really, she sent me a message Sylvie, through a messenger."

"What, you mean a person, a real messenger person, not the app?"

"That's right, a strange guy, an older gentleman, very distinguished looking, sharply dressed, showed up at the station today asking for me. During my first break, Luke told me that a guy was waiting for me with a message from Crisper."

"From Crisper?" Sylvie thought for a moment, then said, "Isn't that what Dr. Eavers and Fohr were talking about on your program way back about DNA and stuff?"

"Yeah, it was a codeword Sylvie so that I would meet this strange person. So when I went out to meet him, he didn't say a word to me; he just reached out his gloved hand and passed me a note. While I was looking at the note, he disappeared out the door…vanished!"

"Ho…lee," Sylvie whispered; this is like right out of a spy novel! What was in the note?"

"Trouble Sylvie, trouble," Wes replied.

"Wes, I need to see your face, trouble, what sort of trouble?" Sylvie sat up and said, "Oscar, light on!"

The bedroom light came on instantly as Sylvie instructed Oscar.

Wes then sat up cross-legged, facing Sylvie and grabbing her by the shoulders, "Babe, this is serious. Remember I said that calling Dr. Eavers might have some risk? Well, it does. The only difference is that she contacted me before I contacted her, but she's given me a way out if I so choose."

"Is this to do with us being able to maybe have a baby? Is it Wes, is it?"

"I don't know, I don't know Sylvie. Look, here's what was in the note. It said that something has happened with The Forever Bug, something big. The note said that the story needs to get out; the world must know. If Dr. Eavers or Fohr were to talk about it in the open, they might never be heard from again, and they would be in danger. The note said that they trust me, and I could be in a position to break the most incredible piece of news in human history.'

"What are you going to do, Wes? This is unbelievable! You were right, you were right! You said up in Algonquin that if you called, we'd be walking a dangerous path. State secrets and the whole ball of wax Wes. These two world-famous doctors, they believe in you, Wes, they believe you can spread the word of something incredible that they're not allowed to talk about."

"Sylvie, I've been thinking about this all day. I know their note said that they would be in danger, but she didn't indicate anything about me being in danger. Babe, my radio program hasn't been muffled or imposed with restrictions. It's still free speech here in Canada, and unless I'm told by the RCMP or CSIS that I can't talk about something, well, I'm going to talk about it! One more thing, I'm confident that neither Dr. Eavers nor Dr. Fohr would jeopardize my safety. I just don't think they'd put me up to anything illegal without warning me about it first. My concern, babe, is that my actions will get them in trouble, but I bet you they've figured out that part too."

"So what are you going to do, Wes?"

"The note said that if I wanted in, I need to say a special phrase next Monday right after my intro statement for the Westernman show. They'd be listening, of course, and if they hear me say the phrase, I guess that will be confirmation that I'm in, and they'll contact me again."

"Okay, so what's the special phrase," Sylvie asked with wide eyes.

"The air sure is crisper now that fall is here," Wes said.

"Are you going to say it?"

"I will say it, but only if you're on board with this

babe. You know we could be on that path to the unknown and danger,” Wes replied.

“Yeah, and a baby!” Sylvie added.

“All right then, babe, I will reply, telling the doctors that I’m in, and hold on tight, Sylvie, we may be in for the ride of our lives!”

<><><>

Dateline: Monday, October 21st, 12:00 PM – 2047
Toronto Ontario – CHYI Radio Station

“You’re listening to Wes Ternman, and you’ve got the *Westernman* show coming at you from above the 49th parallel direct from atop the CN Tower in the land of the free and the greatest city in the great white north and North America; Toronto Canada. We’re broadcasting around the globe on F.M., AM, shortwave, and Globalnet sat-systems. A special shoutout to our Canuck listeners on moonbase 5 beaming at you with laser-line radio.

Well, here we are well into October already. I’m noticing the trees around Toronto are vibrant with color. The air sure is crisper now that fall is here.”

At 12:04 PM, just four minutes after Wes opened his show, Luke Stenner spoke into Wes’s earpiece.

“Wes, that guy from last week is here again. He said he’d wait till your first break.”

Wes wasn't expecting this immediate response. Wes did something he rarely ever does. After his program lead-in promo, he went to a two-minute commercial break and stepped outside his sound booth. It was the same gentleman, the elderly well-dressed man, just like Luke said. Wes was about to say something when the man raised his hand, then motioned, waving Wes's effort off. Once again, he reached out with a gloved hand, passed an envelope to Wes, tipped his hat, and left the building.

With envelope in hand, the tension and curiosity were overwhelming, but Wes stood his ground. He folded the envelope and placed it into his jeans front pocket where he knew it wouldn't be pulled out accidentally. Wes would wait till the show was over and open the envelope with Sylvie back home.

"Okay, we're back; you've got the Westernman show coming at you!"

The next three hours were the most challenging hours of radio Wes had ever had to endure in his thirty-eight years as Westernman.

***

CHAPTER FOURTEEN
2047

ICELAND

Dateline: Monday, October 21st, 4:03 PM, 2047
Toronto Ontario-The Ternman Home

Once again, Wes was torn on his way home. Torn between reading the note now or waiting to open it with Sylvie. He chose to just hang in, get home, and open it together. Wes well understood that this second note would need to be destroyed but not having read it yet, he told himself he could not yet know that for sure. Wes could hardly wait to get home. He knew Sylvie would be on pins and needles waiting for him.

It was 4:03 PM when Wes finally walked through the front door of his home in Lawrence Park.

Sylvie was so anxious for Wes to get home, she was counting down the minutes. When Wes walked in, Sylvie was waiting.

"Wes, I've been beside myself all afternoon. I don't know how you can take the waiting and all this cloak and dagger stuff. It's driving me crazy, and I'm just a witness to this; you're the real participant, God, I'm so glad you're home. Did anything happen today after you said the phrase?" Sylvie asked as Wes walked in.

"Trust me, I've been on pins and needles all day long as well. Yeah, something happened, like almost right away. That guy from last week, well, he showed up like a minute after I did my opening promo and then added that phrase, *the air sure is crisper now that fall is here*," Wes replied.

"Yeah, I heard you say it, Wes, you worked it in just right."

Being able to talk to Sylvie was a massive weight off Wes's shoulders. Wes started to calm and reached into his jean's pocket.

"I brought the envelope he gave me home, babe. I wanted to open it with you," Wes said.

Sylvie just stood looking at Wes and suddenly covered her mouth in a shocking response. "Oh my God, Wes, you have the note with you?"

"Yeah, it's right here," taking the envelope out of his pocket and unfolding it. Come on, let's sit down and see what it says," Wes said, walking over to the living room couch.

"Oscar, make me a vodka tonic with lemon on ice, Sylvie, want a drink?"

"I think I better join you in this one, yeah," Sylvie replied.

"And a glass of merlot for Sylvie," Wes said.

"Coming right up," replied Oscar.

"Okay, let's see what's in this envelope," Wes said, sitting down.

Just as Wes was about to open the envelope, Oscar was over with Sylvie's merlot.

Sylvie took it from Oscar, saying, "Thank you, Oscar,"

"You're welcome, Sylvie."

"You don't have to thank him, you know, he's a robot," Wes said.

"Yeah, I know, but he's kind of become like a person around here now, you know?"

A moment later, Oscar was back with Wes's vodka and tonic. Wes reached up and took it from him, saying, "Thanks, Oscar,"

"You're welcome, Wes," Oscar replied.

Oscar then walked back to an out of the way spot, faced Wes and Sylvie, bent his head down, and assumed his ready position.

"You see!" Sylvie said, nudging Wes. "Open it already!"

"All right, here we go."

Wes then opened the envelope and took out the

note.

Wes cleared his throat and started reading it out loud, with Sylvie sitting beside him. Sylvie sipped on her merlot, with her right arm wrapped underneath Wes's left arm. She snuggled in close to his side. Wes read and held the note so Sylvie could read along with him.

"Dear Wes,

We are glad that you have decided to take this next step. Dr. Fohr and I have been temporarily silenced by our government. Our new discovery concerning the Forever Bug is of such magnitude that it has the potential to bring great joy to the world. But there are problems associated with this potential global revision of humanity. Much will depend on how various cultures, religions, and social practices react to this new development. Dr. Fohr and I have been prevented from talking about our discovery. But there is a way. The Fohr-Eavers Research Center has a sister lab located in Reykjavik, Iceland.

We've been working closely with our sister lab over the past twenty years, sharing research that has led us to our recent discoveries on The Forever Bug. Dr. Helga Karlsdottir and Dr. Ragnar Stefansson head up the Reykjavik lab. They've mirrored all of our processes and procedures that we've conducted at the Fohr-Eavers Center. For many years, we've been doing this as a verifying entity to retest and independently confirm everything we do here in Canada. Drs. Karlsdottir and Stefansson are fully aware of our situation here concerning the lockdown and termination of information flow. We cannot disclose our findings at this time until we receive a release from our government. That, however, is not the case in Iceland. There is no information blackout there. You may be wondering why they cannot just go ahead and release the new findings on the Forever Bug themselves and be done with it. They cannot because the Canadian government is laying claim to the information.

You see, the Fohr-Eavers Research Center is a government-funded medical and research center. Therefore, Canada's government is trying to claim patent rights to all discoveries made by Dr. Fohr and me because, to some degree, we work for the government. Our labs at McMaster University in Hamilton and McGill University in Montreal are also government-funded.

The problem is that the courts have ruled on these patent issues in the past. They've always ruled against medical procedures being patented. But our government claims that medical methods accomplished through quantum computing are patentable because proprietary software used in achieving the medical procedure was developed through their funding. Until this is sorted out, we are in lockdown. The lab in Iceland cannot announce a discovery made by Canadian scientists and patents potentially owned by Health Canada.

But the patent thing isn't the main reason the announcement of our discovery cannot be made at this time. Our Prime Minister feels that it would bring about a worldwide calamity, a rush to having babies by millions of couples clambering to get pregnant."

"Oh, Wes!" Sylvie suddenly said. "Wes, we can have babies!" Sylvie exclaimed with excitement.

"Hang on, Sylvie, there's more here; hang on, babe, we're jumping to conclusions. I don't think it's that simple."

Wes knew that Sylvie couldn't control her sudden excitement after hearing that the world could have babies again, so he understood her premature reaction.

"Let me read the rest of this; it's not sounding good, babe."

Wes continued reading…

"That would prove devastating to the global population by accelerating its decline. Yes, you read that right; having babies would accelerate the population decrease. You are asking why, no doubt. That is the part Dr. Fohr, and I cannot discuss, but Dr. Karlsdottir and Stefansson, well, they can discuss it a length. If you want to find out why and tell the world about it, then do the following.

Wes, we want you to fly to Iceland, to the Reykjavik lab, and meet with the two Icelandic doctors. They are waiting for your arrival. This coming week you will receive an official invitation from Drs. Karlsdottir and Stefansson to come to speak with them. The invitation will state that they have some independently verified news concerning The Bug, and they'd be honored if you'd have them on your program as you did with Dr. Eavers and Fohr several years ago. You can consider it as a Westernman special on-location report from Iceland.

Fly out on Icelandic-Supersonic Air next Saturday morning. The flight leaves Toronto International at

11:11 AM, arrives in Reykjavik six and a half hours later, but with a five hour time difference. The flight itself is only an hour and a half long. You arrive just before 5:45 PM Reykjavik time. Drs. Karlsdottir and Stefansson will both meet you at the airport. They will take you to their lab, where you will learn everything you need to know. They will answer any and all of your questions. You will be staying overnight at a facility they have at their lab. You fly out Sunday morning at 11:AM Reykjavik time, arrive back in Toronto an hour and a half later, 7:30 AM, with the time difference.

And finally, to answer a question that might be swirling around in your mind, "why are we doing this? The answer is that Dr. Fohr and I do not believe any government entity, in this case, our Canadian government has the authority or the right to regulate human evolution. Suppose we have regained our God-given ability to naturally conceive. In that case, we should not be denied this fundamental human right no matter what the possible unexpected circumstance might be, and that will be revealed to you by Drs. Karlsdottir and Stefansson.

We will be in touch. Fly safe.
Lillian and Nigel (Crisper)

***

CHAPTER FIFTEEN
2047

REYKJAVIK

Dateline: Saturday, October 26th, 2047
Toronto Ontario

Like every other morning since July 16th, one day after the baby-birth leak, Brad Sommers and his partner Rod Quinn had been waiting and following Wes's every move outside of his and Sylvie's Lawrence park home. It was no different this 26th day of October, Saturday. Their surveillance on Wes was 24/7 for the past 102 days. An overnight team kicked in at 9:00 PM every day for their 12-hour shift. Not much noteworthy ever happened during the late shift. Wes and Sylvie were pretty much homebodies. Mr. Dern of Granger Pharma saw no need to have Mrs. Ternman followed; the target had always been Wes.

In the 102 days since Brad and Rod's P.I. contract with Mr. Dern, there was only one time for two nights back in early October that their surveillance was broken. That was the two-day canoe trip to Algonquin. Rod and Brad managed to follow them through the west gates into the park, but they were forced to break off after that. There was no way they could have followed them to their campsite. In fact, there were a few ways in which Wes could break surveillance without him even knowing it; one was a camping trip.

Brad and Rod were experts in their craft. They knew well how to avoid detection in their daily pursuit of Wes Ternman. Changing vehicles every day was a requirement for one. Staying well behind two or three cars was the rule. Rod had tagged Wes's and Sylvie's vehicles right at the beginning of their agreement with Mr. Dern. Even if Rod lost sight or contact with Wes's car, they'd always be able to catch up; their tag tracker would bring them back in line. It was most helpful if there were turns involved in Wes's destinations.

It was 9:03 AM Saturday morning; Rod and Brad had just relieved their overnight surveillance team. This was no ordinary surveillance setup. Staking out a residence for days and weeks on end, waiting in cars wasn't going to work from street level. Soon residents along the street would take note of strange overnight vehicles, and when winter seasonal parking restrictions kicked in, their methods would need to change. The negative surveillance variables were many, and Cumberland P.I. pointed out the weaknesses that would need to be overcome to avoid suspicion of the surveillance teams camping out on Wes's front door. One month after Cumberland P.I. services started watching Wes's home, Michael Dern solved the street level surveillance problem by purchasing two homes opposite Wes and Sylvie's house. The two homes Michael Dern purchased he then set up as short term corporate executive housing. This then provided the opportunity to keep watch on Wes's comings and goings 24/7 with the ability to engage in pursuit should Wes decide to leave the house.

On this day, Rod and Brad watched and waited for something to happen. At 9:10 AM, a taxi drove up in front of Wes's house.

"Rod, a cab just pulled up to the house," Brad said to his partner as he surveyed Wes walking out his front door.

"Now Rod, we're outa here, the game is on," Brad said to his partner. "Looks like our pigeon is on the move with an overnight bag," Rod and Brad were in their vehicle and two cars behind Wes's taxi.

"He's got to be heading to the airport if he has an overnight bag," Rod commented to his partner.

"I think you're right; that would be my bet."

Rod and Brad followed Wes's cab as it arrived on the departures level of Pearson International. The cab pulled over to let Wes out.

Brad pulled up just ahead of the cab. Rod would follow Wes into the terminal while Brad parked the car.

"I'm on him Brad, he's by himself so far, hasn't met up with anyone," Rod spoke into his watch.

"All right, I'll be right there, just a couple of minutes away."

"I'm staying back; I know where he's going. He's checking in at the Icelandic Air counter."

"Iceland! What the fuck?" Brad replied.

"Yeah, this sure as hell is a curveball!" Rod replied.

"It'll be probably five or ten minutes; he has a few people ahead of him."

"Well, we're fucked. Look at the departures board," Rod spoke.

"Yeah, I see that, Icelandic Air – Supersonic! 11:11 AM to Reykjavik."

"I have to call Mr. Dern," Rod replied.

"Yeah, you better, this is big!"

Michael Dern down in Philadelphia wasn't expecting any calls from Rod at all, especially on a Saturday. He took the call immediately.

"Michael Dern."

"Mr. Dern, Rod Quinn, Cumberland P.I. here."

"Yes, what have you got for me, Rod?"

"Our pigeon is about to fly, sir," Rod replied.

"Okay, and where is he going, do you know?"

"Well, sir, Brad and I are watching him check in right now at the Icelandic Air counter. He is flying out in an hour to Reykjavik, Iceland!"

"I see," Michael replied.

There was a silence for a while.

Then Rod asked, "Mr. Dern, are you there?"

"Yeah, I'm here. There's a Learjet Charter outfit at the Toronto Airport. I can have a charter ready within the hour," Dern replied.

"No, Mr. Dern, that's not going to do it. The Icelandic Air flight is supersonic. The flight time from Toronto to Reykjavik is only an hour and a half in duration. He'll be in Iceland four hours before we would, even if you could charter a Lear in the next hour. I'm afraid we'll lose him as soon as he boards," Rod replied.

"Yeah, yeah, you're right, I forgot about the supersonic service, damn!"

There was another twenty seconds or so of silence on Michael Dern's end.

"All right, leave it with me, for now. But I want you to be at the Toronto Airport for every arriving flight from Iceland in the coming days. I want to know exactly when he gets back to Canada," Dern said.

"Yes, we will be here for all incoming flights, that's so long as his returning flight is to Toronto," replied Rod.

"It will be; I just checked. All flights between Canada and Iceland originate and terminate in

Toronto," Michael replied.

"No, I get that, Mr. Dern, but from Iceland, he may fly out to some other destination, like someplace in Europe, and be returning to Canada from Paris for all we know," Rod said.

"Probably not, since he has a radio show to do on Monday; just hang tight at the airport over the weekend for arriving Icelandic Air flights."

"All right then, Mr. Dern, we're on it," Rod replied.

Well, that was it! Iceland! Michael Dern thought. As soon as Rod told Michael where Wes was heading, Michael knew immediately that he'd been right all along to have Wes followed. Medically speaking, specifically drugs research and facilities, Iceland was no Mayo Clinic or Harvard. It was still famous for one very highly specialized facility, and that was the Ultra Deep Virus Repository (UDVR, pronounced as *Oodvar*) outside of Reykjavik. The general public had no idea it even existed, but the scientific community and drug companies knew it well.

The repository is similar to the Doomsday Vault on Spitsbergen Island, part of Norway's Svalbard archipelago in the high arctic. It is dubbed the Doomsday Vault because it holds the world's most extensive collection of agricultural biodiversity. It is a seed safety deposit box deep within a mountain, storing more than 900 thousand food crop varieties. If there ever should be an apocalyptic global catastrophe and mankind survives, agriculture could be restarted. The facility in Iceland is thought to be the world's most secure repository vault for virus storage. Every known virus ever discovered has a copy stored deep in an underground vault some 500 meters deep bored into Iceland's granite. It is considered to be the safest biohazard storage facility on earth. Part of the vault storage complex has a smaller ground-level research center with the state of the art facilities and computing power.

After ending the call with Rod, Michael whispered to himself, "That had to be it, and Wes Ternman was heading to the Ultra Deep Virus Repository."

Icelandic Air – Supersonic, touched down in Reykjavik right on time. 5:45 PM. The sun had just set ten minutes before Wes arrived in Iceland, so he couldn't see much from the air coming in. The airport was 31 miles from Reykjavik city center, but Wes wouldn't be going to town on this trip. This wasn't a sightseeing or shopping trip. Wes's future career in radio may well hang in the balance of what was to occur this evening. He wasn't really sure what to expect.

Having been cleared through customs, Wes exited into the arrivals terminal section, and the first two people he laid eyes on; a man in his 50's it looked like, and a woman in her 40's maybe. Wes wondered if either one had begun their age reversals yet. The man and woman were holding a sign positioned between them that read, *Crisper*.

Seeing the Icelanders holding the Crisper sign, Wes couldn't help thinking back to what Sylvie had said; *this is like right out of a spy novel!*

Wes approached the two smiling Icelanders.

"Dr. Karlsdottir, Dr. Stefansson?" Wes asked.

"Yes, yes, welcome to Iceland, Wes, please call me Helga; this is my husband Ragnar, we are pleased to meet you!"

Suddenly Wes felt good; he felt relieved. Dr. Karlsdottir and Dr. Stefansson seemed so genuine and disarming. Even in the first fifteen seconds, there was a certain Icelandic warmth emanating from them both.

"And I am very pleased to meet you as well Helga, Ragnar, a pleasure, I'm sure," Wes replied.

"Our car is close by. Do you need a few minutes, perhaps before we continue on? Restroom maybe?" Ragnar asked.

"Yes, as a matter of fact, if you don't mind, I will leave my bag here and just let me freshen up. I will be right back," Wes said.

Wes hit the men's room, degreased, and was back in three minutes. Having washed his face and then cooling off with ice-cold Icelandic water had him invigorated. The flight had only been an hour and a half, and he was in Iceland. *Wow,* Wes thought, *I wonder what the next few hours hold?*

"We are going to the facility directly. I'm afraid you will not have time to do any exploring around

Reykjavik this time since our schedule is so tight, Wes," Helga said. "Is this your first time to Iceland?"

"Yes, my first visit and most unexpected, I must say."

"Well, the world is full of unexpected developments. We discover them often in our line of work," Helga replied.

"It will be about just under an hour to the facility. We will drive by the outskirts of Reykjavik and another fifteen minutes or so to Mosfellsdalur, a smaller town," Ragnar said, then started laughing.

"Smaller town, ha! Reykjavik is already a smaller town! Its population is only one hundred thirty thousand—nothing like Toronto or even Halifax. But we are unique! Reykjavik and Iceland hold many treasures. You know Wes, 100% of our electrical power needs are provided by renewable energy. Hydropower and geothermal power. Iceland burns no fossil fuels. Now that all transportation is battery-powered, we maintain the world's least carbon footprint per capita. Oh, and of course, we have the whole reason for your visit," Ragnar added, looking straight at Wes sitting across from him and Helga.

"You know Wes, Ragnar, and I have been fans of your radio program for many, many years. You have a big following here in Iceland. Ragnar and I might not catch your show every day fully, but we usually have it on playing in the background. You have the most interesting guests. We really like your program because you don't let anyone get away with funny stuff. If a politician or perhaps a leader of industry tries skirting around your question with unclear answers, you call them out!" Helga said. "And good for you!"

"Yes, yes, last week, I believe on Wednesday, right Helga? You had that Ambassador fellow on your show from North Korea, what was his name again…ah Ambassador Kim Choi, yeah that was the guy, Choi. Honestly, Helga and I couldn't understand why he agreed to come on your program. Eventually, after you'd had enough of Choi's B.S. when he denied the mass graves and had no explanation for the labor camps, you kicked him off your show; we loved that! He must have known that he'd be in hot water for not answering your questions!" Ragnar said.

"Yeah, a few days after I had that murdering bastard on my show, my producer told me he was called back to North Korea and replaced with a different North Korean ambassador to Canada. I'll never understand why Canada decided to establish diplomatic relations with that country. I figured that things would change after Kim Jong-Un's rule, but I guess prison camps and forced labor for dissidents still go on there."

Hearing Ragnar and Helga going on about the Westernman show really surprised Wes; they were fans! Now he was even more relaxed; this territory was becoming friendlier and friendlier by the minute. He was drawn to Helga and Ragnar. But then again, it was only human nature to feel being flattered by people who like what you do.

"Well, here we are, Wes, welcome to *Oodvar.* UDVR Wes, Ultra Deep Virus Repository. Our lab, our home, our offices, and the administration center and visitor accommodations are all located in the main building, in five separate wings," Helga said.

"Ragnar will get you settled in, show you to your suite, and we can meet in our dining room for dinner just after that, say in fifteen minutes?"

"Sure, that'll be fine."

"Ragnar and I were toying with the idea of introducing you to some traditional Icelandic cuisine, but to be honest, it's probably not something you would have gravitated towards," Helga said.

"So, we're not going to subject you to those delicacies this evening," Ragnar added. Then laughingly said, "Unless, of course, you're fond of horse and fermented shark."

"Okay, I think I might want to pass on that," Wes replied, with a smile and a grimace.

"But I think you will enjoy a few of our other traditional main dishes. We have delicate langoustine Icelandic lobster and pan-fried salmon steaks as the main course," Helga said reassuringly.

Dinner conversation was mainly about Wes's career and his radio talk show, his public life in Toronto with Sylvie. The conversation was not all on Wes's side of the map; Helga and Ragnar talked about life in Iceland, their careers, and how Ragnar had started age-reversing six years ago when he turned 61.

He was 55 now in Bug years.

Helga was 47 in real years and hadn't started her reversal yet; she was still a good 16 or 17 years from beginning her Bug years.

"It will be strange for us, Helga said; when I'm 63 or 64, and my Ragnar will have reversed by then to 38, I will look like I could be his mother! Maybe he will look for someone younger!" Helga added, nudging Ragnar.

"Well, my mother was 71 in 2025 when she started her reversal, and look at her now! She's 49 in Bug years and looks younger than I do! My God, things are really all upside down all over the world! Ragnar commented.

"Come, Wes, let us relocate to the library and talk about why you are here in Iceland," Ragnar said. "Cognac Wes, schnapps, or perhaps a glass of port?" Ragnar offered.

Helga entered the library holding a cognac glass, smiled at Wes, and took a seat in one of the three French provincial style high back chairs placed around a Spurlin claw coffee table.

"Okay, that sounds nice, a glass of port, please, Ragnar," Wes replied.

"Absolutely; I will join you in a glass of port as well."

The three of them clinked glasses.

"Once again, welcome to Iceland," Ragnar said.

"I must say, Ragnar and Helga, I couldn't have pictured a more friendly, inviting environment to speak with you. This room is perfect. The warmth from the fireplace is most calming. Your invitation for my visit to Iceland was to interview the two of you on the breaking new discoveries about the Forever Bug, so let me grab my audio recorder, and we can start."

Wes was back in a minute with his autonomous recording device, placed it on the coffee table between the three of them. "Okay, we're all set. I'd like to conduct this talk not so much as an interview but rather like a normal fireside chat. I will probably end up playing it in its entirety on The Westernman show. Allow me to make a brief intro, and then we can have a normal friendly, informative conversation on why I'm in Iceland. In fact, we can totally ignore my recording device. It is an AI recorder; no need to worry about it picking up your voice; it auto-detects and amplifies directionally," Wes said. "Does that sound all right with you?"

"Yes, yes, sounds fine, Wes," Ragnar replied with Helga nodding in agreement.

"Okay then, here we go. Lead in – Westernman Show Reykjavik Iceland October 26th, 2047.

I'm just a few miles outside of Reykjavik, Iceland, at the Ultra Deep Virus Repository. UDVR pronounced Oodvar. The Oodvar holds all the world's known viruses in the most secure facility on the planet in vaults 500 meters deep underneath Icelandic granite. This facility is an independent verification entity working in cooperation with the world-renowned Fohr-Eavers Research Center in Montreal, Canada. The Oodvar is privately funded, receiving corporate endowments from donors interested in keeping scientific discoveries at the cutting edge of technology. I have been invited by Drs. Helga Karlsdottir and Ragnar Stefansson to their facility and research lab to discuss the recent developments concerning The Forever Bug. Iceland is unique for not imposing information restrictions on medical discoveries shared with research centers worldwide. That fact may become most significant as time moves on.

I sit here with Dr. Karlsdottir and Dr. Ragnar, who has graciously invited me to dinner in their home adjacent to the Oodvar. The three of us are now comfortably situated in their library and about to have a fireside chat concerning the many-faceted game-changing effects on man's destiny brought about by The Bug." Wes then paused a moment.

"Dr. Karlsdottir, Dr. Stefansson, thank you for the invitation. My listeners and I are anxious to hear your new discoveries awaiting the human race," Wes said.

"Dr. Stefansson and I are most pleased that you were able to accept our invitation. We chose you and your radio program The Westernman show, which we've both been fans of, by the way, for many years, so that we could carry on where Drs. Fohr and Eavers left off in 2036 on your program," Helga replied.

"Yes, it was unfortunate how things turned out, but thankfully Dr. Eavers and Fohr were choppered to safety."

"And now the reason you are here, Wes. The headline that hit the internet on July 15th; Canadian woman gives birth in secret at the Fohr-Eavers research center. Full story to follow. What we are about to tell you is what happens, not how it happens. The how it happens part will be discussed at length by Drs. Eavers and Fohr with you on your follow up radio show. You see Wes, once the world learns what can happen, the how part will become secondary, but without the how, the what part cannot exist."

"But it's all to do with babies, natural birth, is that right?"

"Well yes, partly, there's a lot more to it, Wes, game-changing circumstances, game-changing daily life, and game-changing ethical considerations. The decision to bring a new life into the world will bring on far-reaching results of monumental proportions to humanity's destiny. Wes, we, and by we, I mean humans, specifically Dr. Eavers and Dr. Fohr, have discovered a way to modify or perhaps better said, manipulate the Forever Bug's workings on our human DNA," Ragnar said, paused, and nodded to Helga.

"But first things first, Wes, Helga said, taking over. Wes, the research into The Forever Bug, its effect on human DNA, and The Bug's continuing mutations have been ongoing ever since its discovery. The Bug's presence has brought about profound changes to life on earth. We aren't here to discuss that at this time; we are here to let you know what new discoveries we've learned since. What we end up doing with these new possibilities will be decisions that society will have to weigh and individuals grapple with. The consequences are not light; we can assure you that!" Helga said, nodding her head and with a burdensome look overcoming her face. She continued.

"Over the years, the scientific community, with Dr. Eavers's and Dr. Fohr's leadership, have made strides modifying The Bug's effect on our DNA. One set of research criteria and experimentation brought about the ability to disable The Bug's effect on human infertility. That resulted in Baby Alpha being born on July 15th. The modification allows a man and woman to become potent and fertile, enabling loving natural conception. In other words, Wes, you and your wife Sylvie could have a baby should you choose to do so," Helga explained, sipping on her brandy.

"That sounds wonderful, a breakthrough, people around the world will rejoice with this news, no?" Wes commented.

"You'd think so, but it's not so simple," Ragnar then replied. "When that news broke, it was immediately squashed because of what happened soon after. As time passed, people chalked it up to a late in-vitro birth and then forgot about it. The shutdown was successful."

"So why was the news squashed?" Wes just sat and listened. He took a sip of his port.

"Tell him, Helga."

"Wes, the baby's mother and father, they are dead." Just saying those words sent Helga's emotions surging, and she couldn't help but shed a tear as she said dead. She wiped her eye with a tissue. "Yes, Wes, the young couple, Cole and Wendy Smith, died shortly after Wendy gave birth to their beautiful Baby Alpha. Their baby Wendy, named after her mother, is doing fine and being cared for by the couple's parents, grandparents, who are both in their age reversing years, putting them into their 40's. They are more than capable of raising their granddaughter," Helga finished saying and looked over to Ragnar.

"Oh my God, that is so so sad! So you're saying having their baby killed them both?" Wes asked with a terrified look overcoming his face.

"That's not all of it Wes, there is much more," Ragnar replied.

"There's more?"

"Yes, two people had to die for Cole and Wendy to regain fertility. For Wendy, a woman had to die so that Wendy could overcome her Forever Bug induced POI, premature ovarian insufficiency, so her body could produce estrogen to release eggs. Same for Cole, a man had to die so that his body would stop producing anti-sperm antibodies so that he could become potent again and fertilized Wendy's egg. Cole died shortly after that as well."

"What do you mean two other people had to die?"

"Perhaps I worded it incorrectly. It wasn't two particular people or specific individuals for the sole purpose of giving Cole and Wendy the ability to get pregnant, no. I meant that two people had to die recently to perform a medical procedure on them while the Forever Bug virus was still active in their bodies. I'm not going to get into the specific procedure that needs to be completed no later than 15 minutes after death, but yeah, a man has to die, and a woman needs to die. It could be any man or woman anywhere who dies, but a minimum amount of tissue must be extracted within fifteen minutes, preferably sooner if possible. Donor tissue is required from both a male and a female," Ragnar added.

Suddenly hearing what Dr. Stefansson just revealed, Wes's eagerness to have a baby with Sylvie suddenly disappeared. Wes, although not showing it, was personally devastated. *How could he ever break this news to Sylvie?* He thought.

As Wes was thinking to himself about Sylvie, Helga then took over from Ragnar.

"Anyone dying on planet earth after 2025 died as a result of an accident, foul play, suicide or sentenced to death. Those dying from foul play or suicide are seldom reached in time by medics and accident victims; only 10 percent at best are reached in time. Those unfortunate souls put to death by our legal system or any other country are not eligible candidates," Helga finished and looked over to her husband.

"Oh my God," Wes said again. "We can have babies, from the dead, then we too end up dead? This is horrific!" Wes added. "No wonder the government has put a muzzle on this information; this is devastating!" Wes commented, stunned!

"Wes, hear us out; it gets better, and then it gets worse again. But if we are careful, it could be manageable for those who take this road," Helga said.

Wes couldn't imagine how it could be manageable, especially if it gets worse!

"How does it get better?"

"Nigel Fohr and Lillian Eavers have never stopped their researching of The Bug. How it works, the effects it has on our DNA. The rounds of mutations it undergoes every year. So they discovered how to make us fertile again, but the unexpected and devastating side effect was too horrific to let the world know. With Cole and Wendy Smith dying shortly after Wendy gave birth, they shut things down, but I said the research is ongoing. Nigel and Lillian found the reason the couple died. The procedure for making Cole and Wendy fertile resulted in negating the Forever Bug's anti-aging element. Not only that, it accelerated the aging process, not the anti-aging but the normal aging. The procedure actually ended up hyper-aging them both and, of course, no age reversal. They were both just in their late 30's reversed Bug years, but then within two months, they aged to their real years. Their bodies couldn't deal with the stress and gave out. They both were on their way to becoming 60. Dr. Eavers and Fohr will get into how and why that happened; the main thing to keep in mind, for now, is that things have changed. They've been able to slow the aging down. Their quantum computer modeling has suggested a reduction in the aging acceleration and can guarantee at least thirteen years of life, disease-free for both parents. That is *the good,*" Helga said.

"One other discovery was that Dr. Eavers and Fohr have had success in tweaking The Bug to begin age reversal at 40 for everyone should they wish to make that adjustment. That too is a good thing."

"And the bad?" Wes asked, taking his forehead into his hand, not believing what he had just been explained.

"Yes, well, the bad," Ragnar said. "The bad works like this. The baby will have inherited The Forever Bug's ability to age reverse and at *the Forever Younger* age, kicking in at 40 or so and reversing back to 25, repeatedly," Ragnor said.

"And what's bad about that?" Wes asked, "isn't that good?"

"Yes, that is good if the baby can survive the years. You see, although the offspring will have age reversal, it loses its disease fighting capability. All newborns will again be subjected to all manners of diseases. Sicknesses that the human race had thought were left behind for eternity. But no, those diseases will still haunt us all over again—measles, polio, leprosy, meningitis, cancer, heart disease, all of it. The Bug can rejuvenate our cells to not die but cannot prevent our cells from becoming infected with the disease. If that happens, the cells die, and the person dies. If by chance we can keep our newly born humans disease-free, then we have hope," Ragnor concluded.

"Wow, amazing! You are saying then that for one human to be born, four will die. The two are needed to harvest the tissue, one woman one man. Then the parents of the newborn will only live for a period no longer than thirteen years, and on top of that, the child may be taken as well by disease. Is that it?" Wes asked.

"Yes, I'm afraid you have it right, Wes, that's it," Helga said as she finished her brandy.

***

CHAPTER SIXTEEN
2047

OSCAR

Dateline: Sunday 7:45 AM, 2047
Toronto Canada – Pearson International Airport

"Our pigeon has just arrived back in Toronto this morning Mr. Dern," Rod informed Michael Dern in Philly.

"All right, good work, least I know he's back. Nobody flies to Iceland for a day unless it's to secure information only available face to face." I can assure you it wasn't to visit geysers," Dern replied.

"I'm sure he didn't go because he wanted to see geysers, that's for sure."

"Face to face is how my new set of instructions will need to be delivered. I will fly up to Canada tonight. I want the two of you to meet me at the Kitchener/Waterloo International Airport. I want to make this trip as quick and short as possible and not looking to deal with Toronto International's complexities. I will get back to you later this morning about my arrival time. We will meet on my plane for your further instructions," Dern said.

"That'll be fine, Mr. Dern," Rod replied, then

added, “Ballpark time?”

“Probably after midnight.”

The call ended.

“Holy shit!” Rod exclaimed to his partner Brad. “Dern is flying up from Philadelphia tonight to meet with us, tonight!” Rod exclaimed again.

“We don’t have anything for him; why the hell would he want to fly up here for nothing?” Brad asked.

“He said he wants to meet face to face because he has new instructions for us. I guess he feels it’s important enough for us to hear it directly out of his mouth.”

“Well, this ought to be interesting.”

“Yeah, but he’s flying into Kitchener/Waterloo, wants to avoid the hassles at Pearson International. We can do that, it’s only an hour drive, and if we take the tube, it’s about fifteen minutes.” Rod said.

“Whatever, but our pigeon is on the move; we need to see if he goes straight home; I imagine he will.”

“Sylvie, I just landed ten minutes ago; I should be home in time for breakfast.”

“Great, I can hardly wait to see you, Wes. Do you

have good news?"

"I have news babe, do I have news!" Wes exclaimed, expressing a tone of disbelief.

"I just got back from taking Smokey out for his walk, so I'll be here went you get home; love you, babe, see you shortly."

"Love you too, see you in 30,"

"The two Icelandic scientist-doctors couldn't have been more gracious, Sylvie. They were the perfect hosts for my one night in Reykjavik. Actually, they're a few miles outside of town, sort of semi-remote. They live right on the UDVR site, have their home right there, offices lab, everything! Had a great dinner with them, sort of a get-to-know-you opportunity before the heavy stuff came. Sylvie, when I say heavy stuff, I'm not kidding! I've actually had to put it out of my mind. I think about it too much, babe, and I might go nuts," Wes said, trying to hold things back, but it wasn't really working.

"Wes, babe, was it that bad? Can we have babies?" Sylvie couldn't resist asking.

"Sylvie, I have it all here, all of it. I'm going to play it all for you. Do you want to hear it now or later?"

"Now Wes, now!"

"Okay, I've replayed it last night and then again

before they drove me back to the airport in Reykjavik. Now I will hear it for the fourth time." Wes replied. "You better make yourself comfortable; I don't want you falling off any chairs."

Sylvie looked at Wes with wide eyes, "Oh God!"

Wes placed his recording device on the breakfast nook table. He took a seat across from Sylvie, then said, "Play recording Westernman Show Reykjavik Iceland October 26th, 2047."

Wes watched Sylvie as she listened. Sylvie sat through the entire replay and hadn't said a word. When it was over, Sylvie then broke down with tears and openly cried, sobbed like a seven-year-old. Sylvie was devastated. Wes stood up from his seat and went to slide in beside Sylvie, hugging her, bringing her close, caressing her head gently kissing her hair. It wasn't working. Sylvie was in shock, seemingly her dreams wiped away. Wes would need to let her cry it out.

"Four people need to die, Wes? Four? And then maybe the baby too? Wes, the world is going to end before we know it!" Sylvie said with broken words trying to speak through her crying.

"I know, babe, I know," Wes whispered. "I don't know what to say."

There was silence for a minute or two.

"But Sylvie, the world must know. The world must be made aware that humans can have babies again."

"But not like this, Wes…not like this!"

"Time will tell, baby, time will tell. Maybe this isn't all. Maybe there is more that we don't know yet," Wes said.

"Sylvie, we both need time to process this. I'm just as devastated as you. When Helga and Ragnar finished telling me what they knew, I felt like I would be sick to my stomach. I wasn't able to sleep at all last night, Sylvie. Babe, it's going to take time."

"We're here, Mr. Dern; Brad and I are here in the terminal," Rod said, speaking into his watch. It was 12:50 AM Monday morning.

"Come on down to the corporate jets gate; I've issued you a passcode, KWRDBDGRGR. That'll get you through the door and out onto the tarmac. My Lear is the only one currently in the jetway parking zone; the stairway is down," Michael Dern replied.

"Be right there, Mr. Dern," Rod replied.

"Okay, let's go; he's here and waiting for us."

Brad and Rod walked to the corporate jets gateway door. Rod entered the passcode into the keypad. The door unlocked, and a minute later, Brad and Rod were on board Michael Dern's corporate Learjet.

"This is most unusual, Mr. Dern; you must have

something extraordinary you want to discuss with Brad and me," Rod said.

"I do, boys, I do. Have a seat, won't you?"

"What is it we can do for you, Mr. Dern?" Brad asked.

Michael Dern just sat, not saying a word for almost thirty seconds. His being silent was starting to feel a bit uncomfortable. Then suddenly, Michael Dern spoke. "I need to take this to the next level, gentlemen. In fact, I'm not going to ask you if you can do it; I will assume you can. You need not answer me; I will know if you are successful. All I've had you do so far was keep an eye on our pigeon. This latest piece of information was important news for me. Our pigeon flying to Iceland and coming back the following morning allowed me to fill in more pieces of the puzzle. I want to show you my appreciation. Here is a bank draft for fifty thousand dollars; consider it a bonus for work well done," Dern said, handing over the bank draft.

Rod accepted the draft and looked at his partner Brad with an expression on his face, *like, really*? Rod couldn't help but think that Dern was setting them up for something. "All right, Mr. Dern, we certainly appreciate it this. We strive to do a thorough job for you," Rod replied.

"I know you do, boys, I know you do."

"What's this you were saying about you wanting to take this to the next level?" Brad asked.

"Well, here's the thing. Although the information about our pigeon flying off to Iceland was beneficial to me, I want more. In fact, I'm not sure I can tell you exactly what it might be, just that it would have something to do with The Forever Bug. You know our friend did that radio show back in 2036 where he got into some hot water and had to have his two guests choppered out to safety, right?"

"Yes, we know that; we figured you hiring us had some relevance to that event," Rod replied.

"Boys, I need something more concrete, something only our pigeon knows, maybe he's sitting on, maybe he's got it tucked away someplace, a safe place. Maybe it's something under his pillow if you get my drift," Dern said, suggestively raising his eyebrows.

"It'll be Bug related information. That's what I'm looking for. Something the world might not know about yet, but our pigeon does.

If you could get me something you think I can use and it proves useful to me, there's another couple of hundred thousand dollars in it for you two, each. That's four hundred grand, plus the fifty I just gave you makes almost half a mil, but it needs to be significant. Yes, I know I'm asking for you to go on a wild goose chase, but that's kind of the thing you do anyway, although this goose might be harder to catch," Dern said.

"That'll be all boys. Now I need to get back to Philly," Dern said and showed them off his Lear.

That was it. Dern didn't say another word after that. As soon as Rod and Brad stepped onto the tarmac, Dern's Lear was being guided back by the ground crew.

"Jesus Christ, Brad, fifty grand just like that!"

"And another almost half a million to come," Brad added.

"Yeah, well, not so sure that I'm cool with that other part. Sure, the two hundred grand for each of us is fucking tempting, I'll admit that, but you know what he wants us to do, right?"

"Under his pillow, yeah, right, he wants us to break into Wes's house and snoop around; that's serious shit."

"No shit, it's serious shit!" Rod replied.

"But a half a million, Rod, just for taking a look and maybe picking up some info!"

"Yeah, I know Brad, we need to think this one through good."

"Well, we already know one thing; their house has old school security, like no security. They don't seem to have much security in place at all. Wes and his wife still have locks, an old fashion lock on their front door. It's a key lock, no high tech involved there. I bet either one of us could pick that thing in a minute. I imagine their side door is a key lock as well," Brad said. "The only thing remotely electronic is their garage door. Christ Rod, we've both watched Wes and Sylvie fumbling with the key to their front door. They use it every day to come and go; it's always a key. Lawrence Park is one of the safest if not the safest neighborhoods in greater Toronto. I don't think there's been a burglary reported here for over a year. Robberies, well, you can forget about those. If you're caught robbing a house with occupants present, well, you can kiss your ass good-bye for a good twenty years, burglary not so much," Brad added.

"Fuck! A half a mil!" Rod exclaimed, watching the highway lights go by on their early morning drive back to Toronto.

"Okay, that's it, she's just pulled the car out of the garage. She's gone back into the house; let's hope she's getting the dog." Rod said, looking out the window of the rented house three places down and across the street from the Ternman home.

"All right, I'm out of here, will get in the car to follow her after she pulls out. If we're going to do it, this is the time, now or never," Rod added.

"Right, we've gone over this a few times, side door only. If I fail getting access through the side door, we abort," Brad said.

Rod headed out and was waiting in his vehicle for Sylvie to leave.

"That's it, Rod, she's got her dog with her now; she's in her car and backing out of her driveway," Brad spoke into his watch.

"I'm on her," Rod replied.

The plan was for Rod to follow Sylvie to know when she'd be making her way back home so he could warn Brad in time. Brad, dressed in uniform as a Hydro One meter reader holding a reading device, then emerged from his house's back yard and proceeded to walk to the few other buildings pretending to read electricity meters. He visited each house, then crossed the street and visited all the homes. When he came to Wes's house, Brad went to the side and quickly took out his lock-pick tool. Having practiced for the past two days on picking several locks, Brad felt confident that this would be no more difficult. Brad started in, making as little noise as possible.

But the little noise Brad made trying to pick the lock was noise enough.

Oscar's highly tuned awareness sensors immediately located the picking noise coming from the home's side door. Oscar had first become aware of Brad approaching the house from the street but had assessed Brad at a threat level of zero since Oscar registered him as a Hydro One meter reader, a common occurrence. Things changed, however with this newly added sound Oscar was detecting. His AI placed Oscar into *alert* mode, home intruder response watch.

Oscar activated his fiber gripping adhesive skin, not unlike that of a gecko, and relocated to the side door foyer. Oscar's infrared vision clearly showed Brad's image through the door as Brad was crouched down and in the act of picking the lock.

Oscar then entered his *intruder apprehension* mode. His state of the art autonomous AI ran calculations and decision logistics.

The choices were three.

A: Do nothing.

B: Warn the potential threat to disengage and retreat.

C: Allow entry and apprehend for law enforcement to arrest.

His algorithms decided on option C: Neither Sylvie nor Wes or Smokey were currently at home, so there was no risk of them coming under threat. Oscar determined that the potential intruder had not selected Wes and Sylvie's house at random since no other homes were targeted. Oscar's AI further determined that the intruder was impersonating an electric company employee. The AI concluded that apprehension was justified to ascertain the reason for the home invasion.

He suddenly leaped up on the ceiling, sticking himself horizontally, spread eagle above the side door entry, and waited. The picking sound continued. Oscar's head had 360-degree rotation capability. He rotated his head, so he was looking down at the door as it opened.

As Brad opened the door and walked in, he spoke into his watch, "I'm in."

Just as Brad closed the side door behind him, Oscar released his gecko grip on the ceiling and dropped down onto Brad.

Brad was no lightweight; 39 years old, just one year away from age reversal. He stood 6 feet 2 inches in height and worked out regularly, but with Oscar dropping on him like a ton of bricks, he had no idea what hit him and collapsed onto the floor.

Oscar switched into his apprehend/defense mode. His telescopic legs extended his 5 feet two inches to seven and a half feet. His arms and torso followed to balance out his body. Oscar's bionics equipped him with night vision, infrared, and zoom lens capabilities; he could spot an ant a mile in the distance. Truth be told, he was a fighting machine disguised as a 5 feet 2 inches high domestic butler. He could become lethal should the need arise. That would not be needed at this juncture.

Oscar stood, his feet glued to the floor. He picked Brad up off the floor like he was a feather, and with one arm extended, he gripped onto Brad's neck. Oscar's robotic fingers wrapping entirely around with the tips of his fingers pressing on Brad's Adam's apple and then tightening. Brad was completely immobilized and in shock.

Oscar then said, "Intruder, be advised. Under Canada Criminal code section RSC 1985 Section C amendment 201-1 2040, I hereby legally and forcibly detain you for breaking and entering. I am further authorized under the said section to extract pertinent information to assist law enforcement officers. I have scanned your physical condition and determined no injuries sustained and no sensory incapabilities.

You are capable of speech. You are hereby given 30 seconds notice to state your full name. Failure to comply will result in severe bodily injury as permitted under revised section 201-2040. Countdown commences, comply now," Oscar said, looking directly at Brad with red glowing eyeballs, and started the countdown speaking, 30, 29, 28, 27…"

Having come to his senses and realizing his immediate situation, Brad concluded that he was fucked, and fucked royally. No wonder there wasn't any security outside. No wonder Wes and Sylvie entered with a key. They didn't need perimeter security when they had a Class10 robot. This was something he and Rod hadn't considered. There weren't many of these units around even in 2047. But sure as shit, one was holding him by the throat and threatening.

Brad spoke into his watch, "We're fucked, Rod, a fucking Class10 bot has me by the neck and threatening to choke me," Brad said.

"Oscar kept counting, 19,18,17, 16…and by the way, please do not call me fucking, 14, 13, 12 …"

"Fine, fine, my name is Brad Sommers." *What the fuck, did this robot just fuck with me? Don't call me fucking, WTF?* Brad thought.

Oscar lightened his grip on Brad's neck but did not let go. Brad relaxed some, knowing the immediate danger had been averted.

"My polygraphy sensors affirm your response as being true; the answer is accepted," Oscar said. "With the same authorizing statute as quoted, I require to know the reason you were seeking unauthorized entry. You must comply with a truthful response. Failure to do so will once again initiate information extraction procedures."

Brad had heard about these Class10 bots. They

were pretty much foolproof. If you didn't comply, you were toast. You couldn't escape from them, hide from them, or fuck in any way with them. They pretty much could tell if you were telling the truth or not. Brad had no choice; he'd have to come clean, totally clean, and perhaps law enforcement and the courts would go easy on him and Rod. Brad was happy to give up Mr. Dern to save his own skin and maybe, just maybe, bargain for a lighter sentence. Rod and Brad had already decided that Dern was a snake in the grass. Someone the authorities most likely already had on their radar.

"Class10 bot?" Rod asked, his voice coming through on Brad's watch.

"You heard me, Rod."

"All right, you have to come clean, totally. Tell it everything it wants to know; we're fucked. Tell him everything, Brad, I mean it; if you don't, it will know, and it will hurt you," Rod said. "Tell it everything, also about Granger. The cops will probably want to know about him anyway. Better to get the info out there now. Besides, if you don't tell the Class10 bot, it will know you're holding information back. It will ask you if that is all you know. If you lie, it will detect it. These things are fucking smart, Brad."

"I was hired to look for information about The Forever Bug. We believe your owner may have pertinent information he obtained on his recent trip to Iceland on The Bug that our client wants to know," Brad said.

"Your client? What is the relationship? A business relationship?" Oscar asked.

"Correct, I am a private investigator, my company is called Cumberland P.I. Services. My partner Rod Quinn and I were hired by Mr. Michael Dern, CEO of Granger Pharmaceuticals. I was trying to get information for Mr. Dern that he believes Mr. Wes Ternman has."

"All right, I have detected your answers as being true. Additional information extraction methods will not be required; I will detain you until law enforcement arrives. We will remain here."

The time was now 3:12 PM. Wes was on his way home, and Oscar could call Wes now without interrupting or getting him all excited at work. Oscar first notified Wes and, by law, was required to notify law enforcement.

There were no exceptions; all manner of detentions undertaken by robots had to be passed on to law enforcement. After Oscar called Wes, he then notified the Toronto City Police Department. Both Wes and the cops were on their way. Sylvie was still at the dog groomers with Smokey, and Rod too was heading home and would wait for the police to come knocking.

Oscar had extracted all the information that would ever be required from Brad.

Wes's earpiece blipped, indicating an incoming call. Wes answered. "Oscar?"

"Yes, Wes, it's me, Oscar, having a nice day?" Oscar asked.

***

CHAPTER SEVENTEEN
2047

A RULING

Dateline: Wednesday, November 13th, 2047
Hamilton Ontario Canada – McMaster University Health Sciences

"Nigel, I had to call you right away. I just got into my lab here at McMaster, and in my hand, I have a courier packet from our lawyer in Ottawa," Lillian said with anticipation in her voice.

"Lillian, I'm so glad you called because I was just about to call you. I got mine as well, arrived a few minutes ago. Have you opened your packet yet?" Nigel asked.

"Not yet, but I'm about to."

"Me too, let's see what we have."

Although being in two different cities, Drs. Lillian Eavers and Nigel Fohr were connected as if in the same room.

"This will be it, Lillian, this will be the ruling from the supreme court of Canada, I'm sure of it."

"Let's open the envelopes, then we can cry or

rejoice together," Lillian said.

"Ready, Nigel?"

"Ready, go ahead, read it; I'll follow," Nigel said.

Lillian began reading the letter from Harrow, Ruff, and Cranshaw law offices, legal representative to The Fohr-Eavers Research Center, Dr. Lillain Eavers, and Dr. Nigel Fohr.

Dear Lillian and Nigel:

The Supreme Court of Canada has ruled on Patent Challenge case FCA 339 Fohr Eavers vs. Health Canada. The court has ruled in favor of Health Canada in a 6 to 3 decision. The court has ruled that the data protection provisions' constitutionality is sound in claiming ownership to the digital computation and specific software required to activate the DNA mutation's efficacy. The process itself is not granted patent rights, but the means in delivery is so granted. The Fohrs Eavers Center retains the patent for the process but not for the critical computer calculations required to deliver the medical procedure.

This leaves the entire process and procedure split. The Fohr Eavers Research Center will retain the rights to licensing the procedure. Still, Health Canada owns the patent on the computer software required to compute the drug design needed to achieve efficacy.

Rubin Harrow
Attorney at Law

Harrow Ruff and Cranshaw

“Jesus Christ!” Lillian exclaimed! “Clear as mud!”

“Well yeah, you know what courts are like and laws in general. They always love to clarify things by issuing rulings that end up sounding or looking like spaghetti. But the second sentence in the letter says it all, Lillian. The court has ruled in favor of Health Canada in a 6 to 3 decision. Hey, but Health Canada didn’t get it all. We retain rights to the actual process of doing the procedure; we just don’t have the rights to the computation required to get the formula right. So, it’s split. We have half, and they have half,” Nigel said.

“Right, but we didn’t want any of it. We’re not interested in holding onto any of this information. The world needs to know what to do and how to do it to make babies. Our half we can let the world have for free. I believe our government is looking at this from a monetary perspective. I’m sure Health Canada will want to license the computer software out to pharmaceuticals so they can start manufacturing the drug needed to achieve efficacy, activating the transplanted tissues. That’s if our government ever decides it’s okay to have babies again.”

“Oh, I’m sure they will Lillian, I think they just wanted to prevent us from going public until they were able to secure the patent rights. You can rest assured they’ll want to start licensing procedures with the world’s drug companies almost immediately and other countries as well. When it comes to government, there isn’t a whole lot of morality in the mix. Sometimes I wonder if our government has any morality left at all. Now that we've been able to guarantee at least 13 years of parenting, they'll be eager to go ahead. You know there will be hundreds of millions of couples ready to accept 13 years so they can experience the joys of a baby girl or boy."

"I agree with you, Nigel, the thing about it is... there won't be millions and millions of dead people around to fill the desire," Lillian responded.

"So are we crying or rejoicing?"

"I think we can rejoice, Nigel. Now that the government has its patent, we can talk freely about how the human race can have babies again. I'm sure the government will lift their lockdown on the research center and unmuzzle us as well. Give it a few weeks, and we'll be home-free."

"Oh, I think we'll be home-free much sooner than that! I'm betting our friend in Toronto is itching to get the word out. I'm thinking it will be before the week's over."

"Interesting times we live in Nigel."

"That it is Lillian, that it is."

***

CHAPTER EIGHTEEN
2047

THE REVEAL

Dateline: Friday, November 15th, 12:00 PM
Toronto Ontario Canada – CHYI Studios – The Westernman Show

"Ladies and gentlemen, listeners and loyal fans of The Westernman Show, this is Wes Ternman, your host for the past 38 years. Every weekday since that first Monday on June 1st, in 2009, I opened The Westernman show with the same intro-promo as when my show debuted on CHYI. The now-familiar wild west themed music in the background depicting a showdown at the OK corral. My dialogue remained the same until 2035, when our fellow Canadians established Moonbase 5 and started beaming our laser-line audio program.

You will have noticed already that for the first time in 38 years, the familiar opening musical notes weren't there; instead, you hear my voice. There is a reason for that, and the reason is change. The human race, ladies, and gentlemen is about to undergo a shift in its future like we could never have imagined. The changes that the Forever Bug brought about twenty-two years ago is about to bring on another monumental change. Today's radio program will air without commercial breaks for the first two hours so that we can convey this world-impacting paradigm shift about to overtake the planet.

A little more than three weeks ago, I received an invitation out of the blue to visit Reykjavik, Iceland. I was asked to come to do an interview at the UDVR. The UDVR, or Oodvar, is the Ultra Deep Virus Repository. Yeah, it holds all the viruses and pathogens known to mankind. But more importantly, I was to receive new information on The Forever Bug. The joint directors of the UDVR, Dr. Helga Karlsdottir, and her husband, Dr. Ragnar Stefansson, had contacted The Westernman Show, offering to share this new development with me and for The Westernman Show to then broadcast it to the world. They picked this program because of the relationship I have with Dr. Nigel Fohr and Dr. Lillian Eavers of the Fohr-Eavers Research Center in Montreal. The information I was to receive is something that the Fohr-Eavers Research Center was not allowed to share with Canadians, but Iceland had no problem disseminating this major shift in human evolutionary development.

I also want to tell you that two days ago, on Wednesday, my home was burglarized. The intruder was detained and subsequently arrested. The intruder's interrogation revealed they were searching for anything they could find related to my visiting Iceland, the UDVR facility, and whatever could be found about the Forever Bug. Another disturbing element of home invasion is that the intruder was contracted by a major drug manufacturer to do the snooping around. The drug company, for the time being, shall remain unnamed. Because of our home invasion, I now have 24-hour security provided by the RCMP. I need not tell you how upset I am about this, but I am not about to back down now or ever.

I wish to thank Dr. Karlsdottir and Dr. Stefansson, and Iceland's government for allowing this information to become public knowledge.

Here ladies and gentlemen is my full interview as it happened on Oct 26th with Drs. Karlsdottir and Stefansson. It runs for approximately one hour. After this has played in its entirety, we will replay it again for the second hour uninterrupted. In the third hour, I will take listener call-ins. This is a Westernman program special broadcast."

Wes then let the recorder play.

I'm just a few miles outside of Reykjavik, Iceland, at the Ultra Deep Virus Repository. UDVR pronounced Oodvar. The Oodvar holds all the world's known viruses in the most secure facility on the planet in vaults 500 meters deep underneath Icelandic granite. This facility is ...

Today's show was also the first time Wes hadn't said a word for two hours after his initial lead-in. It didn't take long before the lines were all lit. Calls were starting to come in from across the globe. The Westernman Show social media was exploding. The *likes* had reached several million in just the first half-hour. Luke Stenner figured that all 195 countries worldwide had tuned in to Wes's program, perhaps even exceeding the radio audience of the July 20th, 1969 moon landing. Wes had instantly become the world's most famous celebrity and The Westernman Show the number one radio show on the planet. The world was tuning in."

About twenty minutes into the second hour of the

program and the replay of Wes's recording in Iceland, Luke Stenner signaled to Wes that he had an incoming call from Dr. Eavers and Dr. Fohr. Wes was only too happy to take it.

"Dr. Eavers, Dr. Fohr, I didn't think you'd be calling. When we spoke on Wednesday, you had said everything was looking okay with the government, and you were expecting a release soon."

"That's why we're calling Wes. The release from CSIS just came through this afternoon, a little after 1:00 PM. We are cleared and can now speak openly about everything we've discovered. We are not permitted to disclose the chemical formulation and atomic structure of the procedure. All that is handled by the government-owned software, which needs to run on quantum computers anyway. Even Dr. Fohr and I couldn't calculate it in a thousand years if we wanted to; the computer does it all," Lillian said.

"Wes, Dr. Eavers, and I would like to come back onto your show and tell the world how all of this works, so people have an understanding of not just what happens but how it happens. Both of us feel that the sooner the world knows, the sooner sound decisions can be made by those who would like to have a baby. We cannot delay the good people of our world to be denied their God-given right to have children." Dr. Fohr added.

"Whenever you want, the entire three hours are yours," Wes said.

"How about this coming Monday? Let's get the

news out to the world as fast as we can, Wes," Lillian replied.

"Absolutely, absolutely, Dr. Eavers."

"All right, Wes, we will be in Toronto for your program on Monday. In fact, we will arrive the night before. If for any reason you feel you'd like to meet before the program, Nigel and I will be at the Hilton downtown." Lillian added.

"Well, then, if you'll be in town Sunday, why don't you and Dr. Fohr join Sylvie and me for dinner at the Budapest restaurant in the village? Sylvie and I always go there every year to celebrate our wedding anniversary. Sylvie was born in Budapest; we got married there back in 2010. This is the best we can do next to being back in the city of love. We'd be honored to have the two of you as our guests. The restaurant is on Yorkville Avenue.

"We'd be delighted, so long as Sylvie is good with it," Lillian replied.

"Oh, I'm sure she'll be thrilled to know you will be joining us. My Dad Cam and Sylvie's Mom Maggie will be with us." Wes replied. "We'd love to have you."

"Sunday it is then, time?"

"It's at 8," Wes replied.

"See you at The Budapest restaurant at 8:00 PM," Lillian replied.

"Okay, we're back. Ladies and gentlemen, my producer Luke Stenner, tells me the world has been listening for the past two hours. According to Luke, our computer call has logged over a million attempts to connect with the station's call-in line. I'm sure the past two hours have been both informative and perhaps even frightening. We have yet to determine what these new developments have in store for people worldwide in the coming year and decade. We'll be right back after this two-minute commercial break, but stayed tuned because I have another piece of news sure to grab your interest even more.

If the last two hours wasn't enough breaking news for you, then you may want to listen up. I just received confirmation directly from Dr. Nigel Fohr and Dr. Lillian Eavers that they will be my guests for the full three hours on next Monday's Westernman Show. If you want to know the *how* behind the *what*, be sure to listen to it. I can guarantee you it will be a must-listen three hours of radio. That's right, you heard me. Dr. Eavers and Dr. Fohr, The world's top experts on The Forever Bug, will be here next Monday, be sure to tune in.

And now I'll take some call-ins. I know you've been waiting and holding for the past two hours. I will try getting in as many as I can.

You've got The Westernman, Jimmy from Port St. Lucie Florida, go ahead, what's your question, Jimmy?"

***

CHAPTER NINETEEN
2047

BUSTED

Dateline: Friday, November 15th, 3:18 PM, 2047
Kawarthas Ontario Canada – Buckhorn Lake

"I'm sure I don't have to tell anyone what this call is all about," Dr. Mark Canning said.

He thanked everyone for taking his conference call request. Even Ernst Heiko, CEO of Steiner Corporation of Germany with Bavaria being six hours ahead of Ontario, accepted Mark's request to join the virtual Bug Chamber conference call. Everyone else was on this side of the Atlantic. Mark was able to get all six members to join in.

"I don't know what we're doing wrong, but there's something we're not doing right. I can tell you that!" Mark said.

"What do you mean, Mark?" Michael Dern, CEO of Granger Pharmaceuticals, asked. Dern was trying to play his *I'm stupid card* to deflect any further thinking on his side.

Dana Blackman, of course, picked up on it right away, and she wasn't having any of it, especially after having heard Wes tell his worldwide audience that his house was broken into. Dana knew well what that was all about and just exactly who was the stupid mastermind behind that brilliant move. Dana now wished she would have just told Dern right there and then on his plane to take a flying leap. Still, she wasn't part of it, but that bad taste in her mouth about Dern just became more bitter.

Dana responded. "Michael, has your head been buried in the sand for the past three hours? You surely have been tuned in to the most important news story in the history of the world! Have you not heard? What Mark is trying to say is that here we are, seven of the most influential people in the medical world and who's at the front of the line when it comes to breaking news about something that could make or break all of us? No, it's nobody in this august body of wizards; no, it's Wes Ternman, a radio talk show host in Canada for Christ's sakes. I, for one, am embarrassed as all hell for feeling so inept." Dana said, not holding back one bit and placing the group on notice.

"Dana, Dana, this radio jock has an in with Fohr and Eavers, obviously," Dern replied.

"Right you are; why is it that you're not the one with the in, or anyone else…why must we be informed about breaking Bug developments from a radio talk show host? And one more thing, what's this about Wes Ternman's home being broken into on the instructions from a drug maker? Now that's something this group cannot tolerate and must condemn whichever company it may be big or small," She added.

"I have some news," Dr. Stephen Bird, CEO of Merit Pharmaceuticals, piped in.

"Whatchya got Stephen," Mark asked.

"Well, first, I have to say I am in total agreement with Dana. We should all be licking our wounds for being scooped by Wes Ternman on this Forever Bug development. We need to get out in front of this thing and be more proactive in what's going on at Fohr-Eavers. But having said that, something else happened yesterday, in fact, and I'm wondering if anyone else was contacted."

"What are you talking about, Stephen?" Mark asked again.

"What I am talking about is Health Canada forwarded an offer for Merit Pharmaceuticals to license quantum computing software needed to produce the drug that will make it possible for humans to become fertile again and to make babies. That's what I'm talking about, and I jumped on it immediately! Merit's legal team is now in the process of reviewing the licensing agreement. We expect Health Canada to sign the licensing contract in the coming days; that's what I'm talking about."

"Holy crap! They're not wasting any time, are they?" Mark commented.

"No, they're not," replied Willy Hollman of Permacare Health; "They contacted me as well."

"Anyone else?"

"Yeah, Mark, me too," Keith Shultz of Durham Chemistry said.

"Yup, me too, Mark, offer to license said software came in later yesterday afternoon here in Germany," Ernst Heiko of Steiner Corporation added. "And one more thing, Prime Minister Helmut Riser, of Luxembourg is a good friend of mine. I spoke to him a few hours ago, and he tells me his government has also been contacted by Health Canada, offering licensing arrangements for The Bug Drug software. That's confirmation right there that we'll have an added layer of competitors; government health departments. I'm sure some governments will be looking to partner with drug companies. We will have our competition like never before it would appear," Ernst said.

"I'm not surprised Ernie, this is much bigger than anything before. Just think, humans will now be able to reproduce again! What about you, Michael? Did Granger receive an offer?"

"Ah, ah, yeah, yeah, I got the offer yesterday as well," Dern said, lying.

Dana jumped on the opportunity to pin Dern to the corner he just painted himself into.

"Michael, this group has huge collective bargaining power; you realize that, right?" Dana asked.

"Yes, I imagine we would. We're a force to be dealt with, five of the major drug producers in the western hemisphere and Europe," Dern replied.

"That's what I was thinking, and since your company, Granger, is the largest in North America, what is Health Canada charging for the annual licensing fee?" Dana asked.

Dern hesitated, his face suddenly tensing up. It was noticeable in the video.

"I'll have to look into it Dana, I can't be sure," Dern replied.

"You can't be sure? You can't be sure if it was five hundred dollars annually for the license or fifty million dollars for the annual license; you mean you don't know? It must have been in the offer. Did you not read it?"

"Like I said, Dana, I will have to review the offer," Dern said.

"Michael, why don't you come clean, because I'm about to, right here and right now!" Dana replied.

Everyone on the conference call was suddenly stunned.

"You didn't get an offer from Health Canada, did you, Michael?"

They didn't make you an offer because your company was named the company that hired the P.I.

guy arrested for breaking and entering the Ternman home. Am I right? Health Canada has cut you out of any future partnerships or deals. Isn't that right, Michael? Tell the group, I'm sure they'd like to know," Dana said.

Michael Dern then ended his connection, his screen went blank.

"Whoa! What was that?" Mark exclaimed!

"So listen up, everyone. This isn't exactly something I'm proud of, but I got snookered into Michael's little private web spun to snarl me into some game he was trying to play. When we all last met at your place, Mark, Michael caught up with me just before flying out from Peterborough Airport. He said he wanted to talk to me about solidifying our business relationship. I listened to him since his company is my hospital network's most important drug supplier amongst a few other products his company provides. He talked about not wanting to bring you, Mark, into this because he was protecting you."

"Protecting me? From what?"

"How did I know you were going to ask that question?" Dana said, with a little laugh to lighten the last few minutes.

"Yeah, so he said because you were Canadian, and so was the Fohr-Eavers Research Center, etc., etc. he didn't want to jeopardize you by casting a possible shadow on you if his plan was to go awry," Dana said.

“His plan?”

“Yeah, he had put a tail on Wes Ternman, the radio show host. He felt that tailing The Westernman would eventually yield him some inside information on The Bug that Michael had no access to. Even if by accident Ternman might end up revealing something useful. Well, it seems that day came when Wes Ternman flew off to Iceland.” Dana paused a Moment and let that sink into everyone still on the call.

“Go on, Dana,” Mark said.

“I told him on his plane that there wasn’t much I could do about his having Ternman followed; that was his choice. I also told him if anything even remotely illegal comes of this, I will not be part of it. I will not be interested in his company’s continued relationship with Finacare Health Systems. It became apparent to me having listened to The Westernman Show earlier today that Dern’s company, Granger, was the unnamed drug company who put the P.I. guy up to breaking into Wes’s house.

When it became evident that everyone here received an offer to license the software from Health Canada except for Michael, well, that was confirmation for me that he was 100% behind ordering the break and enter to snoop around Wes Ternman’s house. That gentleman is why I called him out on it this afternoon. I want no part of his shenanigans or his underhanded way of doing things. I find him unscrupulous and dishonest. In fact, he lied to me. I believe Greed is his company’s and personal driver, and I think he’s up to no good. I say with Health Canada having cut him out, we ought to cut him out as well. Unfortunately, that may only drive him deeper into the dark side of our industry, and we all know that exists," Dana finished.

"Oh, and one more thing. I am happy to establish closer relationships with everyone at this table. Which I am sure will be a much healthier and prosperous relationship and more than make up for any losses our company might experience as a result of severing ties with Granger and Mr. Michael Dern," Dana added.

"Damn, I sure didn't expect anything like this!" Ernst Heiko added.

"No, I don't think any one of us did!" Mark commented.

"Well, I'm looking forward to Wes's program on Monday. I'm already excited to hear what Dr. Fohr and Dr. Eavers will reveal to the world," said Dana.

"I'm sure we all are, hell the world is! I've got to hand it to Mr. Ternman; he most definitely knows what he is doing. He's become the de facto voice of The Forever Bug for the entire world," Mark said.

"Let's hope there aren't more crazies out there looking to squeeze information out of Mr. Ternman that he doesn't have. I'm sure he is just as baffled and surprised by his sudden rise to fame as we are. Although let's give him some creds, he's got a megaphone, and we don't. With Eavers and Fohr on his Monday show, his megaphone will be put to good use, good on Mr. Ternman, I say," Dana commented.

"Ditto that," Keith Shultz of Durham Chemistry

added. Everyone on the conference video call nodded with Shultz in agreement.

“All right, that’ll do it for today; we got a hell of a lot more than I bargained for, that’s for sure. Let’s see what falls off the tree on Monday,” Mark said and ended the virtual meeting.

***

CHAPTER TWENTY
2047

BUDAPEST IN TORONTO

Dateline: Sunday, November 17th, 8:00 PM, 2047
Toronto (Yorkville) Ontario

"Wes, I'm so looking forward to meeting Dr. Eavers and Fohr. This is such a surprise! I'm thrilled you invited them to our anniversary dinner, and I'm even more thrilled they accepted!" Sylvie said, unable to restrain her excitement as the four of them rode to The Budapest Restaurant in the village.

"Oh, my God, Mom, these two people are the ones making it possible for Wes and me to have a baby! Well, maybe. I know I shouldn't be jumping to any conclusions, but it will be so incredible to meet them!"

"Count on my son to come up with great ideas! This was a doozy, Wes; I'm looking forward to meeting these two Nobel Prize winners myself! It's going to be hard to find something to say. Like what do you say to two Einsteins sitting at your table?" Cam commented.

"I'm sure it will be fine; besides, after Dr. Eavers and Dr. Fohr take their first taste of our Hungarian dishes, they'll turn into country folk like they just walked in from the great plains of the Puszta," Maggie added.

"We're a bit early, but let's hope our table is ready," Wes said as his vehicle pulled up to the valet parking.

"All right, it doesn't look like Lillian and Nigel are here yet; that's good; I can meet them as they arrive and bring them to the table. It will be less awkward for them, I'm sure," Wes added.

The four of them entered The Budapest Restaurant and were immediately welcomed by the maître d' in both English and Hungarian.

"Good evening, ladies and gentlemen. *Jo estet kivanok,*.... Janos then recognized Sylvie and Wes. Janos, a tall Hungarian, with a darker complexion, one of Roma (Hungarian Gypsy descent), had been the maître d' at The Budapest for the past twenty years. Ah, Mr. and Mrs. Ternman, what a pleasure to see you again!" Janos said with enthusiasm.

"I understand you are celebrating your wedding anniversary with us. It is our honor to have you grace our establishment again," Janos said, welcoming the Ternman party.

"Thank you, Janos. We've been looking forward to coming again, we wouldn't change our annual tradition. I'd like to introduce you to my father, Cam, and this is Sylvie's mother, Maggie," Wes said.

Janos greeted Cam and Maggie with handshakes.

"I see you have a table reserved for six. Follow me; we have a perfect table set for you."

After they were seated, Wes walked back to the restaurant's foyer to wait for Nigel and Lillian. They arrived not thirty seconds later.

"Dr. Eavers, Dr. Fohr, so nice to see that you could make it."

"Wes, we wouldn't have missed this for the world. Both Nigel and I are so taken that you invited us to your anniversary dinner and to The Budapest Restaurant; how lovely Wes, how beautiful!" Lillian replied.

"And it's Lillian and Nigel, Wes, please drop the Dr. We'd appreciate that. Formalities are long behind us, I should think," Nigel added.

Janos took Lillian's and Nigel's coats, and Wes escorted his two friends to his table to make the introductions.

As Wes approached the table, Cam, Maggie, and Sylvie stood while Wes did the introductions. Shortly after everyone was seated, Janos came over to the table and said, "Wes and Sylvie, the owners of the Budapest Restaurant, Ferenc and Bella Folyo, would like to extend their congratulations on your wedding anniversary. We hope you enjoy this complimentary bottle of pink Hungarian sparkling wine from the Tokaj region along the shores of the Danube. They regret not being here this evening to personally welcome you back again."

Janos then proceeded to open the sparkling wine. Cam then made a toast to his son and daughter in law. The evening was off to a great start.

"This is our first time at this restaurant Lillian said. Oh, and by the way, Nigel and I were so pleased that you invited us to join you. Truth be told, most if not all of our friends are in the medical field, doctors, scientists, well, you know, all very boring after a while. It is a breath of fresh air that we can break away from that crowd and spread our wings a little with exciting people like yourselves. Why, with Wes and his radio program, he brings the world to our ears, expanding our minds every day. Sylvie I understand, you have international customers for your ceramic artwork; how wonderful! And Cam, you must have some blockbuster stories about your life, I'm sure, especially having raised Wes. Maggie, I'm sure just sitting here inside this restaurant brings back countless memories of your life in Budapest. I hope you can share some of that with us," Lillian said.

"But this restaurant, my word! This place is fabulous," Nigel said. "I had heard of it, but I had no idea I'd be sitting in a virtual world this evening. My God, this is spectacular!" Nigel was utterly blown away by the realism.

The Budapest Restaurant in the center of Toronto was not what one might expect walking inside. One complete wall which ran along the hundred and sixty feet length of the room from floor to the ceiling ten feet high was a LED television screen in full 12K 3D. There were tables set along the length of the wall. Projected onto the screen was a six-hour delayed live view of the majestic Danube and the glittering lights of Europe's most beautiful bridge, the Chain Bridge, as seen directly from the Budapest Restaurant in Budapest, Hungary. There were seven more Budapest restaurants like this one in Toronto around the world, all synchronized to the view from the anchor restaurant in Budapest. The cities of Paris, Tokyo, Sydney, Singapore, London, Buenos Aires, and Dubai all had an identical setup. Being inside the restaurant was like being in Budapest at precisely the same time, but in Toronto's case, with a six-hour delay, to set the ambiance and time simultaneously.

It indeed was magical. London England's Budapest Restaurant would be on a one-hour time delay since it was only an hour behind Budapest time. No matter which restaurant you were seated in, and no matter what time of the day, your virtual wall-sized view would be precisely the same time in Budapest as you were sitting in whichever city around the world. Magical it truly was, the next best thing to being there. If a riverboat happened to cruise under the Chain Bridge at 8:10 PM in the evening in Budapest, and you were seated in Toronto at 8:10 PM Toronto time, you would see the riverboat cruising under the Chain Bridge in real-time but to synchronize with Toronto time. The restaurant overlooked the Danube, and the Buda side of Budapest, with the stunning and majestic Buda Castle and Fisherman's Bastian. Few city vistas could match the old world charm that this thousand-year-old city offered.

After dinner, and when everyone enjoyed their desserts and wine, an ensemble of Hungarian Gypsy musicians strolled over to the table.

Wes motioned to the bandleader, and the violins played the song Sylvie and Wes danced to on their wedding night; it was a tango, *Kiss of Fire*.

"My darling," Wes said as he stood up, holding out his hand for his lovely wife to take. Sylvie then took Wes's hand and stood. The band leader stood back his troupe to make way for *the* couple of the evening. Wes then wrapped his right arm around Sylvie's waist and made his move for Sylvie to follow….The violins played, and the band leader sang the most passionate lyrics ever put to music…

"I touch your lips, and all at once, the sparks go flying
Those devil lips that know so well the art of lying
And though I see the danger, still the flame grows higher
I know I must surrender to your kiss of fire

Just like a torch, you set the soul within me burning
I must go on; I'm on this road of no returning
And though it burns me and it turns me into ashes
My whole world crashes without your kiss of fire

I can't resist you; what good is there in trying?
What good is there denying you're all that I desire
Since I first kissed you, my heart was yours completely
If I'm a slave, then it's a slave I want to be
Don't pity me, don't pity me

Give me your lips, the lips you only let me borrow
Love me tonight and let the devil take tomorrow
I know that I must have your kiss, although it

dooms me
Though it consumes me, your kiss of fire.

Wes and Sylvie danced like they danced that night in Budapest on the Danube thirty-eight years ago. When they held their last embrace and their dance was over, the entire restaurant erupted in applause. Cam, Maggie, Lillian, and Nigel were standing and clapping. Cam brushed his eyes to clear away the tears of joy for his son Wes. Cam held on to Maggie with his arm around her shoulders, saying to her, "That's my son and your daughter, aren't they just amazing?" Still wiping his tears away.

After their tango dance of love, Cam hugged his son and kissed Sylvie. Lillian and Nigel came over to hug them both and once again congratulate them on their anniversary.

Nigel then said, "It's so plain to see the love you have for one another; this is your night. Thank you for allowing us to be part of it. Lillian and I have a small anniversary gift for the two of you." Nigel said, "Lillian?"

Lillian then reached into her handbag and pulled out a present, handing it to Sylvie. Wes and Sylvie were humbled that they should receive gifts from Nobel Prize-winning doctors.

"Oh, my," Sylvie said, thanking Lillian and Nigel.

"Open it, go ahead," Lillian said.

Sylvie, then looking at Wes, started undoing the

bow and eventually the wrapping, revealing a beautifully engraved box with Wes and Sylvie's name. Opening the box, delicate wrapping paper gently covered a complete set of handcrafted embroidered colorful lace doilies made in Hungary.

"Oh, look, Wes, aren't these just beautiful? Oh, thank you ever so much; these are gorgeous. I just love this exquisite, intricate work. I can just imagine the hours and hours of work that goes into making these." Thank you ever so much, Lillian and Nigel," Sylvie said.

"Tonight we rejoice, tomorrow we work," Wes said, kissing Sylvie and raising his glass to toast the table of family and friends.

Franz Liszt's Hungarian Rhapsody No. 5 could be heard fading in the background as they brought the night to a close at The Budapest Restaurant on the blue Danube in the middle of Toronto.

***

CHAPTER TWENTY-ONE
2047

MUTATION

Dateline: Monday, November 18th, 12:00 PM, 2047
Toronto Ontario CHYI Radio Station

"You're listening to Wes Ternman, and you've got the *Westernman Show* coming at you from above the 49th parallel direct from atop the CN Tower in the land of the free and the greatest city in the great white north and North America; Toronto Canada. We're broadcasting around the globe on F.M., AM, shortwave, and Globalnet sat-systems. A special shoutout to our Canuck listeners on moonbase 5 beaming at you with laser-line radio.

Well, my dear folks, the day has arrived. It's Monday, and you know who my two guests are this afternoon. From what I hear, a good part of the world has The Westernman Show tuned in. From far off Mongolia to Cameroon, The Cook Islands in the south Pacific, to McMurdo Station in Antarctica, and to the reaches of the northernmost inhabited place globally, the community of Alert on Canada's Ellesmere Island in the high arctic, you're listening.

Dr. Eavers and Dr. Fohr, welcome back to The Westernman Show. It's been eleven years since you last appeared as my guests, let's hope we don't need to chopper you out to safety like back in 36," Wes said and paused.

"My two Nobel Prize winners are back again to follow up on last Friday's program. Three days ago, The Westernman Show revealed to the world what Dr. Eavers and Fohr were not allowed to by our Canadian government. Since then, things have moved along at breakneck speed. The information provided by Dr. Karlsdottir and Dr. Stefansson from the UDVR in Reykjavik, Iceland, has shaken the world. Calls from around the globe have been coming into CHYI studios, to the Fohr-Eavers Research Center, to the UDVR in Iceland, and everywhere I turn, people are talking about babies, babies, babies!" Wes said, paused a moment, and continued on.

"So here we are, at the crossroads. From no babies to babies again…but are we willing to trade off being forever young with just thirteen more years and lights out? Here to shed some light on that darkness are the discoverers of The Forever Bug, its magic, its potential tragedy on the human race and how it all happens, Dr. Fohr, Dr. Eavers, welcome," Wes said, introducing his guests.

"It's good to be back, Westernman; we hope to bring clarity to what's been happening with The Bug and the major mutation that has taken place and, of course, its consequences. We'd like to share information with your listeners around the world about how this mutation came about and what this means to every one of us," Dr. Eavers said.

"Thank you, Dr. Eavers; we are eager to listen and learn. The Bug has changed us, our world, and in many ways, turned things upside down. I understand that it's about to change again and take our planet in a different direction, is that right?"

"That is right, Westernman," Nigel replied, "But we have options this time around."

"Options, what do you mean by that, Dr. Fohr?"

"Not options in what The Bug does, but options we have in deciding what we do in response to what it does, do you follow?"

"I think so," Wes replied.

"Once again, before we get into that, we need to start with where we are at this stage in the evolution of The Forever Bug."

"Okay, I think my enthusiasm in getting to the chase has me putting my cart before my horse," Wes said. "Please, please, go ahead, Dr. Fohr, the floor is yours."

"All right, Wes, I will do my best to keeping it simple and logical. I may have to ask Dr. Eavers to jump in now and then as we go," Nigel replied. "So let's start with recapping some mile markers, okay?"

"That sounds like a perfect idea," Wes replied.

"Year is 2025 – around March or so. People worldwide are suddenly becoming healthier by the day, and by the end of 2025, other than self-inflicted or accidental deaths, no humans die.

The year is 2026 – we notice ourselves not only having fully recovered from all diseases, but we are starting to look better and feeling younger. In fact, all men around the age of 60 have begun their age reversals, but we don't yet have confirmation. At this point, we're all just thinking we're feeling better because we are rid of diseases. The same effect has not yet hit the world's 60-year-old women, but they are also disease-free. Those who are closer to age 64 or 65 are feeling the age reversal kicking in.

The year is 2028 – The world now understands that people, the elderly, have been undergoing age reversal for more than three years, almost four by now, but at this stage, we still have no idea what has brought about this phenomenon.

The year is 2028 still. The world has, for the past three years, recorded decreasing numbers of childbirths around the globe.

The year is 2029 – Classification of Forever Youngers arises. Those born after 1980 start reversal at age 40.

The year is 2030 – The end of natural childbirth, the end of human procreation; in-vitro is still ongoing.

The year is 2030 still – No women on earth now past the age of 65, everyone has started their age reversals.

The year is 2034 – Dr. Eavers and I discover The Forever Bug's hijacking the CAS9 Crisper Technology and incorporating it into its gene-splicing functionality, enabling the regrowth of the Telomeres and thereby preventing aging and bringing on age reversal.

The year is 2036 – End of in-vitro births worldwide.

The year is 2036-2045 – Things are holding steady as she goes

The year is 2046 – Dr. Eavers and I discover how

to bring on earlier Bug age reversal for everyone should they choose to do so, at age 40, but not yet disclosed to the world.

The year is 2047 – Baby Alpha is born through natural conception on July 15th, 2047. The first baby born on earth in 17 years the natural way.

The dates and the related events I listed Wes are the events and facts the world is aware of in general. Over the past couple of years, there have been some significant developments not yet disclosed, which we are about to do on this program today," Nigel concluded.

"Okay, we're listening," Wes replied.

"Dr. Eavers?"

"Thank you, Wes. We want to make it clear to everyone listening that research at our center and, for that matter, around the world into the Forever Bug has never stopped or slowed down. Every year we've made a few little discoveries that, when added up, led to some breakthroughs, one being our ability to offer Bug age reversal for everyone now at age 40, not just for those born after 1980. There have been some other developments as well. Some have nothing to do with research but the shaping of laws and government oversight. One significant effect and law that kicked in not too long ago is the Baby Lottery Act of 2047. I know your listeners will be all over this in the next few minutes, but yes, there will be a Baby Lottery. It has already been enacted into Canadian law but not yet announced.

I guess I'm announcing it now and pre-empting a joint announcement by Health Canada and the Fohr-

Eavers Research center, but so be it. I am no doubt stepping on someone's toes in the government, but I think it's only fair to let your listeners know now that they don't get their hopes up too-too high. I thought I'd throw this little tidbit in there now because it will become crucial with what I have to describe next about The Forever Bug, and the more I get into it, Wes, the more the Baby Lottery will make sense. I'm sure our capable government officials from Health Canada could explain it brilliantly, but we may as well get it out into the open. It's not a law needing interpretation; it's evident and fundamental. But like I say, I'll get into that a bit later as everything else unfolds," Lillian said.

"Well, I'm glad we have the next two hours and fifteen minutes to talk about this. It sounds like we're about to chew off a bigger piece than we can swallow this afternoon, but we'll try," Wes replied.

"By the way, I'm getting reports in from my producer Luke Stenner that virtually the entire country is tuned in to The Westernman show right now. So Dr. Eavers, tell the world what you have for them," Wes said.

"You'll recall, Wes, I had told you back in 2036 that the world needed babies. Why did I say that? Well, it became clear, after the initial few years of euphoria about not ever being sick again wore off, that without new blood, babies, the human race was doomed to extinction. Sure, the majority of the world's population was projected to cycle over and over old to young, young to old. Still, each year, we'd lose a few hundred thousand people globally just because of accidents and suicides; eventually, in a few hundred years, there'd be no one left on earth. So we had to find a way back to procreation," Lillian said.

"You know Dr. Eavers, you are right. For those first few years, all we could think about was how miraculous our fortunes had become: no more diseases, no more deaths. Until the years crept up on us, first five then ten, it finally dawned on us all that we were in big trouble. Schools were closing, no more sounds of children laughing and playing, and we're still in that state. Our Bug years, I'm afraid, have clouded our outlook for a long time, and we're just becoming aware of the imminent danger facing our survival," Wes replied.

"So Westernman, we at The Fohr-Eavres center along with sister labs around the globe have been experimenting day and night trying to make things work again. We finally did achieve success, but it came at a cost," Dr. Eavers said and then took a deep breath to continue.

"Last summer, after thousands of hours of experimentation and failures, we were successful in preventing the Forever Bug from causing POI – Primary Ovarian Failure in women and robbing sperm production in men. Both of those symptoms have been reversed, but like I say, at a cost. But let me explain how we were able to accomplish this. We were trying to find a way to weaken the Forever Bug virus that had embedded itself into our DNA. We needed to find a way to relax its effect and then further engineer only the POI causing genes and sperm-producing cells. Our greatest challenge was finding a way to do that, how to weaken The Bug. We found it. The answer was stem cells, but half-dead or dying stem cells. Where would we find those? From dead people. Mind you, there weren't a whole lot of people killed to be had—very few cadavers. From time to time, we did manage to acquire accident victims on whom we could experiment. The major problem there, too, as they had to be donors. We couldn't just go grabbing recent accident victims and start cutting into them. If they weren't carrying self-approved donor cards, we couldn't have them, but we did manage to get a few.

I want your listeners to understand that just because we no longer got sick, that didn't mean there wouldn't be a need for body parts. Genuine body parts were still much as ever preferred over prosthetics. Accident victims needed replacement of hands, feet, faces, livers, kidneys, and the list goes on.

Our experiments and research found that the cadavers' Bug was dead, as was the body, but then something changed. We received two accident victims, a man and a woman who happened to die in a vehicular accident right outside our research center in Montreal, and they both happen to be victims with donor cards. Within fifteen minutes, we had them in our lab and extracted bone marrow from both the man and woman. You know Wes, bone marrow is where the body manufactures our blood. It's where we find our stem cells and the building blocks to our DNA and such things as T-Cells.

T-cells are white blood cells Wes and are critical to the immune system. They act in determining the specificity of the body's immune response to antigens, those things that are foreign substances in your body. So anyway, they originate in bone marrow but mature in the thymus. They are then sent to circulate in our blood or lymphatic system. Once they are stimulated by antigens, they then start the antibody-producing cells to fight the disease. That's the down and dirty, in simple terms. I brought this up because this part with T-Cells was a side effect we hadn't counted on. Let me explain a little further.

We got to the two accident victims early, within fifteen minutes of death, and were able to extract bone marrow from both. It turned out that the Forever Bug virus itself was still active and doing its job, maintaining the human DNA but not that well. It too started dying soon after the person died, in other words, the body was still warm, and the Forever Bug within the bone marrow was weakened but not dead. Immediately after extracting the marrow, we then cryogenically froze it, allowing us to conduct experiments for several days," Lillian said, then asked Wes, "Good so far, or do you need a review?"

"No, I'm good, might be a part or two that fell off the wagon, but go ahead, I get the gist of it all. I'm sure my listeners are in the same boat. You know, Dr. Eavers, the work you people, and I mean you incredible amazingly gifted people, do is superhuman. I think of you and Dr. Fohr and what you do every day, and honestly, it blows my mind. I have enough of a time trying to understand *the arrow of time*, multi-verses, the tenth dimension, string theory, the big bang, and then to think of all this and what you do well, it's frankly overwhelming and mind-boggling," Wes commented.

"Let me assure you, Wes, it's overwhelming to us as well. But we have incredible technology today that helps us along. When it first started back in 1990, it took thirteen years to sequence the human genome.

Our quantum computers today can do it within two minutes. And Wes, without the computing capability we have today, none of this would be possible. Dr. Fohr and I take apart the human DNA, jumble it all up and then tell the computer to put it all back together with the way we want it, not the way we found it. Just to give you and your listeners an idea of what it involves, our DNA comprises millions of small chemicals called bases. They come in four types, T, C, A, and G.

A gene is a section of DNA consisting of A, C, T, and G sequences. You have about 21 thousand of them inside each cell, and how many cells are there in the human body?"

"I have no idea Dr. Eavers, no idea, billions?" Wes asked.

"Not even close Wes, how does 30 trillion sound? That is why we need quantum computing power. The Bug has wormed itself inside all of our cells, and we need to modify specific cells of those 30 trillion with just the right amount of protein-coding and amino acids to allow humans to have offsprings again. So we know how to do it, but the software to make it all happen is what does the magic. Software such as Cytoscape can visualize molecular interaction networks integrating gene expression profiles. When it comes to cells, Wes, The Bug, acts like a regulator or, better said, a manager. You see, specific cells in the body become old and must die and be replaced by new cells. It's the natural part of the body's recycling of building blocks. That's where those telomeres come into play, remember? Before The Bug, the telomeres were shortened with every cell division until new cells could no longer be produced. The Bug fixed that, then there are cells that shouldn't die, such as brain cells. The Bug kept those cells healthy too. It had to know how to manage all the different compartments. But I'm getting too detailed here already.

That is it in a nutshell, and the way we wanted it put together, in this case, was to take the weakened DNA from the cadaver and combine it with the stronger DNA in a live person, follow?"

"Yeah, I do," Wes replied. "Wow, that is miraculous!"

"Yeah, well, wow is right! But has nothing to do with miracles; it has everything to do with science, Wes. Science and our understanding of the biology that has grown alongside technology have allowed us human beings to jump from that invention of the light bulb in 1879 to quantum computing and the manipulation of our human DNA, reshaping and engineering our very makeup. That I don't call miraculous, I call it incredible! We accomplished all this in the last 168 years. It took Homo sapiens who looked like us a hundred thirty thousand years to progress from stick to lightbulb. I can't begin to imagine the advances to come in the next 168 years," Lillian responded and then looked over to Dr. Fohr, nodding for him to take over.

"But Westernman, there have been some fall-outs," Nigel said. The tragedy that occurred just after Baby Alpha was born, well, Baby Alpha is healthy and growing, but with both parents having passed away shortly after the mother gave birth was a milestone in our history. Cole and Wendy sacrificed their lives in giving new life. With the grace of God, they were both able to greet their new baby into this world, but only to be snapped away a couple of months later, with both dying within minutes of each other. The modified Forever Bug shortened both their lives like a countdown clock precisely eleven months after achieving conception. Thankfully they at least had a couple of months to know their baby. That was fall-out number one.

Fallout number one has now been corrected. We can guarantee a minimum of thirteen years of life to both mother and father after a newborn's birth. Our computer projections have shown a 100% accuracy in this fix, and we stand by the science. Even more incredibly, the software can be tweaked to sequence the DNA, to the precise degradation of cell telomeres to year by year longevity virtually down to the exact day. In this case, we were able to squeeze out thirteen years or 4,745 days driven by the body's natural 24-hour circadian rhythm. It is the body's virtual biological clock monitored by the 20 thousand neurons located in the brain's hypothalamus."

"Dr. Fohr, you mean you're now looking for new couples to take the drug developed to modify The Bug in their systems so they can have babies?" Wes asked.

"Yes, we will be taking names of volunteer couples who have chosen to go this route," Dr. Fohr replied.

"So you'll be just taking names for now but not actually giving out the drug?"

"That's right, we have a limited amount of

opportunities for next year, a year from now, that is."

"What do you mean, a year from now?" Wes asked, not understanding why they couldn't give out that drug now if a couple wanted it.

"Wes, the government, Health Canada officials were to discuss this in an open forum with the nation, but I suppose it's already seen the light of day, so I may as well open the door wide on this," Nigel replied.

"Here's the thing, remember we need to extract viable but weakened Bug virus from bone marrow tissue no later than fifteen minutes after death and then freeze it immediately for it to be viable when needed. Wes, nobody, is dying; we need to wait for accidents to happen, and then EMT's or doctors need to be present. Remember, they all need to be donors as well. So the way this is going to work is with a baby lottery every December 1st.

Each year, all successful extractions from accident victims will be stored and held for the entire year, starting with the first extracted marrow. Unfortunately, one accident victim will only have enough weakened Bug virus to treat one healthy parent. At the end of the twelve months, the government will tally the number of doses it has harvested, perhaps a few thousand if we are lucky in that respect, but sad in others. Say the country has five thousand male deaths and three thousand female deaths."

"Yes, what happens then?" Wes asked, jumping on that question.

"Well, in that case, only three thousand couples will be offered the opportunity to have a baby the following year. The government will pull three thousand couples' names out of the millions entered in the lottery, and only those three thousand will be able to fulfill their dreams of becoming parents. Only they will know the joy of bringing a new life into this world," Nigel replied. "And that will go on year after year after year. There really is no other way.

"I see," Wes replied, understanding but dejected. "Okay, Dr. Fohr, I think we just created a world-wide sigh of sadness. But Dr. Fohr, why can't those extra male extracted bone marrow specimens be coupled with extra female samples say from other countries?" Wes asked.

"Well, Wes, these are the things that will have to be worked out between countries as our societies evolve to address these issues and find solutions."

"But Dr. Fohr, Dr. Eavers, what about the idea of this being a doomsday scenario? Four will have died in the end to produce one baby? Isn't this a mathematical formula for the accelerated extinction of our humanity? With enough babies being born, in a few hundred years, we'll be on our way to depopulating the planet!" Wes commented.

"That won't happen, Wes." Dr. Fohr answered. "Yes, at first the graph will show a sharp decline in the population, for the first couple of generations. For the first twenty or so years, until 2067, say, four will have perished with the technology we have today for every human born on planet earth. The graph will show a sharp decline for the first twenty years, but then those newly added humans to our overall global population will start having their own babies. Remember, the new babies' reproductive systems will be fully functional, and they will become new parents. We will still have a population decline for the second generation in the following twenty years. Still, then with those young people also having new babies, the graph will start its upward trend, and by the fourth generation, approximately a hundred years, we will have achieved equilibrium," Dr. Fohr said with a reassuring voice.

"So, we're not doomed!" Wes exclaimed.

"No, I don't think so," Dr. Fohr replied, smiling and looking over to Dr. Eavers.

"We do have other concerns, however. The new babies will have weakened immune systems. The Forever Bug will have mutated with the infusion and integration of its weaker version. The new people will be prone and susceptible to disease, everything from mumps to leukemia to everything! Doctors will be needed once again, like before. The nice thing is, we will already have all the doctors we will ever need, they didn't die, and they didn't go away; in fact, they've all gotten younger! The Bug still lives in us all; that hasn't changed one bit. For the new generation, well, yes, big changes, but they too still have The Bug; they preserved their abilities to age reverse when they reach 40," Lillian said with a reassuring smile.

"All we need to do is to keep them healthy fighting off the diseases. You see, Wes, The Bug acts in strange and perhaps inexplicable ways. It retains certain properties and loses others. We were able to maintain The Bug's ability to keep the telomeres long. Remember, we talked about the way we saved cells from dying? We elongated the telomeres that prevented the cell from becoming weaker every time it divided, and eventually, it couldn't because its telomeres had become too short after each division. Well, we were successful in getting The Bug to retain that ability. As long as the cell isn't attacked by disease, it will divide and divide forever, staying young, but attack it with a disease, and it will die. That is where drugs and hospitals and medicine come back into the picture. Let's hope we can keep the new humans alive for hundreds of years," Lillian added.

"And as for the parents, well now there is a choice to be made. Many people over the world will figure they've lived long enough, perhaps in their second life already, and soon to reach childbearing age all over again. They may choose to have a baby, live with it, and love it for at least thirteen years and add to the human race's survival. I am sure millions and millions of people will choose that to be their way of seeing their dreams coming true. It's thirteen years now, that is what we can guarantee, but Westernman, we are always marching forward; maybe in five or ten years or even tomorrow, somewhere someone will have discovered a way to turn the thirteen into thirty or fifty. We never give up hope, and we never stop," Lillian finished.

"Dr. Eavers, you're saying thirteen years. I'm still not sure I understand," Wes said.

"No, I get it, Wes, I get it."

"Dr. Eavers, the parents, they won't get sick, but they die anyway?" Wes asked. "How's that?"

"Right Wes, The Bug is still in their system, but it's lost its capability to keep the cells strong and healthy. For the parents, the telomeres have weakened and become smaller by the minute, their cells are dying faster than ever, and the body ages quickly with age acceleration amplified. The new parents will age five times faster than normal. A thirty-five-year-old will look like eighty-five in ten years. The stress load on their cells and body will no longer process the oxygen in their blood, and their bodies will give out. They will die. It will not be a painful death, but it will be fast. Every parent will die looking like they are in their 70's, 80's, or 90's. Wes, the decision to do this will not be simple. And once committed, there is no turning back," Lillian said.

Wes had no idea what to say or how to respond. He had a weight on his mind and a perplexed look on his face. "Well, you heard it, directly from Dr. Eavers and Dr. Fohr. I think our questions, for now, have been answered! As far as Canada goes, Canadian couples can start thinking about becoming parents starting twelve months and about one week from today! The nation needs to wait a year to determine how many of us will be lottery winners next year on December 1st. Big life-changing decisions ahead for us and the world. My guests have been Nobel Prize doctors Lillian Eavers and Nigel Fohr of the Fohr-Eavers Research Center in Montreal, Canada. This is Wes Ternman, and you've been listening to The Westernman Show."

After Wes had closed his program, he had one question that he wanted to ask, so he did.

"I guess I can ask either one of you. Who was the elderly gentleman who showed up at the station delivering the messages to me?" Wes asked.

"Oh, that was Karl, Helga Karlsdottir's father. Hence the name, Karlsdottir – Karl's Daughter. They have a strange naming system in Iceland; in fact, surnames are banned. If you had a daughter Wes, her last name would be Wessdottir or a boy; his surname would be Wesson, which really isn't a surname. It is your first name with daughter or son added to it. Interesting, isn't it?" Lillian replied. "Karl lives here in Toronto, loves the city, but we hire him as a messenger and courier for sensitive information from time to time."

"Well, he's good at what he does," Wes replied.

***

CHAPTER TWENTY-TWO
2047

CORRUPT TO THE CORE

Dateline: Monday 8:00 AM December 2nd, 2047 Philadelphia Pennsylvania USA – Granger Pharmaceuticals Corporation

"Health Canada is not going to budge on this, Michael."

"Did the minister say how long that would be or give you a reason why they are holding off on issuing Granger a license for the software?"

"All she said was that she couldn't comment on an ongoing investigation into Granger Pharmaceuticals. I asked Minister Richardson just that; how long it would be. She didn't answer my question, Michael."

Michael Dern knew precisely what was going on. The Ternman home break and enter and his two hired private investigators' arrest was the reason. Wes Ternman had already made that clear on his program, even if he didn't mention Granger Pharma.

"Well, that's too long! God-damn it! We can't wait for even one more week or day. We need to get out in front of this; otherwise, it will be too late, and we will go from being the largest pharmaceutical in the US to the smallest or disappearing altogether. We need to get approval from those fucking Canadians on licensing that Bug software; otherwise, we are done! I've been CEO of this company for too long, seeing it through twenty-two years of The Bug crisis. I'm not about to let our rivals drive us into the ground just because the Canucks won't grant us a license. We need to find another way, Tim!" Michael Dern said.

"What's this thing about the Canadians conducting an ongoing investigation into Granger? Shouldn't I know about this?" Tim asked.

"Yeah, I guess you should know now that the shit's hit the fan. Back a few years ago, like eleven, I had put a tail on to Wes Ternman, yeah, the radio talk show host. That Westernman program he's got up there in Toronto. The whole fucking world is listening to him now. Dana Blackman and a few others think the tail I put on Ternman was just after the announcement of that baby's birth back in July, but I've been tailing Ternman since 2036. Ever since he had his big radio show with Eavers and Fohr. The guy has become the voice of The Bug ever since."

"Yeah, he's got me hooked as well," Tim replied.

"So anyway, with Ternman being so closely tied in with Fohr and Eavers, I figured it would serve us good to have Ternman followed just in case he slipped up and could maybe lead us to some information about The Bug or lead us to a guy who knows a guy who knows a guy. Get my drift?" Michael paused.

"Okay, go ahead."

"Yeah, so I pushed them to look harder, not just follow. You say you're hooked on his show too. That I take it means that you listen regularly, is that right?"

"Yeah, pretty much."

"So then you caught his show when he told the world his home had been broken into, and it was all masterminded by some big drug company."

"Yeah."

"I'll give you two guesses who that drug company is. The two guys I hired talked to the cops, no doubt, and laid it all out. But they can't prove a thing. Don't worry, I know what I'm doing. Just is I pushed those boys too hard, and they got caught. It did fuck things up though, now we're on Health Canada's shit list, and we're not going to get that software license. We need to change that," Michael said.

This Monday morning at Granger's corporate offices located on the 32nd floor of the Granger Building in downtown Philadelphia it was just Michael Dern and his senior vice president of development and acquisitions. They were in the boardroom that looked out over Market Street towards the liberty bell. Granger Pharma was situated in the medical district's heart, surrounded by hospitals and health care facilities. Just down the street was Jefferson Hospital, Pennsylvania Hospital, and Penn Neurosurgery, just to name a few. Most of the hospitals were at skeleton staff or even closed. Most other hospitals in the city had long been converted to condominiums and apartment complexes.

From what Michael Dern and the rest of the world learned over the past couple of weeks, things were about to change in the coming years. With Fohr and Eavers saying that people will now need treatment for the past diseases, Granger Pharmaceuticals could be back in the driver's seat if he played his cards right. The first step in regaining and maintaining prominence was to secure Granger's reputation. That required the company to secure a license for The Bug quantum computer software from Health Canada, or perhaps another source. Dern opted for the other source at this stage. He could not wait.

"Tim, I don't think we're going to have a choice in this. We can't lose our position as the premier pharmaceutical in this country, and we certainly can't put our stock price at risk. We will have to find alternate sources for the software. It's not looking like Health Canada is going to cooperate with us."

"Alternate sources? What do you mean Michael, there are no other sources," Tim replied, with a look of, *you're not going there, are you Michael?*

"Tim, I know your mind works like mine; that's one of the reasons I picked you as my VP of acquisitions. You know how to acquire things, am I right?"

"That is what I do, Michael."

"Yes, it is. Tell me, Tim, the Canadian government is licensing their Bug software to both corporations as well as government entities, isn't that right?"

"Yes, to certain corporations and to governments around the world as well but with restrictions. For example, Michael, licenses granted to governments will restrict those governments from doing business with certain pharmaceuticals, or their license is revoked. Should those governments break the license agreement, trade sanctions, and tariffs would be imposed, costing those governments heavily," Tim replied.

"What else have you learned about the licensing restrictions? Tim, there must be more to secure the software should a government break the agreement; it can't be just sanctions," Michael replied.

"Yeah, well, there are safeguards built into the software Michael. The software cannot be moved. No, I mean it. The software works off GPS positioning with tenth generation security code verification. For example, say the government of Albania was granted a license. The license would only open the software to operate in a specific spot in Albania. You couldn't just get the software's license and then move it and start making the drug anywhere you wanted to. The software would only operate on quantum computing located in a specific spot designated when it was granted. It would not operate in the cloud or any other virtual space other than a physical location verified about a billion times per second. They have it locked down, Michael."

"Okay, so Tim, I know you have a way around this because I do. But I want to know what you would do if I said to you, no matter what it takes, get me the software to produce this damn Bug Drug."

"That would take two things, and then two more things after the first two for this to become profitable."

"Go ahead," Dern said.

"First two are money and corruption. The next two are more difficult," Tim said. "And the next two I don't know how to acquire," he added.

"I'm listening."

"Right, the money part is no problem, and the corrupt part isn't either. Enough money will corrupt just about anybody, and there are plenty of corrupt dictators in this world, even running countries that are not on the UN's terrorist list or rogue nations. You know the Canadian government will deal with any and all nations so long as they're not designated as terrorist nations or on the UN's human rights watch list. So I think we'd be good there. I am confident we can acquire the software from one of those nations. Just buy out the motherfucker president or king and be done with it. We move in and run the software to produce the drug right where it's designated to operate. It doesn't come to us; we go to it," Tim replied.

"And what about the other two, the more difficult ones for which you have no answers?" Michael asked.

"That would be the need for dead bodies and the need for new parents," Tim said, "And I don't know how to manufacture dead bodies. New parents? Well, there are plenty of those around the world, but without dead bodies, we have no volunteers lining up to become new parents. All the world's accident victims will never be enough to meet the supply of new parents waiting in line to become new Daddies and Mommies. But where to get 15 minute old dead people from, well that's something I don't think anyone has the answer to," Tim concluded.

"You leave that part to me," Michael said. "Just make sure you get me the software, and I don't care where it is. We will go there, do the chemistry there and manufacture the drug on-site. I don't care which country it's in or which dictator you have to bribe. Pick a country where bribery is part of their everyday life. I think you'll find the going a lot easier," Michael said.

"Michael, I have to ask you where are we going to find all the dead people who die just in time for the marrow to be extracted? We'd need thousands dying every year at just the right time! How the hell are you going to find that?"

"Oh, I'm way ahead of you, Tim. I've been planning and gaming out this scenario for a while now. Long enough to find a solution by looking in the right place. Tim, the only thing you need to know is that this facility will be a clearinghouse. You sell it like that, got it?"

"Yeah, got it, Michael, that I can do," Tim replied, sounding relieved.

You'll never guess who told me where to look, Tim. Not in a million years will you ever imagine. The funny thing about it is that this individual told me where to look for just-in-time dead bodies without knowing it. You know who it was?"

"No, who told you, Michael?"

Michael Dern then looked at his VP Tim Kingston and said with a forming smirk, "Wes Ternman did just a few days ago."

Michael's response startled Tim. His eyes suddenly went wide open, and his jaw dropped. Staring at his boss, Tim whispered to himself, "what the fuck!" in disbelief.

Dern then sat back in his chair at the head of the boardroom table. He then swiveled his chair to gaze out the window and down onto Market Street towards the Liberty Bell Museum. Leaning back, he then started chuckling while looking out onto Philadelphia and then said softly but loud enough for Tim to hear, "Oh yeah, there is a way, there's always a way."

***

CHAPTER TWENTY-THREE
2047

A BIG ASK

Dateline: Monday 8:00 AM December 2nd, 2047
Toronto Canada – The Ternman Home

"Wes, baby, you know what today is?" Sylvie asked as she rolled over onto her side to face Wes.

"What, Sylvie, tell me."

"It's the first day in which our country will be making every effort to harvest viable Bug virus enabling prospective new parents to become pregnant, Wes. I wonder how many people in Canada will die this year? One year from today, the winners of Canada's first baby lottery will be notified; that could be us," Sylvie said nervously. She had no idea how Wes would react. She wasn't exactly easing her husband into this conversation.

Wes just lay there beside her for a moment or two, not saying anything. He sighed a deep sigh looking up at the ceiling then blowing out his breath.

"Sylvie, don't think I haven't been thinking about

this. I have. More and more every day, but especially since our camping trip to Algonquin in October. Sylvie, I've been obsessed with it more than you, I bet." He then turned on his side to look at his wife.

"We're both on our second ride babe, we're both getting younger now. I've been on this earth for seventy years, and you sixty-nine. If we have a baby Sylvie, it will mean I'll be checking out around eighty-four or so, you eighty-three, a decent amount of time. More than enough time for love. That is how I feel, and I'm good with that. But babe, there are a lot of things to consider. Oh my God, I've had things in the back of my mind, but now they're front and center."

"I know Wes; I think of those things too. But I have faith in hope. I have faith in what will come in five or ten more years. Dr. Eavers and Fohr say thirteen years for now. I just know they will find a way to turn the thirteen years into twenty or maybe even fifty, just like they said on your program. I can't ask you to die for me Wes, I cannot do that. I love you more than I love my own life, baby, but what I can ask you for is to have a baby with me," Sylvie said with her eyes now tearing up.

Wes, too, couldn't hold it back. He again teared up, answering Sylvie as he softly caressed her face, "I will, baby, I will."

Sylvie moved her body against Wes's, wrapped her arm around his chest, and kissed her husband. "We have a lot to figure out, babe, a lot."

"Sylvie, we might not be lottery winners the first

year. It may take ten years or fifty or a hundred years before we are one of the country's' lottery winners, or we may never win!"

"I know Wes, I know, but we will keep trying until our name gets picked."

"Then there's the future, you know what I'm talking about, Sylvie, our child's upbringing and future. Thirteen years isn't enough; someone will have to step in when we are gone, Sylvie."

"I know, and I've been thinking about it. I'm going to ask my Mom if she would take over from us to raise our child as if it was her own after we are gone."

"That's exactly what I was thinking; I was thinking of asking my Dad, maybe the two of them could, and I know they would love him or her as they love us, baby," Wes said. "You know the ironic thing about this whole picture, eh?"

"What?"

"Depending on when we are successful at the lottery, it may turn out that your Mom and my Dad will be younger than you and I when we pass, putting them at a perfect age to raise their grandchild," Wes said, adding in a little laugh.

"I think we should ask them soon," Sylvie said.

"Okay, let's do that in the new year baby, we'll pick a day in January. Do we ask them together or separately?"

"I think separately, Wes, less pressure," Sylvie said.

"I think you are right."

***

CHAPTER TWENTY-FOUR
2048

PARAGUAY

Dateline: Friday 8:00 AM January 3rd, 2048
Philadelphia – Granger Pharmaceutical Corporate Offices

"Have you narrowed down the countries or maybe better said, leaders?"

"Yeah, we've concluded our due diligence. Crazy, I can even call it that; an investigation would be a better term. The three countries, finalists, shall we call them, were Somalia, South Sudan, and Paraguay. Paraguay turns out to be our best choice. They're not as fucking backward as the African choices, and Paraguay's had the same guy in charge for the past twenty years; there is no reason why he won't be in charge for another twenty. It's the most stable corrupt bribery ridden country on earth. Bribery runs through every fabric in their daily life, from bribing doctors to bribing priests. It's their way of life. Our offer to President Fernando Bolivar will be accepted even before I present it," Tim said, laughing.

"Bolivar?" Isn't that one of their war heroes or something?"

"Yeah, Simon Bolivar, a soldier and statesman. Back in the early 1800s, he liberated six South American countries from Spanish rule. It's quite a famous and common name in South America. It might be that Fernando Bolivar is of the same bloodline, not sure of that, although he claims he is. I think that's what has kept him in power all these years; a bloodline claim to Simon Bolivar. But he's not that righteous, far from it." Tim said.

"Just as soon as you tell me that you have secured a source for the bone marrow, I can get the ball rolling in Paraguay, I'm sure of it. He's already agreed in principle to the humanitarian aid. He's just waiting for the finer detail from me before he goes ahead."

"Does President Bolivar understand we require his Bug license coding? That we are moving in?" Michael asked.

"Yeah, he knows, just need some details, such as how much he stands to make and specifically how things are going to work. The number of people we will have on-site and security concerns. It's all being handled, Michael."

"All right, I know you know what you are doing; I have no doubt about that. Get the ball rolling, Tim, we need that software, and don't worry about the bone marrow supply; I've got that all covered," Michael said.

"I'll fly out to Asuncion this afternoon then. Paraguay is not a puddle jump; it's a fucking twenty-hour trip."

"Well, take a couple of sleeping pills. Go to sleep in Philly when you take off and wake up in Para-fucking-guay," Dern replied.

◇◇◇

"President Bolivar, it's been my pleasure. Our team from Philadelphia will arrive next week, at which time the security requirements and the facility's operations plan will be presented. If all goes as planned, we should be ready to produce the first batch of The Bug Drug by the end of the month," Tim Kingston said, bidding President Bolivar farewell.

"I look forward to doing business with you, Mr. Kingston. I can assure you that all will be in place as you have requested, and my office will do everything to make sure your quality assurance parameters are followed. I am happy that Paraguay can offer a way for anxious want-to-be-parents and baby lottery losers to achieve parenthood. This will be a welcomed clearinghouse facility to service those countries wanting to take advantage of our solution to this global problem. Have a good flight back home, Mr. Kingston."

President Bolivar escorted Tim Kingston from the presidential palace. The deal was done.

◇◇◇

"All good, Michael, we're sending our team in next

week. The facility known as The Paraguay Life Clinic is just on the outskirts of their capital city Asuncion. It has good transportation and infrastructure. Asuncion, as it turns out, has left its sleepy little town reputation over the past ten years and has really stepped up, becoming a moderate South American power. It's certainly overshadowed the jittery and unreliable government in Venezuela and Paraguay has no cocaine or illicit drug problem. Their economy is doing pretty good despite the widespread bribery. But it is the way they live; everyone bribes everyone. Hell, you can't get a cup of coffee served without first bribing your waitress in a restaurant. Me going down there and openly bribing the president, well he didn't bat an eye, Michael."

"What's the final cost? What are we looking at?"

"Five million in drug profits that we will not have because we're sending five million dollars worth of Neoral-B to them as a humanitarian donation. They will reap ten million from that, and that's it. It costs us five million, not a penny more, except of course relocating and housing six of our employees. Actually, it will be twenty-four in all each year. We are rotating them every three months. I can't ask anyone to stay longer than three months," Tim replied.

"Everything is operating above board there, right? It's a legitimate pharma facility with client facility and nearby overnight accommodation, as I asked?"

"Oh yeah, Michael, you need not worry about that. We are golden. Five kilometers from the facility is a new four-star hotel. The international clients flying in to pick up their Bug Drug from The Paraguay Life Clinic will have a comfortable place to stay while they overnight in Asuncion.

Our people will be safe as well. I've arranged for their 24-hour security detail, so there will be some added costs, but minimal, nothing like the operation we would have needed in Somalia or South Sudan. There we would have been spending millions a year just on security, never mind appropriate housing. Paraguay is the right choice. There are a dozen or so countries in the world that do not have laws explicitly covering bribery, Paraguay is one and the best one," Tim said.

"Yeah, well, that's fine and good, just remember we have our securities and exchange commission here in the US and the department of justice overseeing all corporate activities with the Foreign Corrupt Practices Act (FPCA). It clearly makes paying bribes to foreign officials a criminal act. How are you getting around that?" Michael asked.

"Don't worry, we're getting around that," Tim replied.

"How? Tell me again. I want to be clear on this."

"It's like I was saying, we will send five million dollars worth of Neoral-B, our newly patented version of Cyclosporine, the anti-organ rejection drug. We're sending it as a humanitarian donation. The corrupt president then turns around and sells it to the world for ten million over the next couple of years. We hold the worldwide patent and the chemical codes, so there is no chance of generic duplication," Tim answered.

"Okay, that'll work," Michael replied.

"Should I ask from where and whom you secured the bone marrow supply?"

"No, all you need to know is that our facility in Paraguay is a clearinghouse for the world's nonpaired bone marrow units," Dern replied.

***

CHAPTER TWENTY-FIVE
2048

CAM AND MAGGIE

Dateline: January 4th, 9:00 AM, 2048
Toronto Ontario

"Maggie, I hope I'm not calling you too early," Cam said, greeting his son's mother-in-law.

"Oh God no, I'm up with the birds, have been most of my life. I'm just not one to sleep in ever Cam, what's on your mind?" Maggie responded.

"I'd like to talk to you about something that's been on my mind for quite a time now, but it really hit home for me a couple of weeks after that Sunday night at The Budapest Restaurant."

"Oh,?" Maggie said, with inquisition and surprise in her voice.

"Yeah, Maggie, I'd love to buy you lunch today. Could you meet me at The Budapest Restaurant say at 1:00 this afternoon?"

"Back to the Budapest Cam? Are you going to propose to me?" Maggie asked and then started laughing.

"Ah, no, not quite, but I think I will give you something to think about. Will you meet me?"

"Sure, Cam, 1:00 PM it is."

"Great, I'll meet you just inside the door then," Cam replied.

<><><>

"Thanks for meeting me for lunch, Maggie," Cam said as he helped Maggie with her coat.

"Sure thing, I can always use a nice bowl of hot goulash on a cold wintery day like this," Maggie replied.

"Yeah, that table will be just great. Actually, that's the table I was hoping would be available," Cam said to the hostess seating them.

"So, we're back at that anniversary table? What's up with this Cam?" Maggie asked, looking a bit surprised.

"You know I asked you to meet me for lunch because I have something on my mind. I want to talk to you about it, right?"

"Yeah, you said that, Cam, that is why I agreed to come. Well, not really; I'd be happy to have lunch with you any day, even for no reason at all. You and I have always gotten along great, and we have two fantastic kids we love. You're a great father-in-law to

Sylvie. I hope you think the same of me for your son."

"Oh my God, of course, I do. I don't think there are too many families out there with more love to share than ours."

"You're so right, Cam, and that Sunday night here celebrating our kids' anniversary proved that in droves."

"Talking about families and the sharing of love in our small circle is why I asked you to have lunch with me today."

"Oh, family? But our family is so so small, Cam, just four! That's it! Just us four!" Maggie replied.

"Yes, precisely that reason; family," Cam replied.

"Okay, this ought to be interesting."

Just then, their waitress came by to take their lunch order.

"Bowl of goulash for me," Maggie said.

"Make that two," added Cam.

"Coffee?"

"Yes," Cam replied.

"Earl Gray Tea for me, please, sweetheart," Maggie said.

"Coming right up."

Cam took a sip from his coffee and said, "Maggie, in 2025, I had turned 69 years old. We've both been age-reversing for the past twenty-two years. I'm 47 years old in Bug years but really 91 going on 92, and I'm feeling like a 30-year-old. It's remarkable. You too, Maggie, just look at you; you're looking like a picture of health and beauty. You were what, 64 in 2025, right? We celebrated your 85th birthday last year in May, so that would put you at 43 in Bug years, 42 this coming May. Maggie, in another few years, we'll be fit enough to enter the Olympics, I have no doubt."

"Where are you going with this, my dear Cameron?"

"Just listen up, I'm getting to it."

"Your tea, ma'am,"

"Thank you."

"Maggie, think back to a few weeks ago. The Sunday night here on November 17th. It was a wonderful night, wasn't it? I don't think I've ever seen your daughter and my son as happy as they were that night on their anniversary."

"I have to agree with you on that, Cam. I've thought about that since, yeah, you are right," Maggie replied.

"Do you remember that table across from us, right there? That table for four. Do you recall the party sitting at that table?"

"Yeah, I do, of course, I do. I think everyone here that night in the restaurant would remember that table. That table and our table, with Wes and Sylvie's romantic dance."

"Yes, that table of a young family. Probably the only young family in all of Toronto or Ontario even. Looked to me like the parents were in their 30's and the kids, twins, right? Identical, they looked like to me. They couldn't have been more than 11 years old. They must have been in the group of the last in-vitro kids to be born in Canada."

"Yeah, that's how that would have had to play out. A couple of the last two in-vitro kids to have been born in 2036. Good thing she had twins. Otherwise, that one little kid would have found no one to play with. Least those two have each other," Maggie said.

"Yes, yes, but more than that, Maggie, much more than that. After Wes and Sylvie finished their dance and they kissed, you remember how the restaurant erupted into applause with congratulations on their anniversary? You remember that?"

"Yeah, it was a real and wonderful moment, Cam."

"You remember how all four at that table were standing, the two kids clapping like crazy with huge smiles on their faces?"

"Yeah, they sure were adorable."

"You're not the only one who thought those kids were adorable. Sylvie was so taken with the two standing and clapping, she walked over there and knelt down to hug them both, remember? Same with Wes, they shook hands with the parents and hugged those two kids like they were their own Maggie. For the rest of the evening, until the family left the restaurant, Wes and Sylvie couldn't take their eyes off the children."

"I noticed it too, Cam. In fact, I caught them both looking and smiling at the kids at one point; Wes winked at one of the kids. Sylvie caught him doing it and took his hand into hers on her lap. I know where you are going with this now, Cam," Maggie said.

"You know Wes and Sylvie never had kids when they could have for some ethical reasons, or whatever. Too many people in the world. I'm not sure if they ever thought that through.

But now, I tell you what, ever since his radio shows with those two doctors and then his interview in Iceland. Well, Maggie, I think now that Dr. Eavers and Fohr have guaranteed at least 13 years of life to the parents, I think they want to go ahead and enter that lottery thing Canada has going on this year. I can feel it in my bones, Maggie, but I think they might be stuck a little. I want to help them out and get them unstuck."

"Go ahead, Cam, unstuck me too," Maggie said.

"If my son and your daughter feel that they want to bring a new life into this world and love their baby for the first thirteen years of its life; well, I'm willing to take over and keep loving my grandchild for the rest of its life or at least till I'm alive. I will step in and raise it for the next ten or how many years needed. He or she will always be my grandson or granddaughter."

"I can't see it any other way Cam, we'd be the child's grandparents."

"But I think they're stuck, Maggie. I think they'd want assurances from us. They wouldn't want to burden us just because they want to sacrifice their lives; you get where I'm coming from?"

"I'm with you, Cam."

"I want to remove any fears they may have about this and approaching you or me about it. I want to approach them instead and tell them both that if they were thinking of the baby lottery, I'd be all for it and for them not to concern themselves. So what do you think, Maggie?"

"I think you've almost brought me to tears; that's what I think!"

"You're a good man Cam Ternman, a good man. I will join you in this and promise to share in the care of their child should the time come." Maggie then reached out across the table and took Cam's hand into hers.

"You are a good man Cam. Sylvie couldn't have asked for a more loving and caring father-in-law than you. I'll invite you, Sylvie, and Wes over to my place for dinner, and we can tell them Saturday night, after all, just like Dr. Eavers said, the world needs babies, right?”

“Right.”

***

CHAPTER TWENTY-SIX
2048

CHOI

Dateline: January 10th, 2048
Pyongyang– North Korea

"Vice-Chairman Kim Choi, thank you for taking time out of your busy day to meet with me," Michael Dern said as he reached out his hand to shake the hand of Kim Choi, the feared second in command to Sun Kim Koom, Supreme Leader of North Korea.

"Welcome to the people's paradise Michael Dern," Kim Choi replied.

Kim Choi then walked the CEO of Granger Pharmaceuticals into his private offices located one floor below the Dear Leader Sun Kim Koom's governing sanctum.

"My assistants advise me that you have come to make a proposal to the Democratic People's Republic of North Korea," Choi said.

Dern thought to himself, *what a bunch of shit that was…democratic people's republic. More like the doomed people's prison of North Korea would have made much more sense.* But who was he to pass judgment? He was here to make a deal with the devil himself to save his company. Now that he found himself being shown into the lair of the devil's disciple, there was no turning back.

"Tea Mr. Dern?" Choi asked.

Always accept an offer of courtesy, never refuse was the rule when dealing with a dictator or a disciple of the devil. Michael learned that a long time ago. To refuse was considered an insult.

"Thank you, Vice Chairman Choi; I would like that very much," Dern replied.

A few seconds later, a palace servant brought tea on a silver platter, for Dern only. Choi did not partake. Michael found that strange, but so be it. He drank the damn tea.

"I have spoken with our Dear Leader Sun Kim Koom, and he is anxious to have me tell him about your proposal concerning The Bug and what your pharmaceutical company can do for the people's paradise. I also want to thank you for reaching out to me personally about this opportunity. We are not averse to dealing with American companies that value North Korean life," Choi said and waited for a response.

Michael now had to choose his words very carefully. It was game time. He wanted to be blunt but praising at the same time.

"Vice-Chairman Choi, I understand your country has been purging itself from cancer within.

Dissidents, rebels, criminals, and those trying to undermine the Dear Leader's genius. I have a way for you to convert those traitors, those dissidents, those rebels and criminals, the scum of the earth you so despise into great profits for the people's paradise." Michael paused here, taking a sip from his tea, then placed the teacup back onto the saucer, and sat back waiting for a response of some sort from Choi. He got it.

"You want our dissidents' and criminals' corpses?" Choi asked, staring at Michael.

"No Vice Chairman Choi, just their bone marrow, just their bone marrow," Michael replied. This was the moment.

"How much will you pay the people's paradise for this garbage bone?"

"I would require equal male and female amounts of bone marrow every month. It must be equal numbers, male and female. I know The Democratic People's Republic of North Korea was not offered the quantum computer software for The Bug, but I can give the people's paradise access. I can provide you with The Bug Drug if you provide me with the bone marrow."

Choi asked a second time, "How much you pay for the garbage criminal bone marrows?"

This time Michael answered, "I am willing to pay the people's paradise ten thousand dollars for each extracted bone marrow unit."

Michael knew this was an extraordinary amount of money in North Korea. There would be no negotiations. It would be Michael's one and only offer. Right after Michael told Choi what he was willing to pay for one bone marrow unit, he looked for Choi's immediate reaction, even just the tiniest. He got it. It was a subtle twitch of Choi's eye. Michael knew his offer would be accepted. But it was now Michael's turn to ask a question.

"How many units of bone marrow is the people's paradise prepared to deliver each month?"

"The people's paradise had long hope for a way to profit from these criminals, some sort of a profit stream for our country. You can have as many as you want."

"The world wants many Vice Chairman Choi, more than you can supply, I am sure," Michael now pressed.

"How about we start with ten thousand each month for the first twelve months," Choi said, not flinching a muscle.

Michael almost fell off his chair, hearing that Choi was willing to execute ten thousand prisoners each month, but Michael was in it now neck deep. The money was adding up. He was talking real money here, one hundred million dollars in the first month alone. The payment to North Korea for the bone marrow would amount to 1.2 billion dollars in the first year.

Michaels company stood to generated revenues in excess of five hundred million dollars monthly with those kinds of numbers! Six billion dollars per year! Michael planned on charging a hundred thousand per couple. Ten thousand bone marrow extracts would mean five thousand male and five thousand female, making five thousand new parent couples every month. The figures Choi was talking about were astronomical, and without a proper well-implemented startup ramp, such huge numbers were bound to fail.

Michael realized this was much too ambitious, and he let Choi know. On top of that, although Michael's hand was now about to be partnered into genocide of unfortunate North Korean prisoners, a little genocide was better than pedal to the metal mass murder of thousands.

"That sounds like something we could do, Vice Chairman Choi, but not to start with. The bone marrow units can be increased gradually as the process is refined over the coming year. Vice-Chairman Choi, this surgery is a highly sophisticated medical procedure that must have the highest safeguard practices during the bone marrow extraction. You must remember that the marrow must be extracted no later than fifteen minutes after death and entered into a cryogenically frozen state within that period. The number of units you suggest, Vice Chairman, ten thousand in one month, would require over three hundred individuals' daily harvesting. I would recommend we start with a much lower number, five hundred the first month, and ramp up each month after that to ensure unit processing integrity," Michael said, now speaking like the pharmaceutical CEO that he was.

"I see, Mr. Dern, and you must understand never to underestimate the capabilities of the people's paradise to process and rid ourselves of undesirables, cancer as you called it. But I will take your advice. We will start with one thousand the first month, or we have no deal," Choi said with a smile.

This was precisely the reaction Michael had anticipated. He was shrewd enough to put the Vice-Chairman into a perceived winning position, making him feel like he was driving the deal. One thousand units were something the Paraguay facility could handle without any hiccups. Ten thousand well, that would have presented problems.

"Oh, we have a deal all right, Vice Chairman, yes we have a deal. One thousand, the first month will be fine," Michael said.

Choi then stood up and said, "Excellent, Michael Dern, we can do business." Michael then shook hands with the devil's disciple.

With a strange look of inquisition forming over his face and his eyes squinting, he asked Michael, "So how did you come by my name Mr. Dern? I am curious, why not go directly to our dear leader Sun Kim Koom?"

Michael wasn't sure how to respond but figured in this case, he may well be honest. It would also allow him to show Choi that Michael knew Choi could get the bodies he needed even before approaching Choi.

"Vice-Chairman Choi, you were the Ambassador to Canada three months ago, is that right?" Michael asked.

"Yes, that is right, I was."

"You were a guest on a Canadian radio talk show in Toronto. All I can say is that Mr. Ternman's show that day left me with an impression about you and North Korea that subsequently inspired me to contact you. It was The Westernman Show, isn't that right?"

Michael's honesty and bringing up Wes's talk show in Toronto and Choi being kicked off the program for lying about dead bodies and mass graves seemed to shake Choi initially, but Choi answered anyway, knowing he'd been had.

"Yes, that is right. Mr. Dern, you are a shrewd man. I will enjoy doing business with you. I think you and I have much in common," Choi responded.

Michael took that as a dig from Choi, but the deal was done. One devil's disciple dealing with another.

"Mr. Ternman did all he could on that day to embarrass me personally and the people's paradise."

"Well, this might be a form of karma to get back at Ternman if that makes you feel any better," Michael said. "You will ship the bone marrow units to Asuncion Paraguay through Zurich, Switzerland. One shipment of 250 units each week," Dern said. "First shipment to be made in four weeks."

"We can ship it to the moon if you want," Choi answered.

"Shipping the units to the moon will not be necessary, Vice Chairman, but there will be special shipping requirements. As you can appreciate, the shipment coming out from North Korea will need to be repackaged at a midway location. The repackaging will allow for the scrubbing of all North Korean documentation before it continues on to Paraguay. I will send you shipping instructions. Your shipment will be destined for Switzerland, where a third party will repackage, check the temperature control, re-manifest, and medi-seal the marrow. From Zurich, it will then be forwarded to Asuncion, Paraguay.

"And the payment?"

"You will make your weekly withdrawals from this bank account in the Cayman Islands after we receive shipment." Michael handed a banking document to Choi, and the deal was finalized.

"This facility in Asuncion Paraguay, you will be running it, I assume, not the government of Paraguay?"

"That is correct; Granger Pharma will be operating the Asuncion Bug modification facility. The government of Paraguay will only be handling the marketing, advertising, that sort of thing. That will be good for Paraguay, good for the people's paradise, and keep my company clean. Granger Pharmaceuticals only conducts the computer interface to The Bug's DNA mutation sequencing requirements.

"I should like to visit this facility sometime," Choi said.

"Yeah, we can arrange that, but for your information, although you may already know, The Fohr-Eavers Research Center has posted the bone marrow extract and follow-up cryogenic freezing procedures on their medical website. It's free for the world's medical community to have. The software, of course, isn't. That is my end of things. Just get the marrow to Paraguay as agreed, Michael said.

Michael Dern left the people's palace and the people's paradise and flew back home to Philadelphia. He wasn't feeling so good; he couldn't help thinking that he now had a very bloody hand in the death of thousands.

***

CHAPTER TWENTY-SEVEN 2048

MAGGIE'S HOUSE

Dateline: January 11th, 2048
Toronto Canada

"Oh, Dad, you're here too? I thought it was just going to be the three of us. What a nice surprise!"

"Mom, why didn't you say Cam was going to be joining us?" Sylvie asked her mother as Cam, and she walked in.

"Oh, honey, it must have slipped my mind, or I assumed you'd expect it."

"Well, not really." Sylvie then looked at Cam with a smile forming on her face. "Cam's a pretty busy guy, Mom. He's usually in his store till it closes, and this being Saturday, it would be one of the week's busiest days. Your store doesn't close till 10:00 PM, isn't that right, Cam?"

"That's right, Sylvie, but there's not a whole lot of people out buying suits in the second week of January, sweetheart. Everyone's pretty much shopped out after the Christmas holidays, and really this is our quietest week of the year. I bet your ceramic bowl orders have dropped off since Christmas, too, isn't that right?"

"Well, yeah, you're right it has."

"No, my store manager and one sales agent can handle the shop today. We may sell a few shirts and accessories but probably no suits today. At best, a tux rental maybe for a wedding or two tomorrow."

"Well, great, the four of us, dinner and a movie, is it for tonight then?" Wes asked.

"Dinner and a movie, maybe sweetheart," Maggie said, taking hold of Wes's hand and bringing him along. "Come, Wes, come sit beside me, will you, honey?" Maggie patted the semi-circular leather couch motioning for Wes to sit beside her. "You too, Sylvie, come sit beside me; I want the two of you close. Cam's making the drinks. What's it going to be, Wes?"

"Well, okay! Make it a vodka tonic on ice, Dad!"

"Glass of merlot for me, please, Cam."

"And I'll have my usual Cam, sweet gin martini," Maggie said.

Cam brought over the drinks and sat down beside Sylvie.

"Why do I have this feeling that something's up?" Wes asked.

"Well, my dear Wesley, the reason you do is that

there is something up. Something that your Dad and I want to talk to you two about," Maggie said.

"But right now, I want to make a toast to the two most wonderful kids any parent could ever hope to have. To you, Wes and Sylvie. For the much joy that you have brought into our lives. A toast to you and your health," Maggie said, raising her glass.

"Ma-om!" Sylvie eeked out. "What's this all about?"

"Go ahead, Cam, tell them."

"Maggie invited you two over to dinner because we have something we need to share with the two of you. Now, look, Maggie and I think we are right about this, but if we aren't, then we feel that's still perfectly okay. I'm just going to come out and say it and then be done with it. Is that all right with the two of you?"

Sylvie looked at Wes with a *have no idea what's going on* look on her face. "Fine with me," Sylvie said.

"Shoot, Dad," Wes added.

"All right then. You both know how much Maggie and I love the two of you, and we want you to know that if you are thinking of putting your names into the baby lottery and having a baby, well, Maggie and me, we're there for you, son, Sylvie, we're there for you. Whether you live for thirteen years or a thousand, we are there for you and will always be. You can count on Maggie and me to raise your child if the good lord takes you thirteen years later," Cam said.

Sylvie couldn't help herself; she burst into tears immediately and threw her arms around Cam. "Oh Cam, thank you, thank you so much." Sylvie could hardly get her words out.

Wes then turned to Maggie and hugged her as if she was his mother, who passed when Wes was just a teen. "Thank you, thank you, Maggie," Wes said as he hugged on.

"Looks like we were right about it all, Maggie," Cam said.

"Mom, Wes and I didn't know how to approach you about this; oh my God, Mom, you and Cam, you made it so easy for us, how can we ever thank you?"

"You and Wes thank us every day for just being you. My world would be empty without the two of you, and should you have a baby, my world would be that much more complete, honey," Maggie said, kissing her daughter's forehead.

"Dad, thank you for this; Sylvie and I will be entering our names into the baby lottery this week then. May as well get it in there. We've never won any lottery of any sorts ever; maybe this will be different."

"You have to wait a whole year, don't you, son?"

"Yeah, and we can't get too excited. You know how it all works, right?"

"We do, it's sort of morbid in a way, but I

understand it. There really is no other way of doing it, is there?"

"Not that Sylvie and I know of; we take our chances with the rest of the hundreds of thousands of Canadian couples hoping to have their names pulled in December," Wes said.

"Give it time, son, Sylvie, give it time. I bet you another way will come about. Things have a way of evolving. We humans have a way of changing the ground rules. For now, we have what we have, but I'm sure this will mutate as well over time, just like the damn Bug," Cam said.

"Come on, Sylvie, let's you and me get dinner on the table. I think our men are hungry," Maggie said.

"I love you, Mom."

Sylvie then stood up and walked to the kitchen with her mother.

"Come on guys, dinner is served," Maggie said as she placed the center dish of prime rib onto the dinner table.

***

CHAPTER TWENTY-EIGHT
2048

BUCKETS

Thursday, December 3rd, 2048
CHYI Studios Toronto Ontario Canada – The Westernman Show

"You're listening to Wes Ternman, and you've got the *Westernman* show coming at you from above the 49th parallel direct from atop the CN Tower in the land of the free and the greatest city in the great white north and North America; Toronto Canada. We're broadcasting around the globe on F.M., AM, shortwave, and globalnet sat-systems. A special shoutout to our Canuck listeners on moonbase 5 beaming at you with laser-line radio.

Ladies and gentlemen, people around the world welcome. Today we have one of those shows I think will go down in history. I'm looking to see if The Westernman Show can feel the pulse of the world. Look deep within your hearts and minds. I want to know where we stand, how we stand, or even if some of you wish to remain standing at all. Do I have your attention yet?

Oh, it appears I already do, the phone lines are lighting up like it's Christmas, and that's still twenty-two days away. Even more importantly, I haven't mentioned the topic or the theme for today's show,"

Wes said, speaking into his microphone and pausing for a moment.

Luke Stenner gave him the thumbs up. Wes's teaser opening was doing the trick. The thing about Wes's introduction on this day was that Wes was serious. He wasn't joking at all. Wes had every intention of turning today's program into a memorable one. This was a fitting day, and the world was ripe and ready.

Wes then started talking again. "I have to tell you I was thinking about this show for today all of last night. After I kissed my beautiful wife good night, I stayed awake, looking at the ceiling in the darkness. I wondered for the millionth time, I'm sure, just precisely to where our world was destined, where we as a nation and society are heading. Or do we just live day to day and hope for the best.

So why am I struggling with such thoughts? I'm sure we've all had them. I'm sure we've all been there. But that been there done that thing, well that's not something my wife and I can say. No, we haven't been there and done that, but we wanted to," Wes said, pausing again.

"Yesterday was D-day for Sylvie and me. It was Canada's baby lottery winner announcement day. My wife and I had never been there and never done that, but we want to be by God. We had hoped to be among the winners so we could become parents, but it wasn't to be. We have no idea how long it will be in our future before we can say, been there done that. So, how did it all shake out? You all remember the rules, right? Canada set up the baby lottery based on the number of unfortunate Canadians who lost their lives during a full year. But not only that, those poor souls had to be reached within the first fifteen minutes to have the medical procedure carried out before The Bug weakened too much inside of them, in their bone marrow, to be specific. That really cuts the numbers down, folks. Cuts them down dramatically.

I have some interesting statistics here from Stats Canada. I'm sure those of you who entered the baby lottery will find this more interesting than most, but just to give you an idea. Canada's population is 47 million, give or take a few thousand. Out of that amount, 16,718 died accidentally. Another 1,821 chose to end their own lives; they don't come into the mix of eligible deaths for the baby lottery purposes. Of the 16,718 accidental deaths, 10,301 were men but only 3,114 owned donor cards. Now further whittle that down to just 982 reached within the fifteen-minute window and the cryogenic freezing process, and you have your results.

Because bone marrow is needed from both male and female, no matter how many female bone marrow extractions were made, it still only makes for 982 actual pairs. So, 982 out of 47 million. Women dying accidentally were 6,417 but only 2,215 carried donor cards. Almost half, 1,032, a considerable percentage, were reached in time to perform the medical procedure within the fifteen-minute window. As mentioned, bone marrow specimens from both a male and a female are needed. So, 50 female samples were leftover with no male specimen matches. Canada ended up with 982 possible pairs; just 6% of all the accidental deaths were converted to potential lottery winners. According to Health Canada, 3,519,011 couples entered the lottery. The odds of winning were one out of thirty-five hundred. My wife and I were not one of the 982 winners.

Just to clear things up, the extra or unmatched specimens, being the extra 50 female specimens now in the frozen state, will be held in reserve for next year's lottery; maybe next year, more men than women will die accidentally. Ladies and gentlemen, it's a crazy world. Nobody wishes anyone to die, and yet many couples in our society will be checking the death toll every year on December 2nd. If you are a couple out there, who did win. I'd love to hear from you. I'd like to listen to your story," Wes said.

"But we move on. I want to hear from others as well. Several groups of us out there that fall into specific buckets, that's what I will call them, buckets.

Bucket number one. You're the old-timers who were born before 1980, for whom The Bug kicked in beginning in 2025, making you feel young again. You might have been 90 or even 100 in 2025, and now look at you; you're 23 years younger and probably feeling like you could run the iron-man triathlon.

Bucket number two. You're the ones who are the forever youngers, never got past the age of 45 if you were born in 1980, and if you were born in 85 or after, well, you've never been older than 40.

Bucket number three. You're the ones that were born after 2025 but no later than 2030, and you're still young, haven't even started your age reversal yet. You are in a particular position, whereby in another 15 to 22 more years or so, you'll be 40, and your parents might be looking younger than you are. I guess you'll have to deal with that. I am looking at that sort of scenario with my father soon, I think; I still have to figure that out.

Then there is Bucket number four. You are the in-vitro kids, born between 2030 and 2036; some of you might just be turning 12 years old this year, you others, well, in your late teens. There aren't many of you out there, and I can just imagine how hard it is for you. Nobody around really to socialize with; you are truly unique.

So there you have it, ladies and gentlemen, many buckets and many things to think about. We are living in a new age, with society turned upside down. Amazingly, we cope, we adapt, and we prosper. But I want to revisit these buckets.

Bucket number one, you old-timers; my question is, have you lived enough? Are you looking for more years? Or do you struggle with having to go through hardships all over again? Can you do things differently your second time around? If I could only be younger and know what I know today, we've often told ourselves how things would be different. Well, this is your chance. Can you do it, or are you afraid of even a more significant disappointment the second time around? And what about your life partner. You will soon be young enough that you might consider an addition to the family. Would you think of entering the baby lottery yourselves at age 90, in Bug years 30? You know, once you become parents, you will only have thirteen years to live. Are you willing to give it all up to bring a new life into your world? It's funny, isn't it? When looking back on our lives, it's much easier to recall the good times than the bad times. Are you ready to give it all up for a baby, maybe?

Bucket number two, you forever youngers. Do you ever wish you could grow older? Do you crave to know how it feels to know how your father or mother felt at age 64, perhaps? Have you thought of becoming new parents? But you'll only have thirteen years to live, or is that enough, is that time enough for love? Or will you live through two or three cycles and then try for the baby lottery?

Bucket number three, you youngsters and teens, how do you feel about where your future is heading? How do you socialize? Is all of your time spent in hologram rooms to reach out to your peers around the world? I want to hear from some of you, from all the buckets, as many as I can fit into today's program.

You too, the kids in bucket number four. Your group might be the most fascinating. You no doubt have entirely different outlooks on the future and your situation than anyone else. How you perceive our world, I'm almost positive, is unlike anyone in the other buckets.

This is the Westernman Show coming at you from Toronto, Canada, on CHYI.

Taking caller number one this Thursday on the Westernman show. Steve from Saskatoon, Saskatchewan, which bucket are you calling from Steve?"

"I'm in bucket number one Westernman, and I want to die."

"Oh my God, Steve, why, why, would you say that?"

Everyone tuning in to Wes's program could tell that Steve was calling in under great stress. Wes detected it right away in Steve's trembling voice.

"We are one of the couples who won the baby lottery, Westernman. My wife and I are on our second time around, 38 in Bug years. We found out yesterday morning we were winners, Westernman," Steve answered but could hardly get the words out, his voice trembling.

"What's the matter, Steve? What's going on? I can't imagine why you'd wish to die? You just won the baby lottery!"

Steve then started crying on the phone.

"Take your time Steve, take your time," Wes said, trying to calm Steve.

"Westernman, Wes, my darling wife Libby, she was killed in an accident last night coming home from work."

The gravity of Steve's grief and sorrow reached through the airwaves to every listener tuning in to Wes's program. A moment of national sadness swept over the country, felt by millions in Canada and around the world.

"In our first life Westernman, we didn't have a child, this was our second chance, and we won the lottery, a real chance Westernman, and now my Libby is dead."

"Oh my God, oh my dear God," Wes said, but he lost it too. For the first time, he lost it on-air. Wes suddenly felt like he was in Steve's shoes. His eyes welled up, his throat had a lump in it the size of a grapefruit, and Wes started sobbing.

Wes could hardly get the words out, "Ladies and gentlemen, we'll be right back."

***

CHAPTER TWENTY-NINE
2049

STRATEGIES & POLICIES

Sunday, January 10th, 2049
The Ternman Home – Toronto Ontario

Not all nations of the world followed in Canada's footsteps when establishing the strategies behind running their baby lotteries. The Canadian government felt it to be most equitable to run it once a year, giving everyone that same chance. Doling out The Bug Drug one couple at a time, running daily, weekly or monthly lottery draws was akin to turning it into a game. That was not something Canada wanted to do. There was nothing game-like about the unfortunate people who died in accidents across the country. Great sadness accompanied every accidental death. The loss of loved ones always hit hard on families accident or not.

It was the hope of Health Canada and Canadians in general that the collective deaths of accident victims could be joined in one annual day of joy. A day when all those deaths could be turned into giving new life, perhaps to thousands of new parents across Canada.

There were reasons good and bad one might say in the annual method. One significant advantage was that potentially thousands of new babies could be born simultaneously across the country. This would result in children of the same or like ages being able to interact with each other. Canada's vastness would make it impossible to meet in person, but virtual meetings in 3D hologram environments could go a long way in uniting these children of similar ages. Other positive spinoffs could result, especially in schooling, education interaction, and social skills development. It was important for children to be able to interact with other children of their age group. The more countries that followed Canada's methodology, the easier it would become for kids worldwide to grow together.

Countries that chose to go another way and have babies born all year long would realize after the first ten years or so that annually spaced-out births brought about quicker learning and better support groups to address new parents' needs. The concerns were more concentrated, making troubleshooting easier.

After the first year of bone marrow harvesting and the first baby lotteries worldwide were completed, there remained millions of couples around the world who felt a great sense of loss just from not winning. Millions of couples sought to find another way. The Paraguay Life Center in Asuncion, run by Michael Dern's company in secret but marketed by Paraguay's government, was only too happy to offer a solution. In the first month of 2049, Paraguay's government embarked on a social media advertising blitz that would turn the Paraguay Life Center into a lottery-losing-couples' destination from around the world. By January 2049, Vice Chairman Choi had delivered thousands of bone marrow samples in a cryogenic state, making for twenty thousand potential babies to new couples. President Bolivar wanted the world to know that his Life Center had a solution for those who had the means to pay, and he made sure to put the word out.

Sylvie was surfing the internet on this Sunday afternoon when an ad showed up on her computer screen. She didn't pay much attention, but suddenly the ad grabbed her attention like a chameleon's tongue catching a bug.

Reading the ad thoroughly, her heart seemed to skip a beat. The ad had come out of nowhere but now occupied all of her thoughts. She asked herself, *could this be for real?*

Without even looking up from her screen to look at Wes, Sylvie just blurted out, "Wes, have you seen this? Have you heard about this place in South America? This is unbelievable!"

Wes was having himself a lovely relaxing Sunday afternoon sitting in his comfortable chair just off to the side of the large picture window. It was January, snow was coming down pretty good in Toronto. There must have been six inches already accumulated. It was the wet stuff. Typically with snow conditions like these, kids would be busy building snowmen, but not anymore. There were no kids to be building anything anymore. Maybe a few in-vitros here and there, but not here in this part of the city.

Wes was immersed in a spy novel. It wasn't that often he got a chance to read for pleasure. Most of the time, Wes would be researching topics for his upcoming radio shows or brushing up on the news. Today he finally found some me-time to get lost in a world of make-believe.

Sylvie was about to change all that. Hearing Sylvie calling out to him, Wes figured she must have come across something vital for her to interrupt these pieces of leisure time he stole away now and then.

"What is it Sylvie, see something interesting?"

"God, I'll say! We talked about this, Wes, about what happens to the leftover unmatched or unpaired specimens, samples whatever you call it. If you recall, Health Canada said there were 50 female donor specimens that they are holding over in inventory for next year's lottery."

"Yeah, we talked about that and how many thousands of unmatched units there must be around the world. All those nonpaired units could be matched up if countries brokered their units with a central clearinghouse."

"That's right, and that is exactly what this ad is all about, Wes. Some company in South America, Paraguay is acting as a clearinghouse that pairs up all the unmatched units from countries around the world," Sylvie said, now showing more excitement in her voice.

"Well, I'm surprised at that. Remember, there was something about this whole issue at the UN, about all the countries agreeing not to turn their leftover samples into commodities. There was some sort of an agreement for them to hold onto their units so they could grow their own populations over time." Wes replied.

"I remember that too, babe, but then you actually said that it probably wouldn't hold. You said that if some of the poorer countries found a way to sell their samples, that they probably would, like on the black market or something," Sylvie added.

"Yup, and I bet you dollars to donuts that's what this place in Paraguay you say? I bet that's what it is, Sylvie."

"Well, I think it's a great idea, Wes. Babe, I want to look into this. I don't really see a difference where we can get that so-called Bug Drug from. Babe, people, are people all over the world. I don't need a Canadian dying for us to have a child. Heck, Wes, if we look at it from that point of view, I'd rather have more Canadians live, and we can get this Bug Drug from someplace else."

"Sylvie, babe, I have to tell you, you sure make a good argument; I cannot deny that, and you might convince me. Sweetheart, if you really want it that bad, we can look into it," Wes said, taking a moment to think and then added, "I tell you why I want us to think this through."

"Okay, shoot," Sylvie replied.

"If this place in Paraguay is some sort of a black market thing, I'm just not a hundred percent comfortable about it being first on the up and up and second that we're not getting ourselves into something we might regret later."

"Like what, Wes?"

"Like, I don't know, but if it's the black market or even gray market and babe, this place is in where…Paraguay? Well, jeez, red flags start popping up all over in my mind."

"Come here, look at this ad, babe."

"Look, this is the facility; it's a modern medical center. The Paraguay Life Center is run by the Paraguayan government's health and human services department. Their ad lists the services they provide to international couples. The Life Center is an extension of their national health services program, but it caters exclusively to international customers. The Life Center is modeled after their own Bug Drug facility, approved by the WHO (World Health Organization). Look, hon, they've been stockpiling unmatched units from countries around the world. Check this out, their ad then goes on to say that they are now open to meet the needs of hopeful new parents who don't want to play the lottery game of babies any longer," Sylvie said, reading the ad to Wes as they both scrolled through the photos and descriptions.

"Wes, look, here are their prices; they even have a guarantee policy; it's just two overnight stays in Asuncion Wes," Sylvie added.

The ad was starting to work on Wes as well. His interest was growing. "Yeah, go ahead, click on the prices and let's see what their package includes."

"Whoa, it's a hundred grand!" Wes said.

"Yeah, it is, but look, babe, it's all-inclusive, airfare, hotels, medical pre-check, and they guarantee success. It says here that if The Bug Drug doesn't take the first time, they will repeat the procedure as often as necessary until couples achieve success and there are no added costs," Sylvie added, then she stopped and looked at Wes, placing her hand on his lap.

"Wes, we have the money, heck we have the money even if this was twice as much. Wes, just think we could have a baby this time next year." Sylvie said, placing her head on his shoulder. "What do you think, babe, should we?"

"Let's think about it, Sylvie. Paraguay, eh?"

"Oh Wes, I don't care if it's Paraguay or Uraguay or far away, I really don't. And if we can't get pregnant from Canadian bone marrow, I have no problem getting pregnant from Romanian or British or Spanish marrow, makes no difference to me, and you know what, babe?" Sylvie asked.

"What?"

"You can bet our child won't care either; he or she will be happy that we brought him or her into this world to be loved by you and me and Cam and Maggie. That's all our child will care about, being loved Wes, as much as I love you and you love me."

"All right, Sylvie, let's look into it," Wes said.

"You're serious, Wes, really, you mean it, babe?"

"Yeah, I mean it, let's see what this is all about, go ahead, fill out their online form, can't hurt, right?"

***

CHAPTER THIRTY
2049
CONVERGENCE

Thursday, February 11th, 2049
Paraguay Life Center – Asuncion Paraguay

"Vice-Chairman Choi, I received your message as soon as I arrived at The Paraguay Life Center. I recognized your private security line; how can I be of help?" Michael Dern said.

"Mr. Dern, the people's paradise, and I wish to express our appreciation for your cooperation over the past year, specifically your handling of our product."

"I believe the appreciation is returned to you meeting the needs of our quality control, most importantly your adherence to our strict shipping requirements to the repackaging center in Switzerland," Dern replied.

"That is the reason for my message to call me Mr. Dern. We had a shipment returned to The Democratic People's Republic of North Korea, by Swiss Customs," Choi responded.

"Oh? What seems to be the problem, Vice

Chairman?"

"It seems something went wrong with the temperature control. The required minus 18 degrees Celsius constant threshold was compromised somehow. The temperature read 15 degrees Celsius, and it was deemed a hazardous biochemical risk and was not allowed into the country. The entire shipment was incinerated. The Swiss authorities have placed a product watch on all our future shipments. I think we may have a problem developing that needs to be corrected before we look at more shipments," Choi explained.

"Yes, that must be handled as soon as possible."

"Mr. Dern, you are currently in Asuncion Paraguay, how much longer will you be there?"

"I'm here for the weekend. I will be flying out on Monday morning, Vice Chairman Choi."

"That works out perfectly then. The people's paradise is prepared to replace the spoiled units incinerated by the Swiss. I mentioned to you that I would like to see the Life Center in Paraguay at some point. This will be a good opportunity since you are already there. I personally will bring the replacement shipments to you directly, bypassing the repackaging requirements," Choi replied.

"I can be there tomorrow; we have some issues to discuss in person, Mr. Dern."

"All right, Vice Chairman Choi, I will have a driver

pick you up at Asuncion Airport."

"That'll be fine, Mr. Dern; I will text you my arrival time. I will be at the private jets terminal."

"We're going to do it. Sylvie and I have been looking into this unique opportunity for the past month, and we've decided to go for it," Wes said

"All I can say is congratulations, Wes and Sylvie. When are you two flying out?" Cam asked.

"And this is something that can be done in one day?" Maggie asked.

"Yup, but we're taking the weekend package, staying Friday and Saturday night, and there's no better time than this weekend; it's Valentine's Day," Sylvie answered.

"We leave tomorrow morning on Pan Southern Airlines – Supersonic direct to Sao Paulo Brazil, catch a connecting flight to Paraguay, we'll be in Asuncion by 2:06 PM our time, 4:06 PM Paraguay time. It's all arranged, hotel accommodation, our interview at the Life Center, and then the procedure to be injected with The Bug Drug, which will happen Sunday morning at 10:15 AM. We fly out two hours later and be back home in Toronto before midnight," Wes said.

"You're flying out tomorrow?" Cam asked.

“Yup,” Wes replied.

“What about your Friday show?”

“Will be the second time since I’ve been on-air that I will have a guest host,” Wes replied.

“Okay, looks like you’ve got it all covered. How about Maggie and I take you guys to the airport in the morning?”

“Sure, that’ll be great,” Sylvie replied.

“Well, I’m happy for the two of you, now lets hope this works and you don’t have to go back for a redo,” Cam said.

“If we do, it’s all covered, Cam.”

“For a hundred grand, it better be!” Cam said. “Remember, here in Canada, every one of those lottery winners didn’t have to pay a cent,” Cam replied.

“I know, Dad, but we don’t want to keep playing this game every year and then waiting all year long hoping we are one of the winners. We talked this over, and we feel this is the right move for us,” Wes replied.

“All right, honey, I’m glad for the two of you,” Maggie said, kissing her daughter and hugging Wes. “I’m excited for you both.”

“Thanks, Maggie, we’re excited too.”

"Come on, Cam, I think our kids have things under control. Let's leave them some privacy. I'm sure they're looking for some alone time before they head off to become new parents."

"See you two in the morning," Cam said.

"Thanks, Dad, be here for 6:30 AM."

"Will do, son. Are you okay with that Maggie, 6:30 comes early?" Wes asked.

"Oh yeah, I already told Cam a few times that I'm up with the birds. Cam, pick me up at 6:15; will you, my dear?" Maggie said.

"All right, Cam let's get out of here before they kick us out," Maggie said, laughing then, hugging Wes and Sylvie good-bye.

"Welcome to Asuncion, Mr., and Mrs. Ternman. My name is Benedicto; I will be your guide while visiting our city and The Paraguay Life Center tomorrow. On behalf of our President Fernando Bolivar, I welcome the two of you to our modern city of Asuncion and our beautiful country in the heart of South America," Benedicto said as he greeted Wes and Sylvie at the Asuncion International Airport.

"Hello Benedicto, this is my wife Sylvie, and I'm Wes. Thank you. We are looking forward to our visit here to Paraguay. So we're not going directly to the Life Center this afternoon?"

"My pleasure to meet you both. No, I will pick you up tomorrow morning after breakfast at your hotel, which will be a 10:30. This afternoon and this evening is free time for you to enjoy our city and the restaurant of your choice. The Life Center has made advance arrangements at four of the city's most popular and famous restaurants. Let's go pick up your luggage. I will be your driver for your entire stay in Asuncion. You will not have to bother yourselves with calling for cabs; all transportation is taken care of," Benedicto said with a warm smile forming on his face.

Wes then looked at Sylvie and said, "Well, okay, sounds pretty good to me; how about you, babe?"

"Yeah, may as well unwind and enjoy what we paid for," Sylvie replied. "Besides, Benedicto seems very nice."

"Okay, Bene, let's go," Wes exclaimed.

"These are your two private cell phones while you are here for the weekend," Benedicto said, handing Sylvie and Wes a cell phone each.

"There are two numbers programmed in there for your use. The first number is mine, for you to call any time you wish transportation, and the second number is the receptionist at The Paraguay Life Center. Of course, you can use the phone to make any other calls you wish while here in Asuncion."

"Wow, you really have this covered well, don't you? It looks to me like you folks have thought of everything," Wes commented, taking one of the phones, "Thank you, Benedicto."

"Yes, thank you Benedicto, this will come in handy, I'm sure," Sylvie added.

"I will drive you to your hotel. You have been pre-registered, no need to stop by the front desk. These are your room keys; I have one for each of you. All you need to do is place your thumb onto the screen, and your print is digitized to your door for room number 1010. Your suite is on the 10th floor, room number 10. I think you will enjoy the view; it overlooks the city's skyline," Benedicto said, trying to brief Wes and Sylvie.

"Okay, we have arrived. The Hotel Pantanal is one of the finest in all of Paraguay. I think you will enjoy the accommodation as well as the exquisite service of the five-star establishment."

"Well, you're certainly pushing all the right buttons for me so far, Benedicto," Wes said.

"Thank you, Mr. Ternman; we can only hope that we have thought of everything. If you find something, not to your approval, please do not hesitate to use your phone to give me a call. I will fix things."

"You will find other guests at your hotel who are looking to become new parents. They've all been assigned their own special drivers. You will most likely come across your fellow hotel guests a time or two over the coming few days or may cross paths at The Life Center."

"So we just call you whenever we need you, that's what you're saying, right?" Wes asked.

"That's right, Mr. Ternman, after I show you to your room, I will be at your service until you retire for the night and will be at your service again in the morning from 7:00 AM," Benedicto said. "Just call my number when you are ready for dinner."

Saturday, February 13th, 2049

Michael Dern wasn't exactly thrilled about Kim Choi's visit to Paraguay, but there wasn't much he could do about it. In one way, Choi had the upper hand. Choi was the sole source for bone marrow units for one, and second, Michael was now so deep-seated with the North Korean mass murderer he really had no choice. If the word was to get out about Granger Pharmaceutical's arrangement with the people's paradise in supplying the marrow, it would most likely be Granger's end. Michael had managed to keep the real source of the bone marrow hidden.

Even President Bolivar was under the impression that his Paraguay Life Center truly was a clearinghouse facility for nonpaired units from certain countries opting to sell their unmatched bone marrow. Having Kim Choi here in Paraguay at The Life Center carried a certain amount of risk. Michael had to keep a close eye on Choi's movement, but more than that first, he'd need to make things clear to Choi in no uncertain terms yet be discreet about his visit's sensitivity.

"Vice-Chairman Choi, good to see you once again, and welcome to The Paraguay Life Center," Michael said.

Choi immediately looked to establish his ground with a curt reply, but Michael wasn't having any of it this time around.

"I should think the people's paradise would sooner look at this facility as a death center, not a life center, Mr. Dern. This facility only expedites the death of traitors and criminals of the people's paradise," Choi responded.

It does a lot more than that, you little piece of shit; it puts hundreds of millions into your pocket, Michael thought.

"Yes, well, I suppose there are two ways of looking at it. But the customers and clients of The Life Center look upon this facility as hope for new life, not a depot for death, and you must look at it in those terms while you are visiting. Is that understood, Vice Chairman?" Michael replied, causing Choi to suddenly jerk his neck in a surprising look at Michael. *Had Michael just given Choi an order to be followed?*

Michael figured, *you're on my turf now, and you need to behave*. Choi needed Michael as much as Michael needed Choi. Choi being away from his safety zone in North Korea, gave Michael the upper hand for the time being. The last thing Michael wanted was for Choi to be throwing his weight around in The Life Center. This was Michael's turf, and he didn't need Choi to be pissing all over it, leaving his people's paradise putrid scent.

There was a brief period of silence between the two of them. Choi looked at Michael with a gaze conveying a sliver of understanding. Then Choi nodded, seeming to indicate that he got Michael's message loud and clear. Michael knew he himself was no angel, more so an angel of death now that he was entrenched with Choi, but he needed to keep the fires of hell as cool as possible while Choi visited The Life Center.

"Let me take you to The Life Center so that we can start the tour and introduction to the Life Center's state of the art facilities and technology," Michael said.

"I look forward to the tour Mr. Dern, and this container holds the replacement units for the shipment that was incinerated by the Swiss," Choi replied. He seemed to have calmed down in his mightier than thou attitude.

"Good, we'll take that along with us and place it into our inventory, at the center."

A few minutes later, Michael had taken Choi on the facilities tour but entered The Life Center through the technicians' entrance around the rear of the building. Michael wasn't too keen on having Choi come through the reception area and the new parents' lounge.

"Come follow me, Mr. Vice Chairman; we have a viewing area that overlooks our new parents' lounge and reception area; it is equipped with one-way glass. Viewed from the new parents' lounge, the one-way window appears as a photograph depicting joyous new parents holding their newborn baby. Let's have a look and see how many couples are scheduled for processing this morning," Michael said.

Choi followed Michael to the viewing area. It was quite a large room. It was designed to accommodate ten or so couples with all the comforts one would expect. There were complimentary snacks and beverages but no alcohol or spirits of any kind—a variety of juices, soft drinks, and snacks all on a self-serve basis. The lounge was set up with private stations equipped with loveseats and television monitors, providing information on how the initial registration and sign-in process was to unfold on this first day and a short follow up on how the actual Bug Drug was to be administered the following day.

Wes and Sylvie were seated comfortably after being brought to The Life Center this morning by Benedicto and introduced to the facility's receptionist. Wes and Sylvie were situated so that their station was positioned on an angle but facing the photograph. They watched their television screen with the program telling them what to expect in the next hour.

"Seems simple enough Sylvie, It Looks like all they're going to do today is draw some blood for us both, and that'll be it for the day. That's not going to take more than a few minutes. Yeah, there will be the registration process first, but that's just answering a few questions the receptionist will ask, and after that, it's just the giving of blood, and it looks like we'll be out of here by noon," Wes said, taking Sylvie's hand into his.

Wes could tell that Sylvie was a little nervous; he

was trying to comfort her as much as he could. He had to admit he, too, was a bit on the jittery side. After all, this was it. They will leave here tomorrow after being injected with The Bug Drug, and their future will be in the hands of God like they couldn't have imagined just three weeks ago. Wes couldn't help thinking that they broke into the line and bypassed many waiting want-to-be new parents. He felt like he and Sylvie were maybe butting in. He had to put those thoughts behind him. They were now on their way to new tomorrows and, before the year was over, a new baby boy or girl.

"Don't worry, baby, we'll be through this soon. I can tell you're a little uneasy; everything will be fine. Look, they're really taking great care of us so far, wouldn't you say?" Wes said, trying to calm Sylvie's anxiety.

"No, Wes, I'm good, you know it just is, babe, this is it. We walk out of here tomorrow, and according to this video, we will both be fertile in just a couple of days," Sylvie said. "Be ready to spend a lot of time in bed with me, baby," snuggling in next to Wes.

Michael and Choi moved closer to the one-way glass and took a few minutes to survey the room.

"Ah, looks like we have eight couples this morning. The way it works, Vice Chairman, is we make the couples as comfortable as possible. Rather than have them move to a questioning area, we address the couples right there at their private stations. Our greeter will come and sit with them in a few minutes and go through the registration process. We ask them a few questions just to verify their information. We explain that on this first day, all we will be doing is drawing blood from them both so that we can perform the chemistry needed to produce their specific DNA modification to…"

Choi then cut Michael off. "Yes, yes, Mr. Dern. Do you have a patient list for the day?" Choi asked.

"Well, yeah, I suppose I can get one; let me have a look," Michael responded and was back within a minute with a list of new parents visiting The Life Center this weekend.

"Yes, I have it right here," Michael said.

"May I have a look at that list, Mr. Dern? I believe the people's paradise indeed has the karma you talked about earlier when you visited Pyongyang."

"What do you mean, Vice Chairman?" Michael replied, totally oblivious to what Choi was talking about.

Choi looked over the new patient list that Michael handed him and then started chuckling and nodding his head.

"Ah-ha! I knew I recognized that man!" Choi said with sinister glee in his voice.

"You recognized what man Vice Chairman?"

"That man, right there, you know who that is?"

Michael then grabbed the new parents list from out of Choi's hand and looked at the names. Instantly he understood the reason Choi had started chuckling to himself. On the new parents list, the third name down was Mr. and Mrs. Wesley Ternman of Toronto, Canada.

Michael was shocked! Suddenly he felt trapped not only for himself but for the Ternmans. Michael had never met Wes Ternman or his wife. He had listened to The Westernman Show several times. He had almost become a fan over the last few years, but this he could never have imagined in a thousand years, yet here the situation was! What ran through Michael's mind was enough to frighten him instantly. The tables had turned on Michael in a flash, and now Choi was holding all the aces.

Michael cursed himself for not looking over the new parents listing for the weekend. But there would be no need for him to do that. The couples were from all over the world. What were the odds of the Ternmans' and Choi's paths crossing in Asuncion on this day? The chances slim for sure, but the probability of convergence not impossible. If he had only known, he could have made arrangements for the Ternmans to come just a couple of hours later. But no, they had to be here now!

"That man Mr. Michael Dern is the man who kicked me off his radio program," Choi said.

"You know that to be true because his name is on your list. You evidently have never met Wes Ternman; you only listened to his program. You told me that he or his radio talk show inspired you to contact me, isn't that right, Mr. Dern? And now here he sits in your facility with his lovely little wife, waiting for The Bug Drug." Choi said with a big smile on his face, looking for revenge. "Well, what, luck! We will make sure to give him a special one," Choi added with an element of pure evil in his voice.

This was going to be a big problem, Michael knew. Choi wasn't about to let this go, and he was right.

"You know, Mr. Dern, that Mr. Ternman kicked me off his radio show, and that caused massive embarrassment to the people's paradise and to me on a personal level. Now I will return the honor to Mr. Ternman and his wife. The people's paradise will have its pound of flesh at long last!" Choi said, looking out the window at Wes and Sylvie as they sat next to one another with Wes's arm over Sylvie's shoulder.

Just then, The Life Center receptionist arrived at their station, introducing herself, and began the questionnaire to finalized the registration process. Choi and Michael watched. Three minutes later, Wes and Sylvie were escorted to the lab for their bloodwork. That was the last Dern, and Vice-Chairman Choi saw of Wes and Sylvie, but the wheels of revenge were set in motion.

"What do you mean about the people's paradise and karma and your pound of flesh?" Michael asked.

"This cannot go unattended, Mr. Dern. The people's paradise and I have been given an opportunity by pure chance to make things right." Choi replied.

"Make things right, how? What do you mean?"

Michael asked but now growing concerned. Michael had no bone to pick with Ternman or his wife. Michael knew he was in partnership with the devil himself but was reluctant to carry out Choi's wishes.

"I will not be moved on this, Mr. Dern. I require your full cooperation in this matter. Do you understand me?"

"Not sure I do, Vice Chairman. What is it you need?"

"Need? What I need, Mr. Dern, is for that man to pay! That is what I need." Choi answered angrily.

"And what do you propose?" Michael asked.

"You will alter The Bug formula. I know that your quantum computer software codes the bone marrow proteins to interact with the new parents' DNA, sequenced to allow up to 13 years of life. You will alter the formula and software sequencing settings to reconfigure The Bug Drug DNA lifespan back to just two years. That is what you will do for both the man and the woman. They can have their baby, but they will live only two years after they leave this facility. Two years will give them both 15 months to be new parents. This is the payment the people's paradise demands. There will be no argument over this. Do I make myself clear, Mr. Dern? Choi said.

"And if I refuse?"

"Then that will be the end of The Paraguay Life Center and the end of your company Mr. Dern and most probably the end of you," Choi replied, with a smile.

"You told me yourself that you have complete control over the computer software, and you set the program up yourself here in Asuncion. Well, Mr. Dern, now that Wes Ternman and his wife have been to the lab and given their blood, you will personally modify the formula as I watch you carry out the procedure tonight after The Life Center closes," Choi said.

Michael Dern wasn't quite sure what to say or do. He found himself to be trapped. How could he argue with the devil when he already agreed to be its partner. Michael couldn't see a way out. Not now. The fires of hell he was hoping to keep cooler just became hotter than it had ever been.

By 9:00 AM Sunday morning, February 14th, Valentines Day, Wes and Sylvie had completed their procedure and were infused with the modified Bug Drug. The telomeres were set to provide only two years of life. Sylvie and Wes were scheduled to die, right down to the day on February 14th, 2051.

"Thank you so much; everyone here was wonderful," Sylvie said as she and Wes bid farewell to The Paraguay Life Center staff.

"Benedicto, we are ready, you can take us back to the hotel, and we just need to pick up our luggage and then on to the airport," Wes said.

"It will be my pleasure to help you find your visit to Paraguay a happy one," Benedicto replied.

"So, everything went well? Mr. and Mrs. Ternman? Did you find anything at all we could improve on?" Benedicto asked in his cab.

"Oh, Benedicto, you have been so marvelous; all the staff at The Life Center couldn't have been more gracious and considerate. Our trip to Asuncion exceeded all of our expectations, and we are leaving here knowing we can have a child in the next year or even sooner!" Sylvie said with much joy in her voice.

"Yeah, it was all good, Bene, we were first up. The serum was already prepared for us. We didn't mind coming in earlier than planned this morning, and thanks for arranging that. The whole process only took maybe five minutes, and we were done. It was like we used to get back before The Forever Bug; it was like getting a flu shot. You remember flu shots, Bene?" Wes asked, now feeling much more relieved that it was all over.

"Oh yes, Mr. Ternman, I remember Flu shots and Tetanus shots, and Hep C and oh my lord, all those shots you had to get to stay healthy. But not anymore! And you, you must be so happy that now you can have a family. I congratulate the two of you on your future baby boy or girl," Benedicto said, smiling and shaking hands with both Sylvie and Wes.

Seven hours later, Wes and Sylvie's Pan South America – Supersonic landed at Toronto's Pearson International Airport. Cam and Maggie were there to welcome them back with open arms. They were home.

***

CHAPTER THIRTY-ONE
2049

DISCOVERY

<u>November 1st, 2049 Philadelphia</u>
<u>Granger Pharmaceuticals Corporate Offices</u>

"Yeah, Michael, we have a situation in Paraguay. Seems the honorable President Fernando Bolivar wishes to modify our agreement with the Paraguay Life Center," Tim Kingston said.

"Well, I'm not surprised Tim, I figured that was going to happen sooner or later. Knowing that the country thrives on bribes, the price was sure to go up in time. Sounds like the time has come," Michael replied.

"He is requesting a personal face to face visit and not a virtual one. Looks like I'm going to have to make a trip to Asuncion and iron this thing out."

"Tell the president that the best we can do is set up a monthly payment into this Swiss bank account directly from The Life Center's account. Don't tell him how much. Just tell him that he will be happy with the payment and that I personally will decide how much the deposits will be each month." Michael said.

"You're not going to let him negotiate?"

"Nope. Tell him that if he would rather have us pull our operation out of Paraguay, that next door Bolivia, his namesake country, will be happy to host The Bolivia Life Center. I hear that the two countries aren't on speaking terms anyway, and the last thing President Bolivar would want is for the president of Bolivia to outplay him at his own game," Michael said.

"Well, that is one hell of a noose you have around his neck, Michael."

"Sure is, I know how to play this game with these dictators; trust me, Tim, he will cave," Michael said. "Oh and Tim, our people down there, they really have been doing a fantastic job; take them some good news, will ya. Tell them that there's a bonus coming their way at the end of this month. I want them focused on their job and nothing else, okay?"

"You got it; I'll be on my way in the morning," Tim replied. "I'm sure they'll be happy to hear about a bonus."

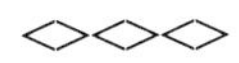

November 2, 4:00 PM 2049
Asuncion Paraguay, Paraguay Life Center

"Mr. Kingston, how nice to see you. I had no idea you were coming. If I had known, I would have arranged for a staff meeting. You know our group here is always anxious for news from the head office or even just gossip from back home," Bill Luckman, the facilities manager, said welcoming Tim.

"Oh, that's okay Bill, I'm not really here to see you guys anyway. I'm here to see The El Presidente. He and I have a few things to talk over. No, I don't want to bother your group. You all have been doing such a fabulous job here, maybe too good a job actually," Tim said with a slight laugh added. "Okay, I take that back, not too good of a job, just a great job overall. I couldn't be happier, and neither could Michael Dern be more satisfied with all that you and your crew do down here."

"Thanks, Mr. Kingston, that is always good to hear," Bill replied.

"Yeah, good to hear is not good enough. Michael has decided to pay all of you a bonus this coming month to keep the shoulder to the grindstone and focus on your assignments. He wants to show his appreciation for the confidentiality you work under and the pressures of living away from home."

"Thank you, the crew will be happy to hear that."

"While I'm here, Bill, I'm going to peek here and there; I want to see for myself the current condition and the shape this facility is maintaining. You have your QC checklist handy? I want to go through it myself."

"Sure thing, Mr. Kingston, it's right here, we just conducted the last one twenty four hours ago, well twenty-five, now, and will be doing another one in twenty-three. We do them just before we close up shop for the day at 3:00 PM. Do you want some company?"

"No, that's all right, Bill, I'll just take my time and go through this list; I know where everything is anyway. You haven't moved anything around, have you?"

"Nope, everything is like you laid it out, just like your plan."

"All right, catch you later, Bill, and if I come across anything, I will have it in my report."

"Okay, sir, have at it," Bill replied.

Tim wasn't much of a checker-upper if the truth be told, but he did want to verify a few things for himself. The main reason was that if anyone asked, he could confidently say that he had first-hand knowledge through randomized checklist item audits he conducted himself. Quality control, temperature control, and basic overall organizational routines were the hallmarks of efficiency in any organization, so Tim wasn't adverse in ticking off a few of those boxes for himself. This inspection would be his first time since the facility opened and started taking on product from around the world.

Tim picked half a dozen items from the checklist, two of which were storage and inventory control. There was a difference. Although inventory had to be stored, it was paramount to follow the proper method. Tim went directly to the temperature-controlled walk-in freezers. He picked out a parka and continued on to the security panel. Punching in his authorization code, the walk-in freezer door unlocked, and Tim entered.

The temperature was reading -18 degrees Celsius, and the temp history showed it had been holding at that level since the opening of the facility almost two years ago. Redundancy was in place with backup generators and refrigeration units. Everything seemed to be in order regarding temperature.

Tim was about to review the FIFO (first-in-first-out) record of the product rotation when he noticed something strange. All of the storage boxes containing the vials of frozen bone marrow looked identical.

First, he figured, okay, all international product shipment was transferred into Paraguay Life Center containers. But then he also figured that it would be an added cost to re-stage the product. The marrow was already packaged according to the strict quality control requirements; why risk product contamination with repacking when the product shipping standards requirements already met the packaging parameters.

Tim decided to have a look inside one of the boxes containing the bone marrow specimens. Each box was precisely the same size container, one-foot square, and eight inches deep. He undid the box latch, lifted the hinged top opening the box, and exposed twenty aluminum vials inside individual slots. The tops of each aluminum vial were marked with a human figure, ten male and ten female. Each box contained enough bone marrow for ten couples looking to get pregnant.

Okay, that all looks good, Tim thought. He was then about to close the top when he noticed something on the inside of the top. It was barely visible, but it was there. It looked like a stamp of some sort, an emblem, or perhaps a crest. It appeared to be embossed or pressure stamped on the inside of the top. If one wasn't' looking for it, you wouldn't even notice. It did catch Tim's eye, causing him to look closer. The lighting inside the walk-in freezer wasn't meant for reading. Everything meant for record-keeping was digitized on display panels so staff could come and go virtually in the dark. Entering inventory FIFO data was all on visual display panels, so lack of ambient light was not an issue. Tim, however, wanted to see what that emblem was all about. He reached for his phone and took a flash picture of the symbol.

Tim's curiosity grew. *What about all these other boxes?* He decided to check a few more. He opened one after another, spending the next half hour inside all four walk-in freezers opening two hundred boxes at random. They were all the same. The current readout showed 250 boxes in each walk-in freezer holding twenty vials each, 5000 vials in each freezer, making for 20 thousand vials in total. That was enough bone marrow specimen for 10 thousand couples and ten thousand new babies. Every box Tim checked had the same emblem stamped inside the top cover.

Before entering the second freezer, Tim already had a bad feeling about everything. Was the emblem a product logo, company logo, or country crest or logo? He noticed right away after viewing a clear image of the symbol on his phone because it had some sort of Chinese or maybe Korean script and the picture of a hydropower dam and bails of bundled rice. Tim decided that it was a crest of some kind from a country, not a box manufacturing factory. It was a country emblem. He settled on that, but then he became more concerned.

No, it couldn't be; no way could all of these bone marrow units have originated from one country; that would be impossible. Tim closed the freezer door and left The Paraguay Life Center. He headed for his hotel, but on his way, decided to call Bill Luckman, the facilities manager.

"Hey Bill, I have a question for you."

"Yes, Mr. Kingston, how can I help you?"

"The bone marrow, where does the shipment originate?"

"Oh, well, I'm not sure, Mr. Kingston, there's some sort of confidentiality thing concerning that. As you know, it comes from various countries that want to pass their unmatched units on to our facility. Still, before it comes to us here in Asuncion, it undergoes quality control and repackaging in Zurich, Switzerland. Everything we receive comes to us from Switzerland, Mr. Kingston, and always has," Bill replied.

"Okay, thanks, I was just curious; it looks like you've got tight control on the inventory and the storage. All checks out good Bill," Michael Dern will be glad to hear that," Tim said, trying not to give Bill a reason to raise any questions.

"Oh, by the way, I want to check on some quality control items at the repackaging center in Switzerland. Text me the name and address of the shipper in Switzerland and their contact information. I will also need a history report of the shipments from day one with the corresponding bill of lading info and digital copies of the Swiss and Paraguay customs clearance docs for each shipment since the very first shipment. Can you get me that, Bill?"

"Sure thing, Mr. Kingston, I can access our database remotely. I'll text the info to you in the next minute or two," Bill replied.

Tim retrieved the emblem's picture back in his hotel room and asked his cell phone search app to identify the symbol. It came back with an instantaneous response.

His phone displayed a clear color image of the embossed stamped photograph he took inside the freezers earlier. The emblem is the crest of the Democratic People's Republic of North Korea. The description displayed on his phone exactly described the stamps on the inside of the boxes. There was the power dam description at Mount Paektu with the power lines and a red star with the five points. The wording on the emblem was in Chosongul characters or text. Tim realized now that all the boxes were, in fact, from North Korea. A feeling of darkness overcame Tim's thinking, and it didn't feel right.

After thinking on the subject for a while, hours, in fact, he still couldn't fathom the idea of all the thousands of bone marrow samples or specimens coming from just one country, that being North Korea. He was hoping that maybe it was just the boxes from North Korea but not the actual vials. Then Tim started thinking that it had to be the vials. All the vials held inside the boxes had to come from North Korea; otherwise, it wouldn't make any sense at all. The vials were all identical, aluminum, each marked with a male or female figure. Inside of each vial was the actually frozen bone marrow tissue. It made no sense to suppose that various countries worldwide would be sending their bone marrow samples to Switzerland only to be opened and then transferred into these uniform aluminum vials. That would be an exercise in stupidity, exposing the medi-sealed marrow's content to the environment, having to move from original cryogenically shipped packaging into another container. That would not only open up the marrow to contamination, but it would also violate biohazard shipping protocols. Tim settling on all the products originating from North Korea had the wheels turning.

The thoughts now whirling through Tim's head, frightened him. He now thought back to asking Michael if he should ask from where Michael was sourcing the bone marrow. *No wonder Michael answered no.* But Tim had to be sure.

The text from Bill Luckman had come in a few hours ago, and Tim rechecked it. The address was Zurich, Switzerland, 1055 Interlaken Road Suite 16. There was a phone number as well. The name of the shipper was Von Wagner Freight Forwarders. At least Tim now had an address and the name of the shipper. To be sure, Tim would have to check this out in person and without Michael knowing about it. Tim still had one more job to do before flying back to Philly. He had to talk with President Bolivar.

"Mr. President, my honor to see and meet with you once again. Mr. Dern sends his regards and regrets not being able to bring you his good news in person," Tim said, greeting President Bolivar at the government house.

"Yes, yes, Mr. Kingston, a pleasure to see you as well. We all know how busy Mr. Dern is, but we both know he sent you because you have no real power to negotiate beyond his instructions to you, isn't that right, Mr. Kingston? He has stripped me of my ability to negotiate with his absence, so let us not play games."

After having discovered the boxes from North Korea, Tim was in no mood for brinksmanship. He almost wished for all this to just go away, but he was here to do a job, and the job was staring him in his face.

"Ah, Mr. President, don't be so harsh on yourself. I assure you Mr. Dern has your best interest at heart and not only your best interest but the people of Paraguay. I'm sure you'd rather keep The Paraguay Life Center here in Asuncion and allow the people of Paraguay to continue receiving the benefits from such a profitable enterprise rather than seeing it move to La Paz Bolivia," Tim countered.

"I'm confident when I say that you would not be pleased with President Cortez of Bolivia purchasing more armament with the revenues that a Life Center in Bolivia could provide. I'm sure you would prefer to seeing Paraguay Life Center remain in Paraguay. Am I not right, Mr. President?" Tim followed.

"But before you answer, Mr. Dern is more than willing to cooperate. He is sending his regards as I have said. Along with his ongoing appreciation in honoring the agreement between your excellency and our company, Mr. Dern will be making a substantial monthly financial contribution to your Swiss account. Further, Mr. Dern hopes this meets with your approval and looks forward to strengthening our interests in this exclusive business venture. Mr. Dern now considers this matter closed." Tim said and added a smile.

"We shall revisit this matter when in the future it requires revisiting," President Bolivar responded.

"I'm glad you are in agreement then, Mr. President. It has been my pleasure once again to have reached an agreement. I will be returning to the airport now. Good day to you, sir." Tim said and left the Paraguay government building.

"Michael, yeah, all is good; I just left the president's office, he'll sit tight for a while. You were right about the Bolivia thing. When I mentioned moving The Paraguay Life Center to La Paz, Bolivia, he wasn't keen on that; there is obviously some bad blood between him and President Cortez. Oh, and you were right about him, not asking about the money. I told him he would see a monthly deposit in his Swiss bank account, and he didn't ask how much. Yeah, you were right on about everything."

"Good job Tim, so you're coming back now?"

"Yeah, I'm leaving Paraguay this evening, but I'm going to take a few days off; I'll see you in the office over the coming week," Tim said.

"All right then, have a good flight and relax some; you've earned it," Michael responded.

◇◇◇

On the flight back from Paraguay, Tim became consumed with the origins of the bone marrow. He was determined to getting to the bottom of it all. He had to know exactly where the bone marrow was coming from. Although he already figured it would be illogical to move all the marrow from various countries into new containers, he was hoping against hope that he was wrong. If, in fact, all the bone marrow stored at The Paraguay Life Center originated from a variety of countries, he would be much relieved. If it didn't, and all the bone marrow was sourced from North Korea, this was a significant problem and an international incident that could be the end of Granger Pharma. Tim shuddered to think of what it could mean. It was unthinkable.

Tim was so driven to finding out the truth that he didn't bother going home after landing in Philadelphia. He caught the first supersonic flight from Philly to Zurich. Tim departed from Paraguay five hours ago, landed in Philly, and then landed in Zurich three hours later. The time was 8:12 AM Wednesday morning, Zurich time.

After landing in Zurich, he realized he was tired. He had been operating on adrenalin. Tim needed to freshen up, at least. He accessed his hotel booking app and requested a walk-in reservation at the nearest hotel to 1055 Interlaken Road, Von Wagner Freight Forwarders. He was booked to register within 60 seconds and was on his way by autonomous airport taxi. Tim was alone. Nobody from Granger, including Michael, knew of his arrival in Switzerland.

Tim checked in to his hotel, grabbed a shower, and changed into some fresh clothes he still had from his Paraguay luggage. By 10:20 AM, Tim was ready to visit Von Wagner Freight Forwarders and was on his way. While en route, Tim researched Von Wagner, accessing the online company management directory. David Mueller was the man he wanted to see; he was on the company website as managing director of international freight and cargo. Tim had the information he needed.

1055 Interlaken Road was a warehousing region, and Von Wagner Freight Forwarders took up one entire building that looked approximately twenty thousand square feet in area. Tim located the front entrance and entered the reception area to be greeted by the desk agent.

"Good morning," Tim said, "Do you speak English?"

"Good morning, sir," A female employee, perhaps 35 years old, replied. "Yes, I do; we speak English, German, and Italian here at Von Wagner sir, how can I help you?"

"Well, thank you, my name is Tim Kingston, our company has an account with you to forward freight every week from here in Zurich to Asuncion Paraguay. I am the executive officer of Granger Pharmaceuticals and the Paraguay Life Center. I would like to speak to Mr. David Mueller."

"I'm sorry, Mr. Kingston, but Mr. Mueller isn't yet here this morning, oh, wait, that's Mr. Mueller now coming in," The desk clerk replied.

Tim then turned to see David Mueller walking in and addressed him immediately.

"Mr. Mueller, good morning; I'm here at just the right time; it must be my lucky day."

"Good morning sir, how can I help you?"

Tim then introduced himself once again.

"I see. Well, Mr. Kingston, I need to see some identification as you can well appreciate before I can help you," Mueller said.

"Oh, I'm sure you do, and let me assure you I have more documentation and verification than you can imagine. In fact, Mr. Mueller, I have copies of all shipping documentation and customs clearance forms processed by your company in service to our corporate account and The Paraguay Life Center in Asuncion."

"Come with me, Mr. Kingston, let's address what you are looking for," Mueller replied.

"That would be great; thank you for your cooperation in advance," Tim answered.

Tim went on with Mueller to his office. Mueller took a few minutes to get situated and then asked Tim if he wanted a cup of coffee.

"Well, I'm going to get myself a coffee. Can I get you one, Mr. Kingston?"

"Sure," Tim replied.

"Tell you what, why don't you walk with me, and we can talk about what you need on the way? The cafeteria is just down the hall; we can grab a coffee there," Mueller said.

Tim and Mueller walked along a hallway to the cafeteria.

"So, what I need to see, Mr. Mueller, is the documentation showing the origins of the shipments that you repackage and forward on to Paraguay, to The Life Center in Asuncion."

"And you have copies of all customs clearance forms for shipments from Von Wagner cleared by Swiss and received in Paraguay, is that right?"

"That's right, I do," Tim replied.

"Well, then all this should be a piece of cake like you Americans like to say," Mueller replied.

Back in Mueller's office, Mueller asked to see copies of Tim's shipping docs.

"How about I just send it to your computer, and you can reference it right there."

"That'll work, Mr. Kingston."

"Okay, let's see. Yeah, all these shipments originate in North Korea. They are medi-sealed shipments meeting all WHO security and safety requirements. All we do here, Mr. Kingston, remove the contents from the outer shipping cover and repackage the contents. We don't actually open the shipment; we just recover it. Any and all markings from North Korea are removed. Those are the requirements as per our contract with Mr. Michael Dern."

"Yes, yes, of course. We had some issues in Paraguay, and I wanted to make sure everything was as it should be here in Switzerland," Tim replied.

"What I would like from Von Wagner is the freight forwarding order for each shipment from North Korca to Paraguay," Tim said. "Can you provide me with that?"

"I don't see why not, Mr. Kingston, we do everything above board here, all very legal and all very much documented," Mueller replied. "We are located in Switzerland, but we don't operate like our Swiss banks. When it comes to international shipping and especially medi-sealed cargo, we play by the rules. All shipments must be traceable and adhere to international agreements." Mueller replied.

"Well, that will do it for me," Tim replied. "But now that I'm here, by chance, did you receive this week's shipment from North Korea yet?"

"Let me check our receiving records for this week; hang on a second."

"Yes, it came in at 4:00 AM this morning; it is scheduled for repackaging this afternoon; would you like to see it?" Mueller asked.

"Yes, that would be great."

"Follow me."

Tim and David Mueller walked out into the warehouse and to the receiving dock area.

"There it is, Mr. Kingston, one crate on that pallet."

Tim walked up to the shipment and proceeded to take several photographs of the shipment along with a video.

"Thank you, Mr. Mueller. Can I see the accompanying shipping documents for this cargo?"

"Right here, Mr. Kingston," Mueller showed Tim on his portable customs clearance device the docs corresponding to the shipment sitting on the pallet.

"All right, forward that to me as well; if you be kind enough, you can use the digital address I used to send you the shipping docs earlier," Tim said.

"Already done, Mr. Kingston."

"Well, that will be all. I want to thank you for your service and cooperation. You have been a great help, Mr. Mueller."

"I have a feeling I have been; I hope you found what you came to Switzerland for. I believe you have."

Tim left Von Wagner Freight Forwarders both

frightened and relieved if there could ever be such a feeling.

He was now frightened for what he discovered and confirmed but also relieved that he got to the bottom of it all. But there was one more thing on Tim's mind that he absolutely had to follow up, and that was Michael's answer to his own question. And Tim would play sleuth just as soon as he got back to his hotel room.

Back in Philly two years ago, in December of 2047, Tim remembered Michael asking him if he knew how he found a way to source the bone marrow. Michael then said that Tim would never guess in a million years. When Michael said that Wes Ternman of the Westernman Show told him how and from where to source the bone marrow, well, Tim was shocked. He needed to follow up on that. He thought about this all the way back to his hotel.

There was another part to Michael's answer about the Westernman show Tim recalled. Michael's exact words were, *Wes Ternman did just a few days ago.* Tim never forgot those words; he was floored when Michael told him. But now those last five little words would make all the difference in the world, *just a few days ago*.

It had been an exhausting past twenty-four hours. Tim needed some rest, but he was driven and so determined. *Another few hours aren't going to matter,* he thought to himself. If he could find the answer, he could then relax and get some much-needed sleep even before he flew back to Philly. One thing that was a lifesaver these days was the supersonic airline service. You could be in San Francisco at 1:00 PM and in New York City by 3:00 PM. The world was getting smaller by the minute.

Now in his hotel room, Tim ordered room service and then set out to research *just a few days ago*. First, Tim checked his meeting schedule history. It was December 2nd, 2047, in the boardroom at Granger corporate offices in Philly. Michael said that Wes Ternman told him a few days ago.

Well, Tim well knew that Ternman would have no idea about where to get bone marrow and certainly didn't think that Michael Dern was buddies with Wes Ternman. No, it had to be something Michael heard on Wes's program not too many days before Michael and Tim talked about it all that day in Philly.

Tim then accessed his phone's live voice assistant saying, "Display all podcasts of the Westernman Show from December 2nd, 2047 going back two months, and list the daily topics," Tim spoke.

His phone displayed the list in date order from latest to earliest and the related topics of each program. Tim scrolled through the list, looking for a clue, and suddenly, there it was. Just a few days before Wes Ternman went on his secret trip, it turns out to Iceland. That was on October 26th, more than a few days ago for sure, but not by much. Reading the list further down, on October 23rd, the Westernman Show podcast listed an interview with The North Korean Ambassador to Canada, Kim Choi. *Bingo!* Tim thought. He selected Wes's October 23rd podcast, and not long into the interview, Tim had what he was looking for and more.

Wes confronted the North Korean Ambassador to Canada for the alleged mass graves and forced labor camps reported by the United Nations human rights watch organization.

Wes had uncontroversial evidence that North

Korea was still practicing force labor and imprisonment of political opponents. Wes had further evidence provided by various NGO's that infiltrated the communist government, estimating a minimum of ten thousand annual executions of North Korean citizens by the ruthless Sun Kim Koom regime.

The evidence was further collaborated and verified by call-in news reporters who then challenged Kim Choi on the air with eye witness accounts from North Koreans who managed to escape to South Korea. The Westernman Show ended up exposing the atrocities still being carricd out in North Korea, which led to Kim Choi being wholly embarrassed and being kicked off the show. Wes accused him of lying and a participant in his own country's domestic genocide. It was one ruckus Westernman Show.

Having listened to it all only confirmed Tim's darkest thoughts. So there it was. Michael Dern decided to contact Kim Choi and make a deal for thousands of bone marrow specimens sourced from the North Korean death camps. That had to be it! It all added up, and it made Tim sick to his stomach. Tim wasn't sure what to do now. He had to think, but the exhaustion had caught up with him. Tim flopped down onto his bed and was asleep within two minutes.

***

CHAPTER THIRTY-TWO
2050

SIGNS

January 3rd, 2050
Toronto Ontario, CHYI Studios

"You're listening to Wes Ternman, and you've got the *Westernman* show coming at you from above the 49th parallel direct from atop the CN Tower in the land of the free and the greatest city in the great white north and North America; Toronto Canada. We're broadcasting around the globe on F.M., AM, shortwave, and Globalnet sat-systems. A special shoutout to our Canuck listeners on moonbase 5 beaming at you with laser-line radio."

"Ladies and Gentlemen, people around the world, The Westernman Show wish everyone a very happy and prosperous new year. Here we are, the year is 2050, another one down, and we're only getting younger. Even if we're getting older, we're getting younger. Wes then thought to himself, *yeah, maybe for everyone else out there but not for Sylvie and me.* I hope everyone listening has reasons to celebrate," Wes said.

"So it's the new year, and I have some new news! I think this may turn out to be one of those shows again; you all know what I'm talking about—one of those shows where the lines will be going crazy and the world will be calling in. So let me tell you a little secret my wife and I have been holding onto for the past year," Wes now stopped and took a deep breath. *He was going to spill the beans, all the beans.*

"Last year, at the beginning of April, we got pregnant! Yes, you heard me right, we got pregnant!" Wes had just let the cat out of the bag and looked at Luke Stenner with a here-we-go expression on his face. The call-in lines started lighting up immediately.

"We had a baby on new year's day, a baby boy. My wife Sylvie and I couldn't be happier, a healthy 3.2-kilogram bundle of joy, we named him after my father, Cam. Cammy came into this world at 11:12 AM on new year's day. I've been holding this a secret, and I'm not sure if I'm going to open a huge and let me repeat this, a huge issue here, but I will let you be the judge. This will go where it will go. I think it may take on a life of its own. For those of you who are regular listeners, you will recall that my wife and I entered the baby lottery the first year it was out, and of course, with the odds being one in thousands, we were not one of the lucky winners. As time moved on, we came across an ad on the internet about a facility in the South American country of Paraguay called The Paraguay Life Center. I'm sure I will be getting calls this afternoon about it. My wife and I couldn't have been the only ones to learn of this facility," Wes stopped for a second or two.

"This facility, The Paraguay Life Center, seemed to be the answer to our shattered dreams of becoming new parents. It is a clearinghouse for unmatched units of DNA from countries all over the world. My wife and I decided this was our opportunity to bypass the annual Health Canada baby lottery. We could, after all, have a baby if we wanted to. All we had to do was fly to Asuncion, Paraguay, and get infused with the baby Bug Drug. We did it. Last February, we arrived in Asuncion on Valentine's Day weekend, an appropriate time of year, and were treated at the Life Center with the drug that enabled us to become pregnant. Yes, we jumped the line, so to speak, and now we have a gorgeous beautiful baby. We are now among the few new parents in Canada. You would think all this sounds wonderful, wouldn't you?" Wes stopped again. With Wes having posed the question as he did, it called for a time-out suggesting maybe all was not as it should be.

"So please let me make it clear that we love our new bundle of joy, Cammy, beyond words. He is healthy, and he's out of the hospital and at home now with my wife Sylvie, but folks, I have to tell you about a couple of things. Do I have your attention? I think I do." Wes stopped again for a couple of seconds.

"We all know by now I'm sure that those of us out there who put their names into the annual baby lottery hat made the decision not lightly. All new hopeful parents willingly sacrificed their longevity in exchange to bring new life into this world, understanding that in thirteen years, it would be lights out. Still, their new son or daughter would have potentially hundreds of years to live so long as he or she remained healthy. The parents would still have thirteen wonderful years to love and be with their child, raise it with all the fundamentals he or she will carry for the rest of their lives. The values and principles you instill lovingly will have shaped him or her for as long as they live. Well, it turns out that that is not the case for my Sylvie and me," Wes paused again.

At first, after our return from Paraguay, we felt

great, I mean physically, and we still do. We feel fine, we aren't sick or anything like that. The Forever Bug, although weakened, keeps protecting us but with one significant difference. My wife and I noticed about five weeks after we got back from Paraguay that we were starting to look older. We were both on our second time around and were in the process of age reversal. We understood that The Bug Drug would cause us to stop the reversal process, and we'd start aging again, but it's coming on fast, like really fast. After we began our age reversals, although it's been only ten years or so, we both started looking younger and younger. My wife and I are both in our 50's now age reversal and were looking like we were in our late 30's or early 40's at the most. Over the last year, we now look like we are in our 60s. We have no idea what is going on, but if this keeps up, in another year, we will have shriveled up looking like prunes in our 90s. We are frightened to a degree. Thinking back on the circumstances associated with Baby Alpha and its parents: we know that Baby Alpha's parents died shortly after their baby was born because they aged so quickly their bodies couldn't take the stress. Both parents expired within days and looked like they were a hundred years old. My wife and I fear that may be our fate as well," Wes added and stopped again.

"Ladies and gentlemen, we took our chances, and we got what we got, but we did get a beautiful baby boy who will go on to a very long and loving life. He will have the best grandparents any child could ever wish for. But there is something else. Make no mistake, once again, we love our baby; however, we get an unexpected surprise when little Cammy was born. I'm sure you are asking, what surprise was that Westernman? Well, my wife and I knew we'd have a bouncing little baby boy or girl, but we didn't expect our baby to be Asian. Yes, little Cammy looks like he is either Chinese or perhaps Korean," Wes stopped again and let that sink into his international audience.

Then he continued. "My wife and I are both Caucasians, but our baby Cammy is Asian. Neither one of us have a racist bone in our bodies, and our baby will receive the greatest love any child could ever wish for, but we weren't expecting an Asian baby," Wes stopped again.

"The reason I am telling the world about our situation is for your information. I am not doing a woe is me, nor am I looking for any kind of pity. We took our chances, and we have lived a good life. I wanted to put this out there so you are informed of what could happen if you choose to go a different route than your country's official baby lottery program, which has been proven safe so far in all the countries of the world using the system."

"My wife and I are good; we both have loving parents who will raise our beautiful son should we perish before the thirteen years come to take us both. I hope my program will give pause to all who are considering The Paraguay Life Center's services. And now, I will take some calls. If there are couples who have used the services of this place in Asuncion Paraguay, I'd like to hear from you."

Wes then took the first call of the day. "Susan in Calgary Alberta, welcome to the program, Susan."

"Oh my God, Westernman, you have me crying, and my heart goes out to you and your wife," Susan said.

"Thank you, Susan, but remember we aren't looking for pity. I just want people to know."

"Westernman, my husband and I went there too. We went to The Paraguay Life Center, and we have our baby. Westernman, we had the same thing happen, we have a little girl, two months old now, she too is Asian Westernman, she too is Asian!"

"Wow, Susan, hang on, I have ten other lines holding, hang on, this might be the floodgates opening."

"Sam is calling from Liverpool, England; hey Sam, do you have a similar situation?" Wes asked.

"Westernman, yes, yes! Our daughter! My wife delivered our baby just two weeks ago, and she is gorgeous but is Asian as well! But Westernman, we're not aging like you and your wife are; we're looking and feeling about the same as we looked last year at this time," Sam said.

"Okay, we're all on at the same time now; I will open a few more lines. I think I'm getting the picture here," Wes said.

"We're not aging either, Westernman," Susan from Calgary added.

"Fred, from Richmond, Virginia, you're on, what's your story?"

"Us too, Westernman, my wife and I decided to go for it, and we got pregnant at the beginning of

February last year, and much to our surprise, our baby boy, is Asian as well."

"Have you and your wife been aging at a faster pace?"

"No, Westernman, we don't look much different than we did last year; I think we're good for our thirteen years," Fred said. "But I have something else you and your listeners might be interested in," Fred added.

"What's that, Fred?" Wes asked.

"Our baby is Asian for sure; my wife and I are African Americans, so now we have a Black Asian child who we love beyond words as well. But Westernman, we wanted to find out more. We sought a local lab here in the greater Richmond area to do heredity DNA analysis on our baby boy. We now know Westernman; he has North Korean genes with heredity pointing to one particular region in North Korea. Our son's Bug Drug donors were from the capital city Pyongyang; that is all we know. At least we can tell him that when he is old enough to understand," Fred said.

Wes was getting a clear picture now as to what was going on. Asian, he could understand. All the donors were of Asian origin, but could it be that all babies born to couples who received The Bug Drug were from North Korea?

"You're listening to the Westernman show coming at you from Toronto, Canada, CHYI; we'll be right back."

"Wes, you have a call from Dr. Eavers on line four," Luke Stenner spoke into Wes's earpiece.

"Dr. Eavers, Lillian, this is a surprise!"

"Wes, Wes, I've been listening to your show. Wes, you and Sylvie, you must immediately come to our center in Montreal; you cannot waste one minute, do you understand?"

"Why Lillian, you're scaring me," Wes replied.

"Wes, what's done is done, we cannot change that, but maybe we can slow things down. The sooner you and Sylvie get here, the sooner Nigel and I can work on slowing down this aggressive aging process you are both experiencing. You cannot waste a moment."

"Well, okay, Lillian, I'll talk to Sylvie after the show and see if we can come up on the weekend," Wes replied.

"No, Wes, not the weekend, not after your show, now Wes. I want you to truncate your radio program now, have someone fill in or put up a rerun show, whatever you have to do, do it now and get your wife to the radio station. I'm sending a chopper for you and Sylvie immediately. It's on its way as we speak. Do you understand me, Wes?" Lillian pleaded

Wes suddenly understood that his and Sylvie's lives were in danger. He's never heard Lillian being so dramatic and urgent as she was. Dr. Eavers had finally gotten through.

"All right, Lillian, I'm calling Sylvie now; we will need to make arrangements for Cam or Maggie to look after our baby in the meantime."

"No, bring your child as well," Lillian answered. The chopper's ETA is 2:55 this afternoon. It will be landing on the helipad at CHYI; just get Sylvie and your baby there, understand me?"

Wes was suddenly alarmed. Lillian had never spoken to him like she just had; now it was Wes's turn to scare the crap out of Sylvie.

At 2:59 PM, four minutes after the helicopter arrived to pick up Wes, Sylvie, and Cammy, it was lifting off the helipad at CHYI studios and on its way to the Fohr-Eavers Research Center in Montreal.

Wes and Sylvie looked at one another with real fear in their eyes for one another. Sylvie held Cammy close to her breasts as the chopper lifted.

***

CHAPTER THIRTY-THREE
2050
OUTING

January 3rd, 2050
Philadelphia

Tim Kingston had become a fan of The Westernman show as he had pretty much admitted to his boss Michael Dern a couple of years ago. Today was no different; Tim was tuning in over the web to catch Wes's program. The significant difference today was that today's program hit home and tore at Tim's vitals. For the past two months, Tim had sat on the information and evidence he collected in Paraguay and Switzerland. The main reason he had not acted was that he really wasn't sure what to do. Tim had uncovered something big, so big that it would be the end of Granger Pharmaceuticals, his job, and the careers of many company employees. People he knew and respected, colleagues, and friends. Tim was hesitant to do anything, knowing he'd be putting them all out of work. But today, the scales changed. Tim's conscience and morals had finally caught up with him.

Having heard now that Wes's baby, along with everyone else's, were Asian and likely all of North Korean heritage, something had to be done before more innocent lives were lost. He had to admit it,

Granger Pharma was the bellows providing the oxygen for the flames burning in North Korean death camps.

But this Westernman show today, with Wes and his wife Sylvie, the way in which Wes presented his personal situation had Tim hating himself for having waited this long. It had already been two months since Tim's discovery of the situation, the crimes being committed to humanity, and the ongoing systematic domestic genocide carried out by Vice-Chairman Kim Choi. Tim had connected all the dots, so he thought, and yet one dot remained unlinked. He hadn't spotted until this afternoon's Westernman's program.

Tim asked himself *why only Wes Ternman and his wife Sylvie were aging quicker and faster than any other parents? Why was it just the two?* The answer was obvious, but it too was so unbelievable. It had to have something to do with Choi and Wes. Choi was kicked off the Westernman program by Wes himself, causing Choi to have egg on his face. Somehow Choi must have found a way of getting back at Wes through The Paraguay Life Center. Somehow Choi must have gotten wind that Wes and his wife were clients of the facility and had one of The Life Center techs or chemists alter The Bug Drug formula causing this premature onset of aging, but how?

Tim decided to make a call down to The Life Center in Asuncion. He was afraid to call, fearing what he would find out but called anyway.

"Mr. Kingston, good afternoon sir," Bill Luckman said, answering his phone.

"Bill, how are you?"

"I'm doing well, Mr. Kingston; what can I do for you, sir?"

"Bill, I need you to look up your client history. I'm looking for some confidential information."

"Yes, sir, what is it you need?"

"Last year, Valentine's Day weekend, you hosted a couple, I believe, Mr. and Mrs. Wesley Ternman from Toronto, Canada. Can you just verify that for me?"

"All right, sir, give me a moment," Bill replied.

"Take your time Bill."

"Yes, that's right, they arrived for the weekend package deal, arrived that Friday, and departed on Sunday after receiving their treatment, that's right, Mr. Kingston."

"Now, Bill, I want you to think back to that weekend, was there by-chance an oriental gentleman there visiting the facility that weekend?" Tim asked, holding his breath.

"Oh, I need not think too hard on that one. There sure was; the Asian man was with Mr. Dern. Mr. Dern was visiting that weekend as well, and he seemed to be giving his Asian friend a facility tour." Bill responded.

Tim was batting a thousand. He had put two and two together and had come up with the magic number. This was it, but he had one more question for Bill.

"Anything else Bill, was there something unusual that happened that weekend, specifically having to do with Mr. and Mrs. Ternman?"

There was silence on the phone for a few seconds then, "Hmm, let me think, no not really, other than Mr. and Mrs. Ternman were pleased that their Bug Drug was ready way ahead of time on Sunday morning. Mr. Dern must have shown his Asian friend how the software sequenced the bone marrow specimens with the drawn blood from the Ternmans to prepare their injections. Yeah, it was ready early, and they were out of here catching the first flight back to Canada on Sunday, I think. They were both pleased, as I recall," Bill said.

"Well, I'm glad they were happy; that's what you and everyone at the facility are there to provide Bill, great service and happy new parents," Tim replied, hardly being able to contain himself.

"Is that it, Mr. Kingston?"

"Just one more question, did you all get your bonuses as I promised you'd be receiving when I was down there?"

"Oh yes, Mr. Kingston, the bonuses came through just fine; we all appreciated that. Thank you," Bill replied.

"All right then, thanks for the information, and keep up the great work; my regards to your crew."

Tim sat, rubbing his face in disbelief. What rotten luck for Wes and Sylvie Ternman. The worst possible fate and merging of coincidences. Tim now knew just how evil his boss really was. All Tim had to do now was to let the Ternmans understand what happened to them and how. That was not going to be an easy task.

Tim's decision to bring the Ternman's into the loop would mean the end of Granger Pharma, the probable imprisonment of Michael Dern, and the closing of The Paraguay Life Center. Everything had to come crashing down. This was not going to be a piece by piece disassembly; everything had to come crashing down in one giant pile. He just had to make sure it didn't fall onto him and take him out at the same time. Tim knew what had to be done. He had all the documentation he would ever need, the photographs, the flight records to Paraguay by Dern, the flight into Asuncion by Choi that had to be on record somewhere, his clearance through Paraguay customs. All of the data was available to collaborate his story. Tim knew he couldn't wait one more minute. The longer he put this off, the more people would die needlessly in North Korea.

Tim decided to make two calls. He picked up his phone and made the first call.

"Good afternoon, The New York Times; how may I direct your call?"

The second call would be to CHYI Radio, to Wes Ternman, but that call would have to wait.

***

CHAPTER THIRTY-FOUR
2050

REALIZATION

January 3rd, 5:12 PM 2050
Montreal Canada – Fohr-Eavers Research Center

Drs. Eavers and Fohr were both waiting on the research center's helipad for the chopper to land. The Bell 430 helicopter landed on the research center's rooftop helipad two hours after lifting off in Toronto with Wes, Sylvie, and Cammy on board.

"Wes, Sylvie, you did the right thing; let's get you all into our lab immediately!" Dr. Eavers said. "We haven't a minute to waste."

Dr. Eaver's alarming comments caused Sylvie great concern. "What is it, Dr. Eavers? What are you talking about?" Sylvie asked alarmingly.

"Nigel and I have been listening to Wes's program this afternoon. When we heard Wes say that both of you were aging rapidly, Nigel and I knew there was no time to waste. Sylvie, Wes, the thing with this Bug is if the formulation for pregnancy is not configured correctly, the thirteen-year duration is corrupted, and the aging process accelerates with each passing day.

But Nigel and I will get into that later with you; the most important thing right now is to evaluate your situation. We need to determine the telomere longevity assigned to The Bug Drug you received in Paraguay. We need to draw blood from all three of you," Lillian said with urgency in her voice.

"Look, guys, we cannot downplay the serious nature of your situation, but if we act now, I mean today, we can still nip this in the bud, okay? So you need to calm down, let's give science a chance to work, all right? Nigel said reassuringly."

"Our baby–will you need to draw blood from Cammy as well?"

"Yes, Wes, we want to make sure there aren't any anomalies in Cammy's immune system and his Forever Bug status. Cammy should have the same Forever Bug life cycle status as you two did before you were injected with the modifying Bug Drug at The Paraguay Life Center. We just want to be sure," Lillian replied.

"The two of you can relax now. You are under our care. We'll get to the bottom of what is going on with you both, maybe all three of you."

"Dr. Eavers, we wanted a baby so so much," Sylvie said, now crying through her tears.

"I know, sweetheart, I know, but you should have checked with Nigel and me before you guys flew off to South America. But let's not worry about that now. What we need to do now before anything else is to determine your condition and prognosis, understand Sylvie? Wes, you understand Nigel and me?"

Sylvie nodded her head, indicating she understood. Wes took Sylvie's hand into his and stroked Cammy's head as Sylvie cradled him in her arms.

"Come on, let's get this done, roll up your sleeves," Lillian said. "We're going to draw blood from all of you. It won't take long before we know what is going on."

"How long, Dr. Eavers?" Sylvie asked.

"It's Lillian, Sylvie; I feel like you're my daughter, sometimes you know? I only wish your mother Maggie was here to give you her moral support; maybe I'll send the chopper back to Toronto for both your mother and Cam. Would you like that?"

"Yes, Dr. Eavers," Sylvie responded through tears once again. "Wes, do you think Cam will come?"

"Oh yeah, both your Mom and my Dad will take Dr. Eavers up on her offer; you can bet on it."

"Good, then call them both Wes, tell them we're sending a chopper for them and to be ready in two hours," Nigel added.

"All right, I will, they'll be shocked, I'm sure," Wes said.

"Dad, hi, Sylvie and me, we're with Dr. Eavers and Dr. Fohr in Montreal Dad, all three of us, Cammy too, we're at their research center. Dad, you and Maggie, you need to come. Dr. Eavers is sending a chopper to pick you both up….

<><><>

Four and a half hours later, Cam and Maggie exited the Fohr-Eavers Research Center helicopter, were greeted by Lillian on the helipad, and headed inside the building to see their son, daughter grandson.

“Dr. Eavers, what is going on?” Cam asked.

“Yes, Dr. Eavers; Cam and I, we’re frightened; what is it we can do?” Maggie asked.

“Look, both of you. Your daughter and your son, they’re in a bit of a pickle, danger to put it bluntly. They’re going to need your love, support, and comfort. We don’t exactly know yet what we are facing, but it could be terrible news,” Lillian said.

“Is it Cammy?” Cam asked.

“No, at this point, we think Cammy is safe and okay. It’s Wes and Sylvie; they’re in an aging crisis; we don’t know how long they might have,” Lillian answered.

“Might have?” Maggie repeated with alarm.

“Yes, Maggie, you heard me right. Nigel and I, we can explain later.”

“Oh my God, Oh my God,” Maggie mused.

"What can we do?" Cam asked.

"What you can do right now is just be there for them. Cam, be your son's father. And Maggie, be your daughter's mother and give them the comfort and love only you two can. Nigel and I may have some bad news in the next hour or two. I wanted the two of you to be here to help them through it. Do you understand me? This is a time both of you need to be strong for your kids," Lillian said.

Cam, then took Maggie's hand into his, and turning to Maggie, said, "Let's go love our children, whatever they may face, we'll face it together."

"Thank you for bringing us Dr. Eavers, thank you," Cam replied.

Cam, Maggie, and Lillian then walked into where Sylvie, Wes, and Cammy were waiting for their prognosis.

"Mom, Mom, I'm scared," Sylvie said, hugging Maggie.

"I'm here, baby, I'm here. Don't worry, whatever it is, we'll get through it together, sweetheart."

"Dad, Maggie, thanks for coming. I think we might have screwed up."

"Life itself is a screwup son, you're just living it. Don't blame yourselves; you did what was in your hearts; we're only human, Wes. We think we're strong, but the truth be told, we're all frail. The bond that holds us strong is what we have here today, son, love, and compassion. Maggie and I are here for you. We'll get through this, no matter what."

"Oh, Dad." Wes lowered his head and covered his face with his palms, speaking through his fingers, "What have we done?"

Cam wrapped his arm around his son's shoulders and said, "There is hope, son, there is always hope; why do you think Lillian and Nigel had you come here right away. They have hope, too, Wes. We're all in this together, son."

Nigel then entered the room, saying, "Come everyone, gather around. I've run an analysis on all three of your DNA. Before I go any further, I want to say that your baby is perfectly fine. The Forever Bug is intact; its genetic structure will provide the aging cycle from young to old and then reverse as you both were before you got The Bug Drug in Paraguay. Cammy's immune system seems to be normal, but as you know, still susceptible to disease. With proper care over the coming years, I cannot see any abnormalities in his ability to fight them off. Your baby is healthy and will live to be hundreds, I'm sure, unless, of course, later in life he decides to have offspring, then he'll be dealing with the thirteen year duration time frame as well."

Everyone listened in silence.

"Wes, Sylvie, something extraordinary is happening with your bodies and DNA. It's almost like things were deliberate, let's call it intentionally designed. The Bug Drug, you both received was specifically tailored to shorten your cell's telomeres to exactly two years from the date you were injected. You received your injections in Paraguay on February 14th of last year, isn't that right?" Nigel asked.

"Yes," both Wes and Sylvie said, nodding.

"When Nigel and I discovered how to overcome the rapid and aggressive aging that killed Baby Alpha's parents within months, we also found a way to scale the thirteen-year extension. It's based on the human body's natural circadian 24-hour biological clock. Our cells operate on that rhythm. We found the formula to configure cell division telomeres daily and extended it out to thirteen years. The quantum computer software can set the daily telomere division cycle to stop at any point, any day of the thirteen years. The software is set to default to the full thirteen years, giving all new parents the maximum life span possible, but the program can be set to terminate cell division at any point or day in the thirteen-year window.

Think of it as a countdown timer. The biological engineer–a doctor can set the computer to formulate The Bug Drug to bring on cell degradation at any time, effectively fixing a predetermined death date," Nigel said and then stopped with a look of finality on his face. "That is apparently what happened to you both in Paraguay; there is no other explanation."

"Oh my God, Wes," Sylvie replied.

"Yes, it's like this; if it was just one of you, then perhaps it could be viewed as an error, a mistake, an accident. But think of it like nine-eleven, the twin towers in New York City. When the first plane hit tower number one, it was considered an accident. But then when the second plane hit tower number two, well, the first plane was no accident either," Nigel added. "Wes, you in this scenario were tower one and Sylvie tower two. Might you have some enemies in Paraguay you didn't know about? Wes, Sylvie?"

Wes and Sylvie just looked at one another with bewilderment and confusion. "Why, why would someone do this to us, Wes, why?"

"Something else," Nigel added.

"What?" Wes asked, "What else could there possibly be?"

"After hearing on your program today that all of your call-in parents' babies were of North Korean heritage, I conducted a DNA test on Cammy. He too has genetic markers that point to his heritage in the Pyongyang region of North Korea."

Sylvie then suddenly turned to Wes, now even more frightened than she already had been. "Wes, remember that North Korean Ambassador guy you kicked off your program a couple of years ago? That guy, could he have anything to do with this?"

"Choi, that was his name, Ambassador Kim Choi," Wes replied. "I don't know, babe, I just don't know."

"It's a good thing you are here. Lillian and I can stop the aggressive aging process. You're both already looking like you're in your late sixties. If the aging process was to run wild in the next year, you'd both pass for centenarians. We can stop you from looking any older," Nigel said and then paused and looked at everyone with a sense of defeat in his eyes.

"But I'm afraid the life span cannot be altered. The Bug is set in stone. Wes, Sylvie, next year, on Valentine's day, be prepared to say good-bye to your loved ones. Of course, Lillian and I will be doing everything we can to find a way."

With Wes and Sylvie sitting on the edge of a lab hospital bed and hearing Nigel's prognosis, Sylvie fell onto Wes's shoulders and cried. She held onto Wes as he tried to comfort her, but all he could do was sit and hold Sylvie. There were no words left to say. Cam lay his hand on Wes's shoulder. Maggie stood looking at Sylvie, holding onto Cammy, cradling and rocking him while wiping tears from her eyes. Sadness filled the room; silence followed.

***

CHAPTER THIRTY-FIVE
2050

HEAD'S UP

Friday, February 11th, 2:58 PM
Toronto Canada – CHYI Radio Station Studios

"You've been listening to The Westernman Show here on CHYI coming at you from the greatest city in the great white north. Toronto, Ontario, Canada. This is Wes Ternman, wishing you all a very happy and love-filled Valentine's Day weekend.

Guys, go out there and get those flowers for your lady. Gals, let your guy know he is your world both night and day. This is a weekend for love, give love, and you will receive it back tenfold. Westernman signing off."

"Wes, you have a call from Tim Kingston, he says he's Vice President of Granger Pharmaceuticals in Philadelphia, and you will want to take his call," Luke Stenner said into Wes's earpiece.

Wes thought for a moment, then said, "Yeah, put him through Luke."

"Wes Ternman."

"Mr. Ternman, thanks for taking my call. My name is Tim Kingston; I'm senior VP at Granger

Pharmaceuticals in Philadelphia."

"What can I do for you, Mr. Kingston," Wes asked.

"Forgive me for being so forward, Mr. Ternman, but in this case, it's what I can do for you and every other parent who used the services of The Paraguay Life Center. Mr. Ternman, I have all the answers you are looking for and all the loose ends that need to be tied. I am about to bring down my company and bring closure to your tragic luck in Paraguay," Tim replied.

"Mr. Kingston, I'm not sure I understand."

"I know, Mr. Ternman, I can understand how I might sound to you like some wacko, but trust me, I am serious as a heart attack. I need to meet with you so that you will understand. I am in Toronto now. I am staying at The Royal York Hotel. I suggest you put aside anything you may have had planned for this evening and meet with me. I could meet both you and your wife, or meet with you alone.

Mr. Ternman, the information I have will bring down The Paraguay Life Center, Granger Pharma and will put our CEO in jail. Most importantly, it will have Vice-Chairman Kim Choi of North Korea being tried in front of the world court in The Hague for systematic murder of his country's citizens and willful genocide."

Wes was taken aback. *Ok, this Mr. Kingston was no joke; he was the real thing.* Tim Kingston had Wes's full attention. When Wes heard the name Kim Choi, Wes knew this was for real. There was no way Kingston could be messing with him.

“All right, Mr. Kingston, I will meet you alone. I’d like to leave my wife out of this for now; God knows she’s been stressed enough over the past month.”

“As you wish, Mr. Ternman,” Tim replied.

“I’ll meet you in the lobby of The Royal York; it’s just a couple of blocks from my studio. How will I know you?”

“Don’t concern yourself about that, Mr. Ternman; I will know you. I’ve been a listener for many years; the whole world knows you,” Tim replied. “Just enter through the main door, and I will come to introduce myself when I see you walk in.”

“All right, that works,” Wes replied.

“Hi babe, hey listen, something’s come up at work, I need to take care of for the weekend. I’ll be about an hour or so late,” Wes said, letting Sylvie know.

“Okay, Wes, be careful honey, the snow’s really coming down.”

“I will Sylvie, love you, babe.”

“Love you too, Wes.”

Wes spoke into his phone’s assistant. “Display corporate profile of Tim Kingston, senior VP Granger Pharmaceuticals Philadelphia, PA.” Just in case Kingston missed him on his entry to the hotel.

"Now display a profile of CEO Granger Pharmaceuticals."

Wes had what he needed for now. Now to see what Kingston had in store for him. Not twenty seconds after Wes walked into the hotel's lobby, Tim Kingston spotted him immediately and approached.

"Mr. Ternman, thank you for agreeing to meet me. I am Tim Kingston. I am sure what I have to tell you will be both revealing and help you and your wife understand what happened to you in Paraguay and how it all came to be."

"Wes didn't quite know what to say or how to respond; he could only come up with one word, "Wow," Wes said, shaking hands with Tim.

"Well, all right, where would you like to talk?"

"Your choice Mr. Ternman, a quiet place in the lounge. Perhaps if you'd like a drink, you might need one after hearing what I have to share with you," Tim replied.

"No, I won't be needing any drinks; I just need to know what happened. I come here all the time; there is a quiet corner up on the mezzanine. The chairs are tucked out of the way; we can have a private conversation there," Wes suggested.

Having situated themselves, Tim started in. "Mr. Ternman, may I call you Wes?" Tim asked.

"Sure, by all means, you don't mind if I record this, do you, Tim?"

"No, not at all; in fact, I would have suggested that you do."

"Wes, what I have to tell you, the whole world will know this coming Sunday. But I felt it my responsibility to let you know before the world knows. Our company's CEO partnering with the devil himself is so heinous and evil that I had trouble believing what I uncovered. But I will share it all with you, Wes, because you and your dear wife ended up being deceived.

I understand your time might be limited, but with some luck, you and your wife might still see the day when Kim Choi is prosecuted for murder, genocide, and willful harm to you and your wife. This coming Sunday, Wes, everything that I tell you here and now in the coming hour will be the lead story in The New York Times, the world will know. With this story's printing in The New York Times, you will see the immediate closing down of The Paraguay Life Center, our CEO: Michael Dern's arrest, and the international arrest and detention warrant for Vice-Chairman Kim Choi of North Korea. If he ever leaves North Korea, he will be detained immediately. Some people at The Times think that Chairman Sun Kim Koom may even give up Kim Choi to save face and keep North Korea's diplomatic status. Canada will sever ties with North Korea immediately after this story comes out. Sun Kim Koom may try to salvage his international relationships by throwing Kim Choi to the lions and the world court."

Wes listened. By 5:15 PM, Tim had told Wes his story, and Wes had it all on his recorder. By 7:30 PM, Sylvie had heard Tim's story. It was Friday night, Valentine's Day weekend, 2050. The snow was still falling heavily in Toronto.

Wes and Sylvie had one more year to live.

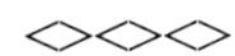

Sunday, February 14th, 10:01 AM, 2050
Nantucket Island - Massachusetts – Dana Blackman's House

One of the most picturesque places to visit in the USA was Nantucket Island, just a couple hours ferry ride from Hyannis. Dana Blackman was looking forward to her usual Sunday morning with the New York Times and her pot of tea. The snow was falling in Nantucket this weekend as well. The Ocean, the beach, and snow made for a serene setting.

Dana went to fetch her copy of The New York Times from the porch. On her way back in and to her living room, she brought her freshly brewed pot of tea and settled in beside the crackling fireplace overlooking the Atlantic on Wauwinet Beach. Dana poured herself a cup of tea, picked it up in one hand, and with the other hand, reached for The Times, read the headline, and promptly spilled the entire cup all over her lap. "My God," she said out loud!

There it was, the headline, above the fold: GRANGER PHARMA NORTH KOREA AND GENOCIDE

The next hour Dana read the entire twelve thousand word article that was sure to sink Granger,

Michael Dern, The Paraguay Life Center and have Interpol on the watch for Vice-Chairman Kim Choi of North Korea.

Almost every line in the news story was a line Dana could hardly believe. Still, the more she read, the more she felt vindicated for having severed her ties both socially and professionally with Michael Dern and his company. Dana's nationwide healthcare network Finacare Health Systems had wholly severed all relations with Granger for over two years. She was confident there would be no spillover from her company's past association with Dern.

But as sure as she was, this would be a prime opportunity to hear from her friend in Canada, Mark Canning. She decided to give Mark a call at his hideaway on Buckhorn Lake.

"Hi Dana, I'm not surprised you called; in fact, I was about to call you!"

"Mark, this is just insane! I had a feeling about Michael, but this? My God, Mark, this is history-making and not good for our industry; it's a huge blight. And to top it off, it's an American company!"

"I know Dana, I know. Here in Canada, our Minister of Foreign Affairs has just put out a statement recalling our Ambassador to North Korea and expelling its embassy staff from Ottawa immediately," Mark said.

"I just hope they catch that bastard in North Korea," Dana replied. "And here I thought the country was starting to turn the corner and become part of the world community in harmony with the rest of civilization. It will be interesting to see how Sun Kim Koom handles this crisis that's just landed in his lap."

"Yeah, what a scandal. Hey, you know the VP, Tim Kingston, the whistleblower, he did one hell of a job in his quest in getting to the bottom of this; he sounds like a decent human being Dana, I'm sure he'll be looking for a job."

"Yeah, Mark, that's already crossed my mind," Dana replied. "I may just give Mr. Kingston a call."

"I really feel for the Ternmans. You know Wes Ternman is an acquaintance of mine; I'll call him later this afternoon; I'm sure he will be inundated with calls from all over the world. I'm sure he's got to be the most listened to radio personality on the planet," Mark said.

"Yeah, it's tragic what happened to him and his wife down there in Paraguay. I can just imagine they left that place filled with joy in their hearts, only to be devastated beyond comprehension a year later. It's still a harsh and cruel world. Mark, let's hope science and technology find a way for them both. I just know that Fohr and Eavers are working on it every day. We can only hope Mark, we can only hope," Dana replied.

"Take care of yourself, Dana, and good to hear from you."

"You too, Mark, take care, bye."

***

CHAPTER THIRTY-SIX
2051

KISS OF FIRE

Tuesday, February 7th, 2051
CHYI Radio Station Toronto Ontario

"Ladies and gentleman, listeners of CHYI and The Westerman Show, it has been my life's pleasure to have been given this platform allowing me to speak with you every day for the past forty-two years. Those who have listened and are aware of my situation, well, you know my time is near; my time and my wife's time. We've had a wonderful life, filled with love and devotion to one another. We leave behind a beautiful little boy who will be loved and raised by his grandfather and grandmother. My wife, Sylvie, and I have no doubt that he will grow up to accomplish great things in his life.

As much as I would like to continue on with The Westernman Show, I cannot. I grow weaker and weaker as each day passes; I need help coming into the studio even now. I will need someone to help me out of my chair when I leave CHYI for the last time today. My wife, she is in the same boat. Our telomeres are giving out with each passing day.

Again, thank you for allowing me to be on your radio, and from the bottom of my heart, good afternoon and good-bye.

Wes Ternman, The Westernman Show, over and out."

As Wes was being surrounded by CHYI radio staff on his last afternoon at the studio, a crowd was forming outside on Toronto's streets. Wes was being helped out of the building by his long time producer Luke Stenner with the rest of CHYI staff following Wes out the door. In front of CHYI studios, the street was filled with thousands of Torontonians and listeners from all across Ontario. As soon as Wes stepped out and was visible to the crowd, the chanting began: "We love you, Westernman, we love you, Westernman."

The crowd of thousands would not stop. The streets in the downtown area of Toronto were wholly blocked with devoted fans as far as Wes could see. Wes was overwhelmed with emotion, and that lump in his throat was back. He threw his arms around his producer Luke to steady himself and waved to the adoring crowd. The crowd of thousands waved back.

"I love them all, Luke, I love them all," Wes said to his friend and producer.

"I know you do, Wes, I know you do, but not as much as they love you, my friend," Luke replied.

And that made Wes lose it again.

"Wes, there's no way you're getting out of here in your wheels this afternoon. We're taking you home in the station's eye-in-the-sky chopper. You know this is being broadcast as breaking news on the local TV channels. I'll call Sylvie to meet your chopper in the baseball park a couple of kilometers down your street. The chopper can land there," Luke said.

"Thanks, Luke, you've been a great friend," Wes replied.

A few minutes later, Wes waved one last time to the crowd of fans before his chopper lifted off, taking him home to Sylvie.

Saturday, February 11th, 2051- Four days after Wes's final Westernman Show
Toronto Ontario – The Ternman Home

"Wes, baby, we only have three more days to go," Sylvie said, trying to turn onto her side to speak but was too weak.

"Yeah, I know Sylvie; I don't know if we can even make it to Valentine's Day; I'm fading fast, babe."

"Wes, I don't want to die here. Wes, I want to die with you under the stars Wes, in Algonquin Park, under the milky way," Sylvie said.

"Me too, baby. I'll ask my Dad to take us. Remember we used to camp on Mew Lake every winter babe, they'll be open this year too. We can stay in one of the cabins. I'll ask my Dad to make our reservations, we can go tomorrow. We can make it there before we die," Wes said, reaching out in the darkness for Sylvie's hand.

"Good baby, good, we can go tomorrow; Cam and my Mom can take us. I love you so much, Wes, good night baby,"

"Good night babe, I love you too."

◇◇◇

Monday, February 13th, 2051- One day before Valentine's Day
Fohr-Evers Research Center – Montreal Canada

"Jesus, Nigel, we've been up all night working on this formula, and we've got nothing. The telomeres aren't budging," Lillian said with dejection in her voice. "They've got today and tomorrow, that's it, and that isn't for sure, Wes and Sylvie might already be out of time. Nigel, we have to find some way, we have to, damn it Nigel, Sylvie is like a daughter to me now, we need to find a way to give them more time! Think Nigel, think!" Lillian was beside herself. They were both stressed out.

Nigel looked at Lillian, his scientific partner, and best friend. Nigel's heart broke for Lillian, as it did for Wes and Sylvie. They absolutely had to come up with something.

"Please, God, please show us a way," Lillian said, sitting and looking at her microscope. She then looked up to the glass shelf behind the counter. There right in front of her, were the three vials of blood belonging to Sylvie, Wes, and Cammy. There was something about the vials. The wheels inside her mind were turning: she was on to something. Lillian couldn't take her eyes off the vials. Then suddenly, the fuel that kept her focused on the vials lit the flame in her brain, and she knew what it was in a flash!

She blurted out, "Nigel! Nigel! Oh my God, are we stupid or what! All this time, Nigel! Nigel, we are Nobel Prize winners, but I think we may be the two dumbest nerds ever born!" Lillian said. "It's been staring us in the face all this time! Look, look!" She pointed at the three vials of blood.

"What, what is it? What do you see?"

"What is that you see there, Nigel?"

"The three vials from the Ternmans," Nigel replied.

"Now go and get me another vial, one with blood from an accident victim and put that vial beside Sylvie's on the shelf."

Nigel then got a vial from an accident victim and set it beside Sylvie's vial of blood.

"All right, now look and tell me what you see! We have been so blind all along! Tell me what you see, Nigel!" Lillian was now frantic.

"I don't know, Lillian! Four vials!"

"No, Nigel, you see, the first vial is accident victim Forever Bug from dead people, weakened Forever Bug Virus. The second vial you see is Sylvie's blood, also weakened Forever Bug because of vial number one. The third vial you see is Wes's blood, also weakened Forever Bug because of vial number one. What is vial number four, Nigel? Tell me! What is vial number four?" Lillian almost now yelling at Nigel.

Then it hit Nigel like a lightning bolt. "Oh, my God!" We've been trying to reformulate weakened telomeres from weakened Forever Bug when we've got perfectly healthy and robust as ever Bug right there; it's Cammy's blood. Cammy has intact Forever Bug telomeres just like you, and I have inside of us! And Cammy's DNA is Wes's and Sylvie's DNA, and it's not weak; it's healthy, strong, and new!"

"That's it, Nigel, we've never tried combining the baby's Bug with Wes and Sylvie's weakened Bug. Do it, do it now. I'm sitting right here by the microscope. I want to see if there is a reaction, do it!" Lillian said.

Nigel then combined Cammy's intact Bug DNA and its fully vibrant age-cycling telomeres with Sylvie's weakened Bug. He passed the plate on to Lillian to load the sample into the electron microscope.

They both then viewed on the monitor, and within fifteen seconds, the virus started mutating, the genes controlling the telomeres were modifying the telomere lengths with no degradation. It was working! Cammy's Forever Bug was replacing all the genes controlling the shortened telomeres in Sylvie's DNA with Cammy's age recycling telomeres

"That's it, that's it!" But it's not just working for Wes and Sylvie. This is the answer we've been hoping to find ever since Baby Alpha and the thirteen-year life limit for new parents. This will bring The Forever Bug back to its full strength in all new parents, Nigel. All they have to do is inject themselves with their newborn's DNA, and they will have fully rejuvenated Forever Bug age recycling as before. This is it, Nigel! This is it! Grab Cammy's blood, and let's go!"

"Air ambulance, this is Dr. Eavers; we have a medical emergency, we need you to file a flight path immediately to Toronto, Lawrence Park, I will provide landing spot details en route," Lillian ordered. Five minutes later, Lillian and Nigel were lifting off from the Fohr-Eavers Research Center's rooftop and on their way to Wes and Sylvie's house.

"We're ten minutes out, Dr. Eavers; I need a landing spot," the pilot said.

Lillian then called Wes's number, it rang, but it went to voice mail. She then tried Sylvie's number, the same thing. She called Wes's number again and, this time, waiting for the voice mail. She was about to leave a message when the phone was answered.

"Dr. Eavers, this is Oscar; I am Wes and Sylvie's robotic assistant. How can I help you?"

Oscar caught Lillian off guard; she wasn't expecting a robot. "How did you know who I was?" Lillian asked.

"Dr. Eavers, you had called here before, and I receive and record all calls whether Wes and Sylvie answer or not answer. I know who you are, Dr. Eavers; how can I help you?"

"Can I speak to Wes or Sylvie?"

"I'm afraid they don't have their phones; they went to Algonquin Park to die, Dr. Eavers," Oscar replied.

"Oh my God, they're not home? They're out winter camping someplace in the park to die?" Lillian asked frantically.

"That is correct, Dr. Eavers."

"Oscar, listen, their lives are in danger; Dr. Fohr and I must reach them immediately. Do you know where they are?"

"Of course, I do; I can take you there if you like. I know who you are, and you wish to save their lives. I will do everything in my mechanical power to assist you. What is it you require?"

"Is Cammy with Wes and Sylvie?"

"Yes, he is, and Cam and Maggie too," Oscar replied.

"All right, we're about three minutes out, but we cannot land there. Do you know of a place we can land nearby?"

"Yes, Dr. Eavers, there is a baseball diamond just two kilometers north of our house; your pilot should spot it easily. I will meet you there in two minutes."

"You can be there in two minutes?" Lillian asked,

a little surprised.

"Yes, Dr. Eavers, I am a Class10 bot," you might have heard of my capabilities.

"All right, Oscar, we will pick you up there."

Oscar then entered into his emergency mode. Powered up fully and exited the house. It was now starting to get dark enough outside that the street lights were on. Once outside, Oscar transformed into his full potential. His body grew to seven and a half feet, his eyes radiated a red laser from each socket, and his entire body lit up like a Christmas tree. He was outlined in light, then started running. Within five seconds, Oscar was speeding through Toronto's darkening streets as a blur of light at eighty-four miles per hour. When approaching intersections, he'd jump across, altogether avoiding traffic. The Class10 bot moved so quickly, people hardly noticed it; Oscar was like a flash that happened to zoom by; if you blinked, you'd miss him.

Oscar arrived at the baseball diamond to see the chopper coming in. He flashed his body's LEDs guiding the helicopter pilot to a landing mark. Oscar then resumed back to his cute little five feet two inches high personal assistant configuration.

"Dr. Eavers, nice to meet you," Oscar said as he entered the chopper.

"Oscar, nice to meet you as well, I am Dr. Eavers, and this is Dr. Fohr; we need to get to wherever they are in Algonquin Park as quickly as possible."

"Nice to meet you also, Dr. Fohr. Yes, I know exactly where they are; I can also give the pilot the GPS coordinates. Wes and Sylvie enjoy camping all year round, and Algonquin is their go-to place. This time we will go to Mew Lake Cabins, they are in cabin number two. Cam made the reservations just a couple of days ago. Like I was saying, I record all incoming and outgoing calls, and I have all the data you could ever ask for."

"Ok great, tell our pilot the coordinates so he can punch them into the flight computer."

"Will do."

"We should be there in an hour and a half," the pilot said.

"I also want to let you know that I have diagnostic capabilities should you be in need. I can take blood pressure, heart rate, brain wave activity measurement along with stethoscope audio with my remote sensing. I can also provide infrared heat imaging and detection." Oscar added.

Monday, February 13th, 2051- One day before Valentine's Day
Mew Lake Cabins – Algonquin Park Ontario

"There it is, but it's pitch black out there. I can see the light from the cabins," Oscar said.

"Where?" I can't see anything yet, the pilot responded.

"That's all right, Captain, I can guide us in; I have night vision as well as infrared, just stay on course; we're good," Oscar replied.

"Damn, I got to get me one of you!" replied the pilot.

"Yes, Captain, we're a lot of fun," Oscar replied.

"Bring us in, Captain," Nigel said.

The sound from the chopper had Cam and Maggie looking out and wondering what was going on. They were both standing by the cabin's side as Lillian, Nigel, and Oscar ran up.

"No time to explain; where are they?" Lillian asked.

"Out back by the fire, they're wrapped up in sleeping arctic thermal sleeping bags, all three of them inside a two-man sleeping bag, their heads are sticking out of the tent so they can watch the stars, that is what they wanted," Cam replied.

"Take us there now, right away! How are they?"

"They both were still alive just a few minutes ago. They're not supposed to die until tomorrow, right?"

"Right, but tomorrow comes in about an hour, Maggie," Nigel replied.

"Oh, my God!"

They all ran to the back of the cabin; a warm fire was keeping the area comfortable. It was a windless night. The stars were out bright, and the milky way was lighting the pathway to heaven for Wes and Sylvie.

"Wes, Wes, can you hear me, Wes? Lillian said. No response from Wes at all. Same with Sylvie.

Oscar then extended his arms, his hands grew larger, and he placed one hand under Wes's neck and another under Sylvie's.

Oscar waited a Moment, then said, "Heart rate is 55 for Wes and 53 for Sylvie. Brain wave activity is minimal; they are either in deep sleep or a semi-unconscious state. Wes and Sylvie are still alive, but they are fading fast, Dr. Eavers."

"Nigel, inject Wes with Cammy's blood now, now Nigel!"

Nigel injected Wes.

"Okay, now do Sylvie."

They waited, one minute, two minutes, three minutes.

"Heart rates picking up on both. Blood pressure now rising from ischemia onset to 80 over 60, still rising in both, 90 over 70 now," Oscar said.

Lillian and Nigel stared at one another with hope

in their eyes. *It worked in the lab*, they thought, and knelt down beside Wes and Sylvie. Cammy was tucked nice and warm between the two of them and fast asleep.

"Come on, Wes, come on, come on, Sylvie, you can do it," Lillian said, caressing their faces.

Cam and Maggie looked on in wonder, now tearing up. Cam wrapped his arm around Maggie as she leaned into him.

"Please, God, please," Maggie whispered as she and Cam stood watching over Lillian and Nigel.

"BP normal now on both, 110 over 84," Oscar said. "Looks like they're coming back."

Sylvie then opened her eyes; a few seconds later, Wes opened his, both still in a haze.

"They're coming back, Maggie, Cam, they're coming back! It's working, thank God, it's working! It was Cammy's blood, Maggie. Cam, it was Cammy's blood! Cammy saved his Mom and Dad! Their baby saved them!" Lillian cried with tears of joy.

Wes was coming to a little quicker than Sylvie and heard Lillian say, "Their baby saved them!"

Wes was slowly coming to. He clearly made out Lillian leaning over him, Nigel, Cam, and Maggie; they smiled and hugged one another. A smile then formed over Wes's face, too, as things began to click in. He then knew that everything was going to be okay. Wes was still too weak to move his body but remembered that Sylvie lay beside him. Sylvie started coming to as well. Reaching out for Sylvie's face, his fingers felt her warm breath and touched her lips.

I TOUCH YOUR LIPS AND ALL AT ONCE THE SPARKS GO FLYING

The End

About the Author

"Frank Julius" Csenki is a hotelier, veteran of the hotel and resort industry. He immigrated to Canada from Budapest, Hungary, during the Hungarian uprising, known as the Hungarian Revolution.

His family settled in Hamilton, Ontario, and later on the Niagara Peninsula, where he and his younger brother both attended high school.

Frank made a career for himself in the hotel business, starting as a bellman and years later as General Manager and Financial Controller for hotels and resorts internationally. Having lived in seven countries and worked a good part of the world, he now writes about the industry that gave him the adventures and career he enjoyed for forty years.

He now lives in cottage country, near Peterborough, Ontario, and writes historical fiction, thrillers, science fiction, and an autobiographic anthology series.

His hobbies are motorcycles and landscape photography.

Comments can be left on his author website.

www.frankjulius.com